Books in the
Captain Lacey
Regency Mystery Series
By Ashley Gardner

THE HANOVER SQUARE AFFAIR
A REGIMENTAL MURDER
THE GLASS HOUSE
THE SUDBURY SCHOOL MURDERS
THE NECKLACE AFFAIR
AND OTHER STORIES
(COLLECTED STORIES)
A BODY IN BERKELEY SQUARE
A COVENT GARDEN MYSTERY
A DEATH IN NORFOLK
A DISAPPEARANCE IN DRURY LANE
MURDER IN GROSVENOR SQUARE
THE ALEXANDRIA AFFAIR
A MYSTERY AT CARLETON HOUSE
(AND MORE TO COME)

Also by
Ashley Gardner

MURDER MOST HISTORICAL
(ANTHOLOGY: INCLUDES A SOUPÇON OF POISON)

Kat Holloway Mystery Series
A SOUPÇON OF POISON
A DOLLOP OF DEATH

The

Alexandria

Affair

Ashley Gardner

Captain Lacey Regency Mysteries
Book 11

Chapter One

In late August, 1818, my wife had me abducted, trussed up, and taken down the Thames to be put on a tall ship bound for Egypt.

Our party consisted of myself, bound and furious; Lucius Grenville, who was funding much of the voyage; our retainers, Bartholomew and Matthias; and one Thomas Brewster, a tough who worked for a man named James Denis.

Brewster and the two lads hauled me, still bound, into my tiny cabin off the ship's ward room, and shut and locked the door.

"Devil take it, Bartholomew!" I shouted.

"Her ladyship's orders, sir," Bartholomew's voice came through the thin partition.

He sounded uncertain, but I had no hope that he'd let me out until we were well underway. It had come to the sad pass that my valet feared my wife's wrath far more than he feared mine.

"Grenville!" I bellowed.

I heard no reply from him, but Brewster's tones came to me. "Mr. Grenville's swallowing his remedies for the voyage," he said calmly. "I'll see to it you're released when it's time, guv."

I knew that though I might coerce Bartholomew in the long run to let me out—after all, my wife, Donata, was safely back in Oxfordshire—Brewster, a former pugilist hardened by a life of crime, never would.

All I could do was fume.

Only when we were a long way out in the English Channel and making steadily for Lisbon did Bartholomew tentatively open the door and cut my bonds.

I had recovered my temper somewhat, but it was more resignation than peace—I'd have no way to reach shore again until we were in Lisbon. There I might jump ship and hie my way back to London and again to Oxfordshire, where I'd enlist the help of Donata's father to prevent her from banishing me again.

I went out on deck, accompanied by Brewster, to plan my escape.

"I am surprised to see *you*," I snapped as I leaned on the railing beside him and watched mist rapidly obscure the dark green line of England. "Do not tell me my wife employed you to keep me to my purpose."

"'Course not." Brewster scowled at the receding coast, looking as unhappy to be onboard as I was. "His nibs sent me. I'm to keep you alive, he says, while you're in foreign parts."

"His nibs" was James Denis, a man who did not bother with the law when he wanted something. Mr. Denis controlled a large part of London as well as many prominent men in England, and now he fought an ongoing battle to control me.

Denis had done much for me, obligating me to him more and more each passing year. But while I'd come to admire his efficiency and unexpected bursts of compassion, I'd also watched him murder a man with his bare hands and flick his fingers to command others to do murder for him.

When Denis knew I'd be making this voyage to Egypt with Grenville, he'd tasked me to go to Alexandria and retrieve an item for him. I had no idea *what* item or where to look for it—he'd told me he'd send me written instructions to be opened when we reached Alexandria. However I'd received no such letter before I'd been dragged from my home.

I glanced at Brewster in sudden suspicion. "You have the letter, don't you?"

"About what his nibs wants you to find?" Brewster gave me a nod. "That I do, Captain."

"Wise," I had to admit.

Denis would know that if I had the letter now, I'd read it immediately and not wait until we landed in Egypt as commanded. Brewster, who was a tall, broad-shouldered man with the solidness of a dock laborer and the strength of a bull, would never give the letter to me until time.

Brewster's first loyalty was to James Denis. I could cajole, plead, threaten, or bribe, but Brewster would never capitulate, and I knew it.

"Mr. Denis is a wise man, sir," Brewster said.

"Ah, well." My hand tightened on the railing as the ship rolled in earnest, a strong wave running under its prow. "Let us simply enjoy the voyage while we can."

"Some of us might," Brewster said doubtfully.

"Mr. Grenville is already in a bad way. Why does he want to go so far from home if it only makes him heave all day and night?"

"Because he's right as rain once he arrives," I answered. "And his restlessness would not keep him in London any longer."

Lucius Grenville, one of England's wealthiest gentlemen and the most famous dandy in London, had invited me on this voyage to Alexandria and beyond it to the wonders of the Nile. Unfortunately, all Grenville's wealth, looks, and fine taste could not save him from his malady of motion sickness. Even a short carriage ride in the country laid him out grievously.

I'd look in on him later. For now we watched the bank of low fog swallow England, the land where my wife, who was heavy with my child, lay.

Donata—formerly the widowed Viscountess Breckenridge—had been ill much of the summer, not weathering her condition well. I'd planned to take her, her son, and my daughter to my boyhood home in Norfolk and continue putting the falling-down house to rights. Donata's indisposition, however, made us retreat instead to Oxfordshire. My grown daughter had returned to France to her other family, while Donata, Peter, and I settled into Donata's father's lavish estate, where she was tended to like a queen.

I watched my wife most anxiously. Donata was thirty, and childbirth was so very dangerous no matter how strong the woman. I'd seen the wife of my former commander lose several children, coming near to death herself on one occasion. Remembering her trials made me sleepless, especially on the days and nights Donata was the most ill.

Donata was not happy to be confined. She was a woman who liked to be up and about, and seethed even as she settled in to be waited on hand and foot. She became peevish and vexed with me, but I was adamant that she stay quiet and not endanger herself in any way.

When I told Donata decidedly one evening that I would abandon my journey to Egypt and remain with her through my child's birth, our marriage nearly foundered.

Grenville and I had already altered our plans from leaving at New Year's to going late this summer, as my child was to arrive in December. I wanted to be back in time for the birth, and I knew I'd scarcely want to tear myself away after that.

Now I'd declared I would stay home and look after Donata during her confinement, and Grenville and I could journey to Egypt next year.

Donata, her body thick and face flushed as she lay on a chaise in her sumptuous bedchamber, had fixed me with an imperious gaze.

"Grenville has been to much trouble making the preparations, Gabriel," she'd said. "You must not disappoint him."

"Grenville will be perfectly at ease traveling on his own," I countered. "He has done so many times before. He will enjoy not having to stop every three minutes and explain things to me."

Donata regarded me in disapprobation. I knew I had been hovering and protective, but until that moment, I had not realized how much I'd been driving her distracted.

"You are a fool, Gabriel," she'd said crisply. "I've borne a child before and know what I'm about. If you leave in August as you and Grenville plan, you will return in plenty of time for the birth. Modern ships keep good timetables. Go, my husband. *Do.*"

I stared at her in stunned anger for a moment and told her stiffly that it was my duty to remain with her, and I'd do so.

Thus began an argument that lasted many weeks.

Some of the reason for my worry was that earlier in the summer a gentleman had sent me threatening letters, followed me about London, and tried to shoot me. Though we'd heard nothing about this man in the intervening months, I did not think he'd give up so easily.

Donata pointed out that not only was her father, an earl, and his retainers perfectly capable of protecting her, but Mr. Denis had promised to hunt for the man and keep him away from my family. Denis had found no sign of him, which likely meant my hunter had left the country, but I could not stem my fears.

We quarreled constantly about the matter until Donata became quite fed up with me.

In the end, she'd resorted to kidnapping. I'd been persuaded to return to London on an errand for her—or so I'd thought. The day after my arrival in London several burly men had entered the dining room in the South Audley Street house where I breakfasted. They wrenched me from my chair, tied me as I tried to fight, stuffed me into a coach, and dragged me off.

Now as I stood on deck, the sun broke free of the gloom that had hovered over England, and the sea sparkled a deep and beautiful blue. I began to laugh.

"Never underestimate the resourcefulness of women, Brewster," I said. "Especially that of wives irritated at their husbands. I suppose Mrs. Brewster would have done much the same."

Brewster didn't smile. "Indeed she would, Captain. In fact, your abduction was her idea. When I conveyed the notion to your lady, she was only too happy to agree."

I imagined Donata's eyes, as blue as the dark sea around me, lighting in enjoyment when Brewster explained the plan.

I laughed again. My homecoming this winter would be quite satisfying.

***

But first, we had to reach Egypt.

The merchantman, owned by one Captain Woolwich, a man for whom I'd been some use earlier this summer, moved swiftly, and we put in at Lisbon after four days to replenish supplies and prepare for the longer voyage into the Mediterranean.

Grenville felt better once we were out of the rocking sea and came out on deck for a look at the town. As I gazed out at the working docks, the sunburned Portuguese men swarming up ropes and hauling down crates, I recalled my last look at this city, when I'd hobbled onboard a ship, in vast pain and furious, my army career at an end.

I'd been a pathetic wretch when I'd departed Lisbon four years ago. Now I was returning as the friend of a generous man and married to a fine lady. I'd been reunited with my daughter and about to become a father again. I counted myself blessed.

"Ports are always dreary," Grenville remarked, watching the smoke and bustle, the forest of masted ships against the pale buildings and twilit sky. "Shall we adjourn into town and take in the sights while they load?"

I was ready to leap down the gangplank and

stride off, or at least limp away, but traveling with
Grenville had already proved to be a different
experience than hauling myself about with the king's
army. Grenville ordered a conveyance as opulent as
one he'd hire in London, and we clopped off into the
avenues, accompanied by our two servants and
Brewster.

The city was lively, the Portuguese coming out
with the sunset to eat and drink with their neighbors.
We dined in a restaurant on a street that rose up a
steep hill, enjoying the balmy evening. I spoke some
Portuguese, as did Grenville, and we ate well on fish
fresh from the sea. Bartholomew and Mathias
slipped away on explorations of their own, while
Brewster waited outside and watched every person
who went in or out of the building.

When we reached the ship again, we found new
passengers on board, a man and his wife who were
off to Alexandria to look for treasure.

Archibald Porter, a slim, wiry man, was a retired
sergeant who'd been a marine—one of the body of
men who were assigned to naval vessels and fought
battles either on land or on the ship itself. Marines
were a tough breed, and we in the army had both
despised and admired them. They'd despised and
admired us in return, and I imagined that Sergeant
Porter and I would rub along well.

His wife, Josephine, was also tough and wizened,
her face brown from their travels. Though she was a
small woman, the strength in her hand when I took it
in greeting was a bit unnerving.

"Your wife stays in England?" she asked me as we
leaned on the railing and watched Lisbon's enclosed
harbor fade behind us. "I had enough of that when
the sergeant was in the war. We go about

everywhere together now, from the cold of Russia to the burning lands of Africa, don't we Archie?"

"Aye, she's a good traveler, is my Jo," Archibald answered without rancor.

"My wife is a bit indisposed at the moment," I said, defending Donata's absence. "She will have a child in December." I could not disguise the note of pride in my voice.

Mrs. Porter grinned at me. "I bore ten of 'em, Captain. All growed now with bitty ones of their own. Never did me no harm. A few years, and your wife will be roaming up and down the world with you, I'll wager. England's a fine enough place, but dull."

"*Egypt* ain't dull, Captain," the sergeant continued. "We're off to dig it up. There's a bit of coin to be had in unearthing treasure. Amazing what these Egyptians did in ancient times. Never knew the inside of a church, the Egyptians, but their temples are astonishing places."

"And what they did with their dead is wonderfully gruesome," Mrs. Porter added. "Wherever you go, you'll no doubt encounter mummies or parts of them—the poor souls are everywhere. People once thought ground-up mummy a tonic for all sorts of ills—can you credit it?" She chuckled. "These same ladies and gents would be shocked by any mention of cannibalism. Takes all sorts, eh, Captain?"

I remembered my father reading that mummy was good for the constitution, but thankfully it was far too expensive for him to procure. A boy at the time, I'd reacted with both fascination and horror.

"Come help us if you like, Captain," Sergeant Porter said. "Find a pretty trinket to take home to your lady."

I wasn't certain what Grenville's plans were for our sojourn, but I thanked the Porters and told them I'd join them if I could. The idea of uncovering treasure that had been tucked away by an unknown civilization eons ago did intrigue me. I wanted to see every part of Egypt, from the Greek city of Alexander to the very ancient and mysterious pyramids.

I bade the Porters good night and went below to Grenville, who'd retired as soon as the anchor lifted.

"Salt of the earth, those two," Grenville said weakly from his bunk. He'd been given the largest cabin in the stern of the ship, which surrounded the ward room. Grenville's cabin held a bunk built to his stature by the ship's carpenter, two large trunks of his belongings, and a tiny window, a light as it was called, that gave out onto the moonlit sea.

"Nothing wrong with salt." I leaned on the doorframe, wishing I could do something to ease his malady. "They have invited us to dig for treasure with them."

"Kind of them. I will arrange for us to do some excavating of our own when we reach Giza. We will have a fine time of it, Lacey." The ship heaved, Grenville's eyes widened, and he quickly put his handkerchief to his mouth. "If I survive, that is."

"Nonsense, the weather is wonderful," I said, unable to keep the ebullience from my voice. "The ship's master is pleased with the voyage so far and anticipates smooth sailing."

Grenville only nodded and gave me a miserable look from his gray face. I took pity on him and left him alone.

Smooth seas we had, as anticipated, all the way to Malta. We passed the mighty rock of Gibraltar, the

English bastion at the tip of Spain. We sailed past that edifice and on through the blue waters of the Mediterranean to put in at Valletta, in Malta.

It was only then that the man who'd shot at me this June made his appearance and once again tried to kill me.

Chapter Two

Grenville and I had disembarked as the ship docked at Valletta to load and unload. We dined with an acquaintance of his in the town, while the Porters went off to explore the old fortress of the Knights of St. John. I rather longed to go with them, but I politely accepted the invitation of Grenville's friend instead.

It turned out that Grenville's acquaintance was an historian who knew much about Malta, the knights, and the Arabs who'd later occupied the island. We spent the evening in lively discussion. The gentleman even lent me books about both Malta and Alexandria to read during the voyage—I'd return them on our way back.

Grenville elected to spend the night with his friend in his fine house, not to mention in a bed that didn't rock, but I chose to return to the ship.

I'd grown used to my hard bunk, and truth to tell, I wanted to walk about the historic town and also hear what the Porters had discovered in their explorations. Leaving the books we'd been lent for Grenville to bring back in his hired carriage, I strolled back to the ship on foot.

It was late, most of Valletta's inhabitants abed. I kept my eye out for thieves and brigands, though I did not walk alone. Brewster and Bartholomew were steps away from me, Brewster with his hand on a knife he wore under his coat. I had my walking stick, the sword blade rattling reassuringly inside it.

Even with our precautions, none of us were prepared when the shadow of a man stepped from one of the tiny side streets and aimed a pistol at me.

In the one second that I saw him, silhouetted against a smudge of lamplight from an open window, I knew it was the same person who'd hunted me this summer. He was as tall as I was, and the familiarity of his stance was unnerving.

In the next instant, I was on the pavement in a noisome alley with Bartholomew on top of me, Brewster's heavy footsteps moving away from us at a rapid pace. I heard Brewster's shouts receding as he moved through the narrow streets.

I struggled up, Bartholomew's weight considerable.

"He's gone," I growled at my robust footman. "A simple warning might have sufficed."

Bartholomew unapologetically helped me to my feet, his strength nearly pulling me off them again. His blue eyes were wide, his face, dirt-streaked. "Couldn't take no chance, sir. Wanted you out of the line of the shot. Besides, Mr. Brewster pushed me."

Brewster had done such a thing before, shoving me aside and taking a bullet meant to hit me. I couldn't hear his shouts any longer, and my heart thumped with worry.

"We'd better make sure he's well," I said.

I took the precaution of peering out into the main street before I simply charged ahead. A hunchbacked beggar scuttled past, but otherwise, the night was dark, the lane empty.

I felt great alarm for Brewster. He'd nearly died when he'd been shot this summer—he would have, if not for the help of a surgeon who was equally as criminal as Denis. The surgeon's skill had healed Brewster, and for that I was grateful, no matter how much of a villain the surgeon might have been in the past.

Brewster tramped around the corner as we reached the end of the lane, upright and unharmed. "Gone," he said in disgust. He spat on the uneven stones. "Like a ghost."

"At least he didn't shoot," I said, my voice severe. "Haven't you learned not to leap in front of loaded pistols?"

"'Tis my task to protect you, Captain," Brewster said without heat. "'Sides, I want that bloke. Want to give him a good clip around the ear for laying me up like that." His hand went to his side, where the bullet had struck and lodged.

Brewster said *clip around the ear*, but I knew he meant to throttle the man, whoever he was. Brewster was the violent sort. He didn't teach lessons; he took revenge.

We said little more as we made our way through darkness back to the ship.

Strangely, what I felt about encountering my hunter again was not fear and anger, but vast relief. If the man who wished to kill me was here in Malta, then he was not in England near my wife or in France where my daughter was.

Whether he'd followed us or chanced upon us, I could not know, but I'd make sure he followed me from now on. I'd lead him to hell itself to keep him away from Donata, Peter, and Gabriella.

We boarded the ship without further mishap, and I asked the mate to keep a special lookout for intruders. He assured me he never took his eyes from the comings and goings while they were in port, and I believed him. Merchantmen had plenty of goods for thieves to plunder.

Even so, I slept restlessly and was sandy-eyed and irritable when Grenville returned in the morning, and the ship made to get underway.

"Good Lord," Grenville said as we met in his cabin and I told him about my adventure.

Grenville was as well-groomed as he would be in a London club, his dark hair combed and crisp, his face smoothly shaved. His suit, a casual one for traveling, was perfectly tailored and likely cost as much as any sailor on this ship made in a year.

"You're certain it was the same man?" Grenville asked, but even as he spoke he nodded, knowing I would be sure. "How the devil did he know you'd be here?"

"We made no secret of the journey." I stepped to the window and looked out, watching the old city recede as the ship made its ponderous way out of the harbor. "The famous Grenville prepares for a voyage to exotic lands. Many a newspaper reported this fact." I turned from the window. "We travel on one of Captain Woolwich's ships—I assume its itinerary is published somewhere."

Grenville sat on his bunk and slid off a boot with the help of a boot jack. This spoke of his agitation— usually he'd call a servant to help him remove any article of clothing.

"Disturbing thought," Grenville said. "So he might be waiting for us to disembark in Alexandria, pistol loaded." He looked up at me. "We can always go back, Lacey. Take an outbound ship to London at the next port. You did not want to come at all— Donata and I rather forced your hand."

"No," I said with determination. "I'm damned if I'll let this fellow decide for me where I will or will not go. I am pleased he's following *me* and leaving Donata and my daughter alone. If he makes his appearance again, we will turn the tables and hunt *him*. Brewster, in particular, would like a word with him."

Grenville opened the small box he kept beside his bunk, removed a goblet and vial, and poured a dollop of yellow liquid from the vial into the glass. His seasick remedy, which he said helped a bit. I'd sniffed it one day and found it perfectly foul.

"I admire your spirit," Grenville said. "But I would recommend caution. We can always change ships and arrive in Alexandria at a different time. Or go to Rosetta instead and make our way back. Keep surprise on our side."

I considered, then shook my head. "If he is intent on finding me, he will. Then I will knock his pistol from his hand and beat some answers from him."

"As I say, I applaud your courage." Grenville swallowed the draught, returned the vial and goblet to the box, then lay flat on his bunk with the look of a man steeling himself to face the worst. "But keep Brewster by your side, won't you?"

A wave heaved under the hull. I rose with it, liking the feeling of gliding along the sea, but Grenville went pale.

I looked at him with concern. "I wish I could help you, my dear fellow. Is there anything I can do?"

"You may read to me, if you like." Grenville slid his handkerchief from his coat and dabbed his lips. "The malady is not as bad these days — I'm more used to the motion." He winced as we hit another wave, belying his words. "Distract me with your studies of nature and the world."

Grenville had brought a library with him, or near enough, which had now been supplemented by the volumes his friend in Valletta had lent us. I had been spending much time already sitting on deck or in the ward room, reading until the words blurred.

I perused everything from Herodotus to more modern accounts of Egypt by French explorers currently excavating on the Nile. I kept myself apprised of the exploits of one Giovanni Belzoni, once a strongman in popular shows at Sadler's Wells and Bartholomew Faire, now becoming known for digging up Egyptian antiquities to send back to England.

I read histories of Alexandria and its famous library, of the oracle in the desert that had told Alexander he would conquer the world. I read of temples and pyramids rising out of the sands and speculations on monuments to dead kings that were still buried.

I read of astronomy and the science of nature in Newton's *Principia*, and more recent studies of celestial mechanics by the Marquis de Laplace, of light by Mr. Young, and the discoveries of comets and other celestial wonders by Mr. Herschel and his family.

Obliging, I fetched the Laplace and began to read out loud to Grenville. I do not know if the mysteries of the skies soothed him, but soon he was asleep. I tucked the book under my arm and went up on deck to continue reading under the warming sun.

***

The voyage continued without mishap. As we went south, toward the coast of Africa, the air grew hotter and dryer. I spent many of my nights on deck, enjoying the cool breezes of the sea and watching the moon and stars.

I contemplated the lands we sailed past, helped keep an eye out for pirates, watched the sailors, spoke at length with the Porters, and read as much as I could.

So entertaining myself, and Grenville when he felt up to it, we lumbered along the coast and came to Alexandria.

I confess that my first glimpse of the exotic land of the pharaohs disappointed me slightly. I had been reading so much about the glorious harbors of Alexandria and its lighthouse that I was a bit taken aback to find the city nothing like I'd envisioned.

The narrow causeway that had been constructed from Alexandria to the island of Pharos by the first Ptolemy's engineers was now a wide isthmus, built up by two thousand years of rocks, sand, and silt. Low stone buildings covered its entirety, which culminated in a fortress on the harbor, itself centuries old—an edifice to keep people out instead of a light to welcome them in. Called Qait Bay after the Mameluke sultan who had built it, the fortress stood where the famous lighthouse had, every piece of that lighthouse now gone.

Sergeant Porter joined me on deck as we rolled past the fortress and eastward toward Aboukir, where we'd land, our ship too large to put into

Alexandria's small port. A flat, very green plain fed by waterways of the longest river in the world opened up to us as we sailed past. Palm trees poked from ripples of green, reminding me that despite Egypt's vast deserts, it was also a very fertile land — had been for millennia.

Our great ship floated to Aboukir, where the French fleet had been routed by Lord Nelson, while Napoleon had been off in the desert fighting Mamelukes and sketching pyramids.

Grenville joined us on deck, more color in his cheeks now that we'd stopped rocking, and looked about with interest. "Old Nappy's quest to conquer the East might have been a military failure," he said, "but it was a triumph of knowledge. There has been no more thorough study of Egypt before or since. Ironic, eh?"

"Aye, he was mad for Egypt, was the Corsican," Porter said. "Good for us, though. He mapped out where all the best sites were. We'll dig it all up for Mr. Salt and England."

Grenville and I exchanged a glance. Sergeant Porter made no pretense that he was after as many antiquities as he could carry back with him. I had to admit, however, that I wouldn't mind finding a few myself, even if I ended up giving them to Henry Salt, the British minister in Egypt.

Offloading our baggage took quite a long time. While I had learned in my many years in the army to travel with a minimum of possessions, Grenville, a wealthy Englishman, brought his entire world with him.

In addition to the two trunks he'd squeezed into his cabin, four others had been stowed below, one of which included furniture. When I'd remarked about his excess of baggage during the voyage, Grenville had regarded me calmly and said,

"You'll be thankful of my things when we arrive, Lacey, mark my words. Accommodations can be spartan in the extreme."

The process of unloading his trunks was slowed by the number of officials who wanted to speak with us. Egypt was ruled from afar by the leader of the Ottoman Empire in Constantinople, closer by the pasha — the governor — who sat in Cairo, and then by city officials of Aboukir and Alexandria. Soldiers in Turkish dress, armed with swords and pistols, swarmed the docks, as did what Grenville called *fellahin*, Egyptian peasants who did everything from carrying baggage or offloading the ships to selling souvenirs to simply standing and watching us.

Grenville was recognized by the officials as the head of our party, or at least as the gentleman with all the money. Grenville began handing out gifts and trinkets — apparently part of his baggage had been snuffboxes, small purses, and other such objects to smooth our way.

I wandered off as he and our footmen became surrounded, and took in my first glimpse of Egypt.

Brewster was directly behind me, his heavy tread audible even over the great amount of noise of the docks. We were still about twelve miles from Alexandria — we'd journey from here to the town in carts.

I took in the sights around me, wanting to remember every detail for the journal I was keeping for Gabriella. Even though this Egypt was not the land I'd read of in Herodotus, it was still strange and wonderful.

The air was soft, the wind from the sea cooling the

day's heat. Walls and buildings of mud and occasionally stone gave way to fields of green spreading as far as I could see. The fields were fairly bare—Grenville had explained to me that we'd arrived at the time of inundation, the Nile in flood. Once the water went down, the farmers would till the fields, which would flourish with rich crops.

At the moment everything was warm and damp, with men lounging together in front of houses or bent almost double in the fields, their long robes tucked around their hips, working on something I couldn't see.

Brewster's scowl told me of his discomfort. He'd never been out of England, and rarely left the environs of London. He'd been to Norfolk with Denis—he'd helped tear apart my home there—and he must have traveled when he'd been a pugilist, but I knew that Brewster was happiest on the streets of London.

"Why don't they were trousers?" he asked, pointing to a group of men in their long plain robes Grenville called *galabiyas*. "Or at least knee breeches. They're like Scotsmen, with skirts that fly up and show off their privates."

"Climate," I answered calmly. "With constant heat, a cotton robe is much cooler than binding clothes like trousers and a coat. In India, men wear similar garments—the heat is even fiercer there. I was once convinced to try the loose clothes of a Punjabi, and found them dashed comfortable."

Brewster grunted a laugh. "Did you crown your head with a turban?"

"I did. Kept the sun off my face wonderfully. Don't worry, Brewster, I won't command you to go native."

"Huh. A right fool I'd look. But maybe I'll find some harem dress for my Em. Wouldn't she laugh?"

"She might wonder what lady of a harem gave them to you," I said with an attempt at humor. "I'd have a care."

"My Em knows I'm her man," Brewster answered easily. "You are the one with the reputation for the ladies, Captain."

I didn't rebuke him, because it was only the truth. I was a man happiest in the company of the fairer sex.

The baggage carts, pulled by donkeys, caught up to us as we strolled along, Grenville tramping next to them with Matthias and Bartholomew.

I was tired enough to perch on the back of a cart, my legs dangling down, by the time we reached Alexandria itself.

The original walls of Alexandria were gone, and even the walls of the old Arab city from the middle ages were crumbling away. The bulk of the houses were on the isthmus, but the quarter where foreigners stayed was near the old walls.

My interest overcame fatigue, and I was out of the cart again. Even with my halting gait, my impatience and eagerness pushed me to the front of the group, moving ahead of even our guide.

So it was that I was the first to round the corner where a Turkish soldier was about to murder a young woman.

He had a sword in his hand, raised at a woman swathed in so much clothing it was difficult to discern where draperies left off and she began. The eyes over her colorful veil, however, were wide with confusion and terror.

The young lady was surrounded by other women,

who were so many plump lumps of cloth. The women wailed and cried, but the soldier ignored them as he swung his sword straight at the younger girl.

His blade was stopped with a clang as it met the sword from my walking stick.

The man swung to me in fury, and I found myself face-to-face with the full strength and rage of a battle-hardened Turkish soldier.

Chapter Three

The soldier must have been twenty years younger than I was, agile and swift. He had no qualms about trying to drive his sword into a foreigner, and proceeded to fight me with a hard arm.

I heard Brewster pounding up behind me, followed by Bartholomew and Matthias, Grenville's voice beyond them. Our Egyptian guide who'd led us from Aboukir began a stream of distressed words, and the women continued to cry out, but the rest of the street had grown suddenly deserted.

My opponent was a very good fighter. He knew exactly how to feint and swing, then parry, elude, and attack. If we'd been fencing as equals, I might enjoy the bout.

As it was, I could only fight for my life, my anger propelling me on. But with my injured knee, which this young man gave me no compensation for, I knew I'd lose.

Brewster had no interest in the elegance of swordplay. He placed himself behind the solider and swung his fist at the man's head.

The soldier whirled with fierce precision, dodging the blow, intent on slicing into Brewster. I smacked the soldier with the flat of my blade, and Brewster balled up his giant fist, this time hitting the man full in the face.

The soldier stumbled, blood streaming from his nose, but he regained his feet with quick ease. Brewster now had a fat knife in his hand, a hard look on his granite face.

The soldier showed no fear at all. He danced aside, his boots kicking up dust, then he spun again and sprinted with astonishing swiftness down the lane. At the end of it, he scrambled up a wall and disappeared among the low rooftops.

It hadn't been only Brewster's blows or the threat of his knife that had driven the soldier away. A gate behind the young woman had opened and men now swarmed out of it, both retainers with swords and also servants. These last began to shout and exclaim along with our guide so that there was a constant riot of noise.

Other men were emerging from the houses around us to see what was happening. With our donkeys, carts, and a few goats and dogs who'd decided to investigate, we were jammed in tight.

The women had disappeared. As soon as the gate had opened, the young lady had been hustled inside by her attendants, and now only men surrounded our party, none of them looking very pleased.

A tall man with a dark, lined face, a neatly trimmed white beard, colorful silk clothing, and a light yellow turban pointed at me and said in French, "You. Come inside."

"No, no," I answered, and then continued in

French, "We are on our way to our lodgings after a long journey."

The man glared stubbornly at me. "Now. Come."

Our guide burst into speech. The tall man turned his head with slow dignity and listened to him without changing expression, then he returned his gaze to me. His eyes were beautifully round and liquid dark, holding the wisdom and weight of age.

"You are English," he said in that language. "My master says you must come inside. All of you." He swept his hand to include Grenville and our entourage, then he turned and stalked through the gate without looking to see whether we followed.

"We'd better," Grenville said. "Refusing hospitality is extremely rude and might cause us much difficulty later."

My curiosity about this man's master and also what was inside one of these houses that turned only blank walls to the street, made up my mind for me. I sheathed my sword and stepped under the gate's very low lintel, Brewster nearly treading on my heels.

We walked through a narrow passage that was cool after the sunshine and emerged into a courtyard. A tiled fountain thronged with vines of brilliant-colored flowers played quietly in the courtyard's exact center. Walls lifted to three stories around us, scrolled ironwork framing windows covered by the climbing vines. The vibrancy of the pink, gold, and scarlet exotic flowers was such a contrast to the house's plain facade that I halted a moment in pleasure.

The tall man we followed strode unceasingly through the courtyard, ignoring its beauty, and ducked through another low doorway to a cool, dim, and tiled hall. Through another open door, I saw a staircase, also covered in bright tiles, curve upward out of sight.

The man led us through the hall to a wider room whose ceiling rose two floors, the windows on the upper level letting in light through slatted shutters. Red, blue, and yellow tiles covered the walls, polished and smooth, painted with flowers and geometric designs.

Carpets of exquisite patterns covered the floor, each overlapping another so the bare spaces were concealed. Low tables had been placed here and there, but I saw no other furniture.

A man came forward from another passageway. He was tall like the man who led us, but his face was younger, rounder, his nose hooked. His hair was black and unruly, his dark eyes wide, his arms outstretched.

"Welcome, welcome," he said in English. "I thank you with all my heart for saving the life of my daughter."

The man came at me, but just before I was certain he'd embrace me, he stopped himself and thrust out his right hand, offering a very English handshake.

When I took the hand, he closed both of his over mine, holding me firmly. "You are a good man," he effused. "I care not what others say about the foreigners. You have proved your worth."

He at last released me but still looked as though he wanted to embrace me. Then he heaved a sigh and turned away, as though reminding himself that Englishmen were embarrassed by such things. "Come. Sit. Karem will bring refreshment."

He led us at a quick and springing pace to an alcove in the far corner, the arch that led to it covered with tile. A window here looked out into yet another tiny courtyard, this one walled around, with another fountain and more glorious flowers in its center. The combination of Mediterranean warmth and cooling breezes helped bring the hidden garden to life.

Our host waved us to cushions strewn around the table. His wide gesture included us all, not leaving out Bartholomew, Matthias, and Brewster, though I noted that the Egyptians in our party, the guide and the men who bore our luggage, hadn't been invited inside.

Matthias and Bartholomew made sure Grenville and I were comfortable before sitting on cushions slightly behind us. Brewster took no cushion at all, only sat down on the floor with his back to a wall, keeping an eye on the rest of the room.

The tall man, Karem, returned with a tray bearing silver cups, bowls, and a tall, narrow coffeepot. The coffeepot was exquisitely made, the silver etched into curlicue patterns, the arc of the spout curved like the soldier's scimitar. The bowls on the tray contained bright apricots and darker dates, and one bowl was filled with almonds.

Karem laid the tray on the table and our host poured thick, aromatic coffee into the tiny cups himself.

Grenville, familiar with Turkish coffee, sipped his with practice, while I raised my cup and delicately took a first taste.

A full, dark flavor flowed into my mouth. The coffee was intense, stronger than any I'd ever drunk, but also complex and many layered. I had heard that the devout Mohammedans drank no wine or other spirits, but I realized now that they had no need, with this wonderful coffee to imbibe.

"Excellent," I said. "As fine a brew as I've ever tasted."

Our host looked pleased, but a flush came over Karem's face and he bowed, ducking his head as though embarrassed. I realized he must have made the coffee, and I nodded at him. He'd spoken to us first in French, so I repeated my compliment in that language.

Karem bowed again, his austerity vanishing. The host said something to him in a soft voice, and Karem bowed to us one more time, then straightened and glided from the table, his dignity intact.

Karem did not go far, however, only moved to another alcove and turned to watch us. I could understand—he did not want to leave his master alone with strangers.

"My name is Haluk Kemal Keser," our host said, bowing to us, though he remained seated. "I say again how grateful I am that you have saved my daughter."

Tears stood in his dark eyes. Haluk did not look old enough to have a daughter who was already a young lady, but Turks often married in their teens and could have a large family by the time they were in their twenties. There was no sign of his family in this empty room, but I knew that Turkish women were kept hidden away in their own quarters.

I'd also heard that harems often had screens through which the ladies observed the outside world and other rooms in the house while remaining obscured from prying eyes. They could be watching us at this very moment, from any of the windows that looked into this room.

I stopped myself from glancing about for them and simply introduced myself, Grenville, and our men.

"I know who you are," Haluk said, waving his hands. "I have heard all about Mr. Grenville from England, and how he travels to see us. Gossip runs quickly in Alexandria, my friends. We hear how he is coming and bringing a dear friend. That is yourself, Captain? You are a soldier?" he asked hesitantly, as though he'd had enough of soldiers.

I shook my head. "Retired," I assured him. "Seeing the world. I must ask why on earth that fellow tried to attack your daughter? Was he a madman?"

Haluk's face fell. "He is the friend of a man called Ibrahim who wanted to marry my daughter. I turned down his suit. Ibrahim is a soldier of a lower order, a man with little honor. He saw my daughter one day, and nothing was for it but that he marry her. I said *no* in the strongest possible terms. My dove had no use for him either—she was very grateful to me for sending him away. As was her mother." Haluk made a face, and I thought perhaps his wife had as many strident opinions as my own.

"This angered Ibrahim, I wager," Grenville said.

"Indeed." Haluk sighed. "These young men in the army are far from home, and when there are no battles to fight, they roam the town, looking for trouble. I wish the pasha would send them off somewhere soon."

"Yes, indeed." I gave him a nod. "I always found it difficult to keep the men under my command quiet when we had no immediate campaign."

Grenville raised his brows, as though he thought my statement unlikely, but it was true. A bored soldier found all sorts of trouble, especially in a country not his own. I did, in the end, have a well-disciplined troop, but only after they discovered that their captain was not above settling a problem with his own fists.

"I will have Ibrahim's friend reported, of course," Haluk went on. "Though it will do little good if the army has need of him." His face softened. "I do thank you, gentlemen, with all my heart. A man is not supposed to be sentimental about his women, but my family is dear to me."

As mine was to me. In this, though we came from very different worlds, Haluk and I had a common understanding.

"Let us banish unhappy thoughts and partake," Haluk said, reaching for the bowls. "Please."

There was no cutlery save a lone silver knife on the table. Grenville reached forward with his right hand and scooped up apricots and almonds, plopping them into his mouth with obvious pleasure.

I followed his example, though Matthias and Bartholomew only drank coffee and did not eat. Brewster watched me closely from his place by the wall as if expecting me to fall dead of poison any moment.

The fruit was sweet and ripe, juices bursting into my mouth. Though I had eaten such exotic foods as these on occasion in London, they were expensive and did not have the bright taste I experienced now.

We spoke a while longer. Haluk smiled when Grenville and I told him how eager we were to see the sights Egypt had to offer, even if the ancient monuments of Alexandria were no more.

"A disappointment our city must be to you, Captain," he said. "It is nothing like the ancients report. Nature and wars have destroyed the glorious city of the Greeks over the centuries. But you must be careful of the charlatans who will pretend to show you antiquities. The Copts will take you to see the wrong things, so that they can help the French carry away Egypt a piece at a time behind your back. The fellahin, on the other hand, will sell you trash at an exorbitant price, swearing the bones of a mouse is from a finger of a king. The Europeans are eager to amass things for their museums and I am afraid are easily fooled."

"Is there no museum here?" I asked. "For the past of ancient Egypt in Egypt?"

"No, no." Again the wave of a hand. "The Egyptians, they do not care for it, only for what money it brings, and we Turks care even less. I am interested in what is under the sand for my own curiosity, but my master, the pasha, he wants to give it all to Mr. Salt and Monsieur Drovetti, even if they battle over it. He seeks to gain favor with the English and Europeans. They will bring guns and other modern things, you see."

Haluk spoke with skepticism that interested me. "You do not agree?" I asked. "That Egypt should not have the benefit of new things?"

"I agree with my master in his ideas." Haluk darted his gaze past us as though fearing someone listened and would report to the pasha. "But I am not certain it can be done. The Egyptians, they are slow to change. Their methods of farming, irrigation, governing—everything—have been the same for thousands of years. The wheel they use to channel water to irrigate their fields was designed by Archimedes himself. These people will not alter their ways because one man wants them to join the new world."

"And why are you here?" I asked. "In this corner

of Egypt? To help persuade the natives to try new ways?"

Haluk flashed us a sudden smile, white teeth in his dark face. "No, indeed, Captain. I am being punished for my sins. My home on the shores of the sea near Smyrna, my friends, I assure you is lavish. This is nothing, a pit that I am ashamed to show you. But I am grateful you have accepted my humble hospitality."

The remainder of the visit was taken up with us assuring Haluk that his home was lovely, and Haluk denying it with every breath.

At long last, we departed, Brewster rubbing his back as he rose from the floor. It was late, the street a blanket of darkness as Karem led us out through the courtyard and the house's front gate.

Our donkeys, men, and baggage had disappeared, though Karem assured us that they had gone to our lodgings. A group of Haluk's retainers with torches escorted us through the quiet streets, looking about cautiously, as did Brewster, but no one troubled us.

We arrived at our lodgings, a narrow house in the foreigner's quarter of the city, without incident. We were the only people in the lane at the moment, all shutters closed, no noise from the houses around us.

Karem bade us good night at our front door, then barked an order at his underlings, who turned and headed into the darkness. Karem bowed with dignity, renewed his good night in French—he seemed more comfortable with that language—and Grenville led us inside.

The house Grenville had let was laid out much like Haluk's but on a smaller scale. Square rooms surrounded a courtyard, and a rickety staircase inside led to more rooms above.

Every one of the rooms I looked into was empty, not a stick of furniture in sight. All the baggage had been left in the largest room on the ground floor, which Bartholomew and Matthias immediately began to unpack.

Grenville leaned against the doorframe and sent me an amused smile. "And you wondered why I brought my own house with me."

I lifted my hands. "I acknowledge that you know more about travels in the Near East than I do. I believe I understand why the pasha wishes to modernize—it is very primitive, isn't it?"

Grenville watched Bartholomew and Matthias work, occasionally lifting something himself and directing where he wanted it to go. Even Brewster, who did not consider himself a servant, unbent to help out with the heavier things, though I suspected this was because he reasoned that the sooner we were settled, the more quickly he could take to his bed.

"The governor—the pasha—is an interesting man," Grenville told me as we sorted through things. "He has laid plans for a canal to cut through from the Nile to the city, so Alexandria can once more become part of the river, as it was in ancient times. He wishes Alexandria to return to its former magnificence. He'll expect us to visit him when we reach Cairo. He's amassing as much power as he possibly can, and he wants to know what every Englishman is doing in his country. I imagine sooner or later he'll make his move to control Egypt completely, independent of the Ottomans."

"But he's a Turk himself, isn't he?" I asked as I set a folding chair near a table Matthias and Bartholomew had assembled.

"Only geographically," Grenville said. "He's Albanian, more familiar with the worlds of Greece and Macedonia than of the more Eastern cities. He was a soldier but quickly worked his way up through the ranks and more or less jostled himself into position to run Egypt for the sultan. Probably not difficult—I don't think anyone else truly wanted the job. But the pasha sees Egypt's potential, on the edge of the empire as it is. He is a powerful man with a powerful personality. Tread lightly around him, Lacey."

Grenville gave me a meaningful look.

I doubted the man would have any interest in me, but I promised to be careful if I ever had an audience with the pasha. I'd likely kick my heels in some antechamber while Grenville, the wealthy and well-connected Englishman, and the pasha visited.

Matthias and Bartholomew at last finished setting up the chambers we'd need, and we retired for the night.

"Captain," Brewster cornered me at the foot of the staircase before I ascended. He said no more, only drew a folded paper from a pocket inside his coat and handed it to me.

Denis's letter. I took it, uncertain whether thanks were in order, but Brewster only gave me a nod and disappeared into his downstairs bedchamber. I clutched the neatly folded paper as I trudged up the stairs.

My bedchamber was a tiny room above the courtyard, lit by one tallow candle Bartholomew had left. Bartholomew had also laid out my nightshirt and dressing gown across the low, folding bed.

The room's walls had once held tiles as beautiful as those in Haluk's home, but years of neglect had ensured that many had broken off or been badly chipped. The window had no glass, only wooden shutters, but I didn't mind in so mild a climate.

By the light of the dim candle, I undressed, got myself into bed, broke the seal on the letter, and began to read what Denis wanted me to do.

Chapter Four

I wish you to locate a book, Denis wrote, *or rather, a papyrus, which once resided in the library of Alexandria. It is a treatise on astronomy by Aristarchus, which postulated that planets travel around the sun a thousand and more years before Nicolas Copernicus dared suggest it. The book was observed by Archimedes and other mathematicians during the Ptolemaic reign but was presumed lost when the library was destroyed.*

However, information surfaced in the seventeenth century that claimed the book had been carried away by a Spartan soldier several hundred years before the library was in any danger. The ancient accounts found spoke of this soldier who told another he'd hidden books where they would be 'safe from the ignorant,' deep in the earth.

It is now rumored that one of the French savants who accompanied Napoleon to Egypt found the book. However, rather than hand it over when the British defeated Napoleon on the Nile, he hid it. The arguments over the stone found in Rosetta overshadowed any questions about an old Greek papyrus, and so it was not noticed. That

Frenchman has since died, and no one knows what he did with his book.

The entire tale might be a legend. However, Napoleon took only the most learned men with him on his expedition, and I believe the French scholar knew what it was he'd found.

I would like you to use your usual zeal to discover this book for me. Find out if any speak of it or have found anything like it. If they have, purchase it, steal it — whatever you must do — and bring it to me. You will be well compensated.

If you can discover nothing of its existence, then that knowledge is valuable as well. I will conclude that the book is legend and be finished with my search. I wish you luck.

James Denis

That was all. I turned the paper over but there were no further instructions, no hints about a place to start.

"Is he mad?" I said out loud. "What the devil does he think I can do?"

Footsteps sounded on the landing before the door of my bedchamber swung open. Grenville stood on the doorstep in a velvet dressing gown, a candlestick in his hand.

"What is it, Lacey? I heard you cry out."

I thrust the paper at him from where I sat in my bed. "Mr. Denis instructs me to hunt for a needle in a haystack, when both needle and haystack might no longer exist. He is having a joke on me."

Grenville's dark eyes glittered as he quickly read the letter. "Ah, the lost book of Aristarchus. I have heard of it." He handed the paper back to me. "If you find it, 'twill indeed be a magnificent discovery. And very valuable."

"Why should he suppose *I* can find it?" I asked in irritation. "A Spartan soldier, information from the sixteen hundreds, one of Napoleon's savants—he is laughing at me." I tossed the paper to my coverlet.

Grenville regarded me thoughtfully. "I believe he concludes that if anyone can find this lost treatise, it will be you. A high compliment to your abilities."

I gave him an irritated look. "So I am to run through Alexandria, perhaps up and down the Nile, asking if any of the men digging for the past have stumbled across a lost treatise on astronomy? I will be a laughingstock."

"Actually, the story has been told in literary circles since Napoleon fled Egypt," Grenville said, far too calmly. "Others have searched for the book—I imagine we'll find men here who have made the attempt. Some might be generous and share their insights. There are gentlemen who are obsessed with finding such treasures, and funnily enough, they are often successful. They carry on when the rest of us fall by the wayside."

"You can certainly believe Mr. Denis has an obsession," I said sourly. "For me running impossible errands for him."

"I believe Mr. Denis cares only for the value of the book, both historic and otherwise," Grenville pointed out. "He knows you have a nose for puzzles, and that I share your interest. He has sent this task to two gentlemen who have far more curiosity than is good for them."

I had to agree that Denis read us well. "I should toss his letter onto the fire and refuse."

"We'd have to start a blaze for that, and it's a bit warm," Grenville said. "Fortunately a large part of the task will involve something at which I excel—

talking to people."

I glanced at him in surprise. "You would help me look for it?"

"I admit, I am intrigued. I'd like to hear what the local men have to say about it. The fellahin, I mean, who know amazing tales. Haluk is a fine enough gentleman, but he's a Turk through and through—I wager he does not know much about the country he lives in, barring his readings about ancient Alexandria. He did not say so, but I imagine the poor fellow is in exile."

I had come to the same conclusion. He'd spoken of his house in Smyrna far too longingly.

"There are worse places to be exiled," I said.

"True," Grenville conceded. "But home is the sweetest place of all. Good night, Lacey."

Grenville shut the door, and I lifted the letter again.

Damn and blast Denis. I hated that he read me so accurately that he knew a foolish quest for legends and lost treasure would suit me. He also knew that I'd consider a book from the famous library in Alexandria worth finding—I'd not be disappointed he wasn't searching for gold.

I put out my candle but my exhaustion had fled. I lay awake picturing myself triumphantly laying my hands on this ancient papyrus and the satisfaction that would bring. Whether or not I'd hand it over to Denis was a different matter entirely.

***

I woke to sunlight streaming through my shutters and a high-pitched, wailing voice singing words I did not understand. I scrambled out of bed, my feet landing on the dusty floor, and made my way to the window.

Below in the courtyard, the Mohammedans among our servants had laid out carpets and were now kneeling upon them and bowing low with such gracefulness that I could only watch in admiration. The goats that shared the courtyard with us milled about the praying men, seemingly unbothered.

I made note of the sight in my travel journal for Gabriella and also wrote of our curious little house here, filled with people but no furniture.

Bartholomew interrupted me to bring breakfast on a tray. We'd arrived in Egypt shortly after the month of Ramadan—of fasting—ended, Grenville had told me, so we needn't worry. There would be food aplenty.

"Not what we're used to," Bartholomew said apologetically, setting the tray on my bunk. "They don't much understand an Englishman's breakfast, these servants. And in the middle of preparing it, there's a man yelling, and they rush away to start bobbing on their carpets." He shook his head, nonplussed.

"The *muezzin*," I told him, turning to the repast. "They call from the mosques several times a day, and the men bend to prayer. You must grow used to it while we're in Turkish country."

"At any rate, they eat no pork," Bartholomew said. "Can you credit it? It's mutton all the time here, and goat."

For my breakfast I had been provided fruit—the ubiquitous dates and apricots—and a thick creamy substance that Bartholomew said came from goats' milk. I ate it heartily, though I wished for some meat to go with it, and washed it down with rather weak tea.

Bartholomew helped me dress, and I headed out

for the first day of my Egyptian adventure.

I met Brewster in the large downstairs room that opened to the fresh air of the courtyard. The men had finished their prayers, rolled up the rugs, and retreated inside to shout at each other in the tiny kitchen.

"They won't give us any ham or meat," Brewster said, disgruntled. "To keep us weak, no doubt."

"Nonsense," I said. "It was only breakfast. I knew fellows in India who ate no flesh at all, for any reason, and yet they were quite robust."

Brewster gave me a level stare. "Begging your pardon, Captain, but I'm already getting a bit weary of your travelers' tales."

I took no offense. "I know I go on a bit when I'm interested. After this journey, you'll have travelers' tales of your own, Brewster."

"If I'm still alive," Brewster said darkly. "Now I suppose you'll scamper all over town looking for that papyrus his nibs wants."

I turned sharply from my contemplation of the courtyard. "He told you?"

Brewster shook his head, no remorse in his eyes. "I read the letter. Wanted to know what his nibs was sending me into."

"The letter was sealed," I pointed out, rather sternly.

"I know it were. I warmed the seal, peeled it from the paper, then warmed it again and stuck it down when I were finished."

Brewster spoke easily, a man explaining his craft, unworried that he'd read another man's private correspondence.

I gave up. "Ah, well, I will no doubt need your help. You understand, then, what I am to look for?"

"Not as such. But Mr. Denis is mad for old books, inn't he? Though he's never been after one as old as this."

"I hardly hope to find it," I said. "But Grenville and I will try."

"Huh. I'll have to follow you down into tombs and things in case this Frenchie buried it in one, will I?"

"Possibly," I said without a qualm. "I planned to go into them, in any case."

Grenville joined us then, garbed in an ensemble practical for the climate. The cloth of his frock coat and trousers was a butternut color, his cravat loosely tied rather than sporting a complicated knot. His valet had not accompanied us—Grenville was using Matthias to perform valet duties, the young man conscious of that rise in his station.

Grenville's face was flushed with eagerness, his bearing more animated than I'd seen in a long while. Perhaps he truly had been stagnating in London, as he'd claimed, and would now come out of himself.

"Shall we explore?" Grenville asked, trying to sound casual. "We've been given leave to wander about the city as we like, as long as we stay away from the mosques, any official buildings where we are not invited, and any ladies, of course."

"Suits me," Brewster said, and I agreed.

Matthias and Bartholomew stayed behind, expressing a wish to put the house to rights, while Grenville, Brewster, and I stepped out into sunshine.

Immediately we were assailed by the myriad sights, sounds, and scents of the busy lanes outside our lodgings. Men swarmed everywhere, calling out to each other, talking, laughing, shouting, arguing. Goats and dogs wandered where they pleased, and donkeys waited patiently while men loaded or unloaded long baskets hanging from the donkeys' backs.

As we left the narrow streets that hugged the remains of the old Arab walls, the wind from the sea brushed aside the smells of cooking food, the marshes beyond the town, and animal and human waste. The sun warmed us, palm trees in the distance fluttered their long fronds, and for the first time in a long while, I felt thawed.

I'd spent many years in the heat of India and then in Spain, and had grown used to warmth. The last four years in London had chilled my bones. Here I could loosen and move—I longed to shed my coat and roll up my sleeves as I'd often done in hotter climates.

However, I was now a proper Englishman, a gentleman's son married to an earl's daughter. I should be as uncomfortable as possible to show the natives here how superior I was.

I laughed out loud at my own thoughts, causing Grenville, Brewster, and the Egyptian men on the street to stare at me.

"If you wish to see where the library was, it is this way," Grenville said, pointing with his walking stick. He said nothing about my strange outburst, but then, he'd grown used to my eccentricities.

We turned our steps in that direction, moving on foot through the old city. Ancient Alexandria had been laid out in a grid, with wide avenues running east and west, north and south, but I found nothing of that in the maze of lanes and crumbling houses we passed through on our way to the harbor. Long ago, the streets had been paved with marble, it was said, so bright that one had to shade one's eyes while moving down the avenues in the light of day.

It had all gone. The glory that had been Alexandria, the city of learning, had vanished under time, destruction, war, earthquakes, and encroaching mud. Alexandria was asleep, waiting to be woken again. The pasha would have a long task ahead of him, I thought.

In this frame of mind, I trundled onward toward the harbor, which was not far from our lodgings. At the curve of shore before the road turned to the isthmus that stretched to Pharos and the fortress, we came to a few tumbledown buildings around an open space. Two giant, square columns of stone lay half-buried in sand, forlorn and forgotten, of interest only to early-rising tourists like ourselves.

The columns were obelisks, though their shape was difficult to distinguish. I brushed a bit of sand from one to see that the fascinating writing called hieroglyphs had been cut right into the stone.

Many of the symbols I uncovered were of birds — from the lofty falcon to a waddling duck, but I saw other things as well — a beetle, a serpent, a seated man, these signs repeated again and again. In a few places, groups of symbols had been set into squares with rounded corners.

I longed to be able to read the hieroglyphs, but even the most intelligent linguists of England and France had not yet broken the code of the ancient Egyptians, the stone from Rosetta notwithstanding. I wondered what tales we'd learn when and if they finally did.

"Bloody interesting, aren't they?" came a gravelly voice.

Straightening up, I beheld the lined and tanned face of Sergeant Porter looking over the stone at me.

His wife, her face shaded by a wide-brimmed hat, stood just behind him.

"Indeed," I said. "I believe these are the obelisks that were brought here from a temple on the Nile by Cleopatra to decorate her monument to Marc Antony."

Porter chuckled. "So you have done your reading. Be lovely things to hand to the museum in London, wouldn't they? But moving them …" He shook his head. "That's the bugger. I'll show you things a bit easier to shift, Captain."

"We're looking for the library at the moment," I said.

"Nothing left of that," Porter said easily. "Less even than here. But we'll walk with you, if you'll have us."

Grenville and I agreed, and we strolled on.

The other foreigners who were up to see the sights nodded cordially at us but didn't attempt conversation. Most of the visitors were French, with a smattering of Englishmen as well as German- and Italian-speaking gentlemen. They wandered about, either greatly interested in the dusty bits of nothing around us, or looking already weary of it.

There were only a few ladies among the visitors. A stout, hardy woman who reminded me a bit of Lady Aline Carrington held a small parasol determinedly over her head as she strode along, a younger woman trailing her, possibly a daughter, niece, or companion.

Another woman entered the scene. She rode a donkey, was surrounded by Egyptian servants, and followed by a tall man with dark hair who looked more Spanish than anything else. She was, I would judge, not much younger than Grenville, with hair of jet black under her hat. Her face was very pale, her eyes a light blue.

"Good Lord." Grenville's eyes widened in alarm, then he swung abruptly around so that his back was to her. "Let us walk swiftly, Lacey, there's a good fellow. Perhaps she will not see us."

I had no time to quiz Grenville about the identity of the woman, because he quickened his pace, moving rapidly around the corner and back into the maze of streets.

Not far from where the obelisks lay, Grenville halted again. "Here," he said, indicating a patch of nothing. "According to ancient maps and legend, this spot once contained the greatest library ever known."

I contemplated the rather small space of ordinary rock and rubble with some disquiet.

Every book in the ancient world had been gathered for the great library at Alexandria, a house of learning. Here, Euclid had written his famous *Elements of Geometry,* which had been drilled into me as a boy in school, and with which men of science like Dr. Newton and Herr Kepler had understood the motions of the planets. This was where the Old Testament had been translated from Hebrew to Greek, a special commission by the Ptolemaic pharaoh for his library. The mathematician Eratosthenes had determined from Alexandria that the earth was round, and he'd calculated its exact circumference well before men had sailed the oceans to prove him correct.

Here on this crumbling space of land, vast knowledge had once rested.

"Makes one a bit humble," Grenville said in a quiet voice. "So much destroyed for so little purpose."

"Indeed," was all I could answer.

Grenville and I fell silent as we contemplated the uneven patch of earth, covered by fallen brick from a much later time. Behind us, toward the harbor, lay the stretch of the new town, built on the land that had begun as a manmade causeway. The sea had receded, and the world had as well.

Even the Porters were quiet, but not, I thought, from respect. They seemed impatient to be gone.

"Why do you not dig here?" I asked Sergeant Porter. "If you could unearth the great library of Alexandria, you would be lauded indeed."

Porter shook his head, large nose wrinkling. "Nothing left of it, and I'm not after Greek antiquities, begging your pardon, Captain. South of here, out in the desert are tombs of bulls. The Egyptians worshiped the beasts back in ancient times, and when the poor bull died of old age, they carried him off to a tomb and encased him in gold and jewels."

"'Struth," Brewster said behind me. "Waste of a good bit of beef."

Mrs. Porter chuckled. "Right you are, Mr. Brewster. But their oddities will be our gain when we find them."

"The Alexandrians didn't leave us as much to find as did the ancient Egyptians," Porter went on. "There are wonders buried in the sand." He swept his arm southward, as though we could see past the tumbledown houses to the deserts beyond.

"Somefink buried here too," Brewster said. He'd moved off to the edge of the clearing and nudged dirt with his toe.

Filled with visions of the ancient library and wanting any scrap of knowledge I might gain about the book, I moved to Brewster quickly. My knee gave a twinge, chiding me for hastening over uneven ground.

Brewster squatted down and reached out a broad, gloved hand to pull back a dirt-encrusted cloth. He straightened up on a sudden, taking a few steps back and thrust out his arm to stop me.

"'S nothing, Captain. None of our business."

I looked past him at what he'd found. Brewster had pulled back a fold of black cloth to reveal a man's hand. Gray with death, the broad fingers were curled as though the unfortunate man had been trying to dig his way out.

I reached with my walking stick to uncover more only to be stopped by Brewster's heavy grip on my arm. "None of our business, guv," he repeated firmly. "Nothing we want to know about."

I shook him off. The Porters and Grenville had joined us by then. Grenville strode forward before Brewster could stop him, thrust his walking stick beneath the cloth, and tugged it back.

The hand was attached to an arm, the arm attached to the torso of a Turkish soldier. He was young, black-haired, and very dead, half his face bashed in and dark with blood.

Chapter Five

My first thought was that the soldier was the young man who'd attacked Haluk's daughter last evening. A second glance told me it was not so. This soldier was of a different build, his face heavier, his jaw more square.

"Good Lord," Grenville said. He drew out a handkerchief and pressed it to his nose. The odor of the body was not pleasant, the warmth of the morning increasing the smell. "What shall we do?"

"Cover it up and walk away," Brewster rumbled. "Let someone else find it."

"Your friend is correct," Porter said. "We don't need the Turks breathing down our necks."

"And leave the poor fellow here?" Grenville asked. "Wouldn't be decent." He had pity in his eyes, though he kept the handkerchief at his nose.

"Or Christian," Mrs. Porter added. She craned forward to study the dead man in fascination—no fainting or hysterics for Mrs. Porter.

"But he ain't Christian, is he?" Brewster said. "He's Mohammedan. Let them take care of their own."

His hand on my arm, Brewster tried to steer me off. He was as strong as one of the bulls the ancients had worshiped, and with my weak knee, he was able to propel me a few paces.

As soon as I recovered my balance, however, I brought up my walking stick and placed it against his side. "Do let go, Brewster," I said, looking him in the eye.

He scowled at me. I had not touched him on the side where he'd been shot—that would have been unsporting. But I firmed the pressure, letting him know I would fight free of him if I had to.

I knew that all Brewster had to do was ball up his giant fist and hit me, and I'd go down. I saw that thought flicker through his eyes and a muscle move in his jaw.

Brewster kept his hand at rest, though I saw his fingers curl. "I'm to bring you home unhurt," he said evenly. "Tangling with the Ottomans is not what his nibs wants you to do."

"I do not intend to tangle with them, only to report the dead soldier," I said. "I promise, the authorities can do as they like after that."

Brewster eyed me with suspicion. I was apt to investigate crimes on my own, no matter who was in charge, even when I was told not to.

The debate was settled for us. There was a clatter of hooves, and a female voice rang out. "Ah, there you are, Grenville. I thought I spied you. I knew you'd be in Alexandria soon. Good heavens, what have we here?"

"Lady Mary," Grenville said, trying to disguise

the note of weariness in his voice. "May I present my friend Captain Gabriel Lacey? Lacey, allow me to introduce you to the dowager Marchioness of Carmarthen. Lady Mary and I are old acquaintances and fellow travelers."

I had heard of the dowager Marchioness of Carmarthen. Her husband's title—now her son's— was Welsh, but Lady Mary was thoroughly English, the daughter of a duke; hence Grenville addressed her with the honorific.

I bowed to her, the rigid politeness that had been drilled into me since boyhood allowing me to do no less. "Lady Mary," I said, as though a dead man did not lie five feet away.

"Good Lord, Grenville." Lady Mary remained on her donkey, the man she traveled with holding a parasol over her. "Fancy introducing me to your chums across a corpse. It is the sort of thing you *would* do. I am very pleased to make your acquaintance, Captain Lacey. I am always happy to meet a friend of Grenville's, no matter what the circumstance."

Lady Mary was about forty, had a round face, shrewd blue eyes that were highly penetrating, a small mouth, and hair of a midnight shade. In her first youth, she might have been quite beautiful, but her looks were fading with time, and her receding chin had not helped her retain her attractiveness. Her eyes sparkled, however, as though she knew what had happened to her face and defied anyone to speak of it.

"Grenville calls us *old* acquaintances, which is very rude of him," Lady Mary said. "However, I will overlook his impertinence in the joy of seeing him again. Now, Miguel, you must summon the authorities about this dead soldier. Killed fighting one of his own, no doubt."

That would be the simplest explanation. Two Turkish soldiers had fought each other, and fought hard. We had already witnessed how easily they turned to violence.

Lady Mary's strident tones and the gathering crowd had made it unnecessary for Miguel to summon anyone. Men in the uniforms of Turkish soldiers came pouring around the corner, followed by Egyptians in long galabiyas. The soldiers saw the corpse, drew their swords, and pointed their blades at us.

Grenville raised his hands. "We only found the poor man," he said to the Turkish soldier who strode to stand in front of the others. "He's one of your men, I believe."

The lead man, likely their lieutenant, began speaking quickly to us in the Turkish language, which I knew not a word of. Grenville, who knew only a smattering, answered in English.

"I assure you, we had nothing to do with his death." Grenville showed his empty palms. "We are travelers, with no reason to harm him."

"Best keep your gob shut, Mr. Grenville," Brewster said in a low voice. "When you talk to the law, they'll twist anything you say around against you. Don't matter if that law's English, Turkish, or Egyptian."

"What utter nonsense," Lady Mary said. She nudged her donkey forward, turned the full force of her gaze to the lieutenant, and began speaking in rapid, and seemingly perfect, Turkish.

I had no idea what she said, but it was effective. The lieutenant's belligerence died into amazement at this female foreigner who deigned to command him in his own language. Even I admitted some bewilderment at hearing the tongue of the Ottomans spoken with such force and ease by a very English Englishwoman.

The Egyptians behind the soldiers, whom I took for the local patrollers, continued to scowl. I had the feeling that they did not much understand what Lady Mary said either. While Egypt had been part of the Ottoman Empire for centuries, the natives, from the little I'd observed and what Grenville recounted to me, still lived much as their ancient ancestors had and spoke Egyptian Arabic.

The lieutenant snapped orders at his men—one with the bearing of a sergeant turned and repeated the orders to the Egyptian men. The Egyptians began arguing until the sergeant half drew his sword. In disgust, one Egyptian gestured with his fingers at a few of *his* men, who came forward and began to remove sand and rubble from the body.

We foreigners drew together in a knot while the Egyptians worked. One of the Turkish soldiers broke from behind his lieutenant, and I recognized the young man I'd fought yesterday.

He paid no attention to me. He walked with quick steps to the body, his dark eyes widening as the Egyptian men flipped the dead soldier onto his back.

The young soldier let out a wail. A string of rapid and distressed-sounding words poured from his mouth, then he abruptly turned on me and drew his sword.

Tears poured down the young man's cheeks. He waved the tip of the sword and shouted at me, his mouth and tongue moving swiftly. While I couldn't understand his words, I understood the gist—he believed I had killed the man.

Brewster shoved himself directly in front of me and lifted a long, fat knife. "Put that sword away, lad, or I'll be feeding it to you."

The Turkish lieutenant rushed over, snarling at the young soldier and at me. Lady Mary tried to cut into the conversation, voice rising as she attempted to reestablish her authority. The Egyptians ceased their task with the dead man and watched with interest.

The young man then swung away from Brewster and pointed his curved sword at Lady Mary. His rage was evident—that a woman, a foreign one no less, should presume to give orders was clearly anathema. His lieutenant did nothing to stop him, and also began to berate Lady Mary. I inserted myself between them, and Brewster put himself in front of me.

Into this madness strode the tall, turbaned figure of Karem, Haluk's majordomo.

At the sight of him, the Turkish soldiers edged away from the confrontation in the middle of the clearing, staying quietly off to the side. The Egyptians backed from the corpse but looked upon Karem in a respectful manner.

Karem began speaking rapidly with the Turkish lieutenant. The lieutenant listened, his expression darkening, but at last he barked an order and made an abrupt gesture. The soldiers relaxed a little and then turned and made their way back down the street toward the Turkish area of town.

That left the lieutenant and the young soldier, who hadn't moved. The young man continued to weep but in silence, his face wet, his eyes holding anguish. I hadn't forgiven him for his attempt to hurt

Haluk's defenseless daughter, but I began to feel sorry for him. The dead man had obviously been a friend.

The lieutenant spoke sharply to him. The young soldier swung back to glare at me, but he sheathed his sword, uttering a grunt of anger as he did so. With one last enraged look, he pivoted on his heel and stamped out of the clearing.

The lieutenant remained. He snapped another order at the Egyptian men who, taking their time, went back to unearthing the dead soldier.

Karem turned to Grenville. "My most profound apologies," he said in French. "That you should be threatened and spoken to so makes my heart grieve. My master, he sent me to look after you, and I am devastated I did not reach you in time to prevent this calamity."

Grenville listened to his flowery apology with equanimity. "Not at all, my dear man," he answered, also in French. "You are not to blame. Whoever caused this man's death is the culpable party."

Karem did not look convinced, but he bowed to Grenville, and stepped over to the body. His expression, when he looked down at it, became still more mournful.

"He is Ibrahim, the unwanted suitor," he announced. "The one who courted my master's daughter and was turned away."

"Is he?" Ignoring Brewster, who was still trying to herd me away from the scene, I hobbled to where Karem stood over the body.

The man had been young, not quite as young as his friend, but only in his twenties, I thought. He'd been handsome, with dark skin, a well-defined face, and thick lashes around his closed eyes. That handsomeness had been marred by the crushing blow — dried, black blood caked his hair and the back of his neck.

I had heard that the Turkish soldier's turban could deflect a weapon, but this man's turban was nowhere in evidence. He had either lost it somewhere, or it had been taken away after he was dead.

"Poor man." A shadow loomed next to me, the outline of a woman with a parasol firmly over her head. "No doubt the blow killed him."

"Indeed," I said to Lady Mary. "The weapon is not hard to guess. It is all around us."

The ground was strewn with stones and bricks from centuries of ruin. One stone must have blood on it, unless it too had been taken away.

My instinct to shield one of the fairer sex from such a gruesome sight was checked as Lady Mary leaned down and brushed the hair from the man's face.

"So young," she said. "What a tragedy. And yet, these soldiers are so eager to fight, to conquer. They are why the Ottomans prevail. Sad that he met his end in what looks like a petty squabble."

"Not with his young friend," I said with conviction. "He was stunned and devastated to find him."

"Yes, these lads do form great attachments to one another," Lady Mary said. "Probably because all the women are hidden away from them. Everyone needs companionship."

Lady Mary looked me over as though wondering whether *I* needed such a thing. I was beginning to understand why Grenville had tried to avoid her when we saw her earlier.

"Come, come." Karem waved his hands at us,

shooing us away from the body. "We will give him back to the army."

The lieutenant shouted again at the Egyptians, who calmly returned to their task. The dead man was fully cleared of sand and we saw his long legs in full trousers and black boots, and his sword still in its sheath.

"Why didn't he draw it?" I asked, pointing to the sword. "He must not have expected the attack."

"Very good question, Captain," Lady Mary said. "What do you think, Grenville? I have heard of your antics in London, helping the Runners bring murderers to trial."

Grenville flushed deeply, the shade of his hat brim unable to hide his color. "You give me too much credit, Mary. But Captain Lacey has the right of it. This young man was not facing an enemy, or else not someone he thought could best him. Likely didn't know he was in any danger."

"And why was he here at all?" I asked. "Karem, will you ask the lieutenant or captain, or whoever he is, whether this soldier—Ibrahim—went missing, and when? I wonder if this happened last night or earlier."

Karem gazed at me with mournful brown eyes. "It is not the business of Englishmen," he said, switching to English. "The soldiers will take care of their own."

"I know," I said, curbing my impatience. "But I am curious."

"The captain is always curious," Brewster put in disparagingly. "Best answer his question, mate."

Karem sighed and began speaking to the lieutenant, who answered in irritation. They argued for a time in Turkish.

Lady Mary frowned at Brewster. "Your servant is impertinent," she said to me.

Brewster gave her a level stare, which made Lady Mary blink, then he stalked to the body, turning his back on us.

Karem swung away from the lieutenant, who continued to speak loudly after him, gesticulating to make his point.

"Ibrahim was missed this morning when he did not rise with the others," Karem told us. "The other soldier, the one from whom you so well protected Haluk's best-loved daughter, was questioned, but he knew nothing. In fact, Ibrahim was to have been punished for his disobedience when he was found. None of the other soldiers left their quarters all night."

So, for what reason had Ibrahim left his billet to wander about the town? To meet someone? He had not drawn his sword, or been afraid.

For what reason would a man sneak away from his quarters and stand in an empty spot in the dark? A rendezvous of some kind was the first explanation and probably the correct one.

With a woman? If we'd been in London, I'd have suspected that immediately. But the Turks and Egyptians guarded their daughters, sisters, and wives with great fervor. Most weren't allowed outside without a horde of retainers or a male member of the family. The penalty for disobedience was harsh, even death.

Likewise, I could not believe a soldier would be allowed to wander the streets when he was supposed to be in his bunk. The British army would flog a soldier for such a thing—I could not believe that the Turkish army would be more lenient.

"A woman is behind it," Lady Mary said. "Mark my words, Captain. Where there is a young man in trouble, a woman causes it."

She spoke with so much conviction I stared at her. "Have you reason to believe so?" I asked.

Lady Mary eyed me shrewdly. "If you are about to say that the fairer sex is gentle and innocent, I can assure you, we are not. I caused much furor in my youth. There is a woman in this—the young man either fought another over her, or he was lured here with the promise of seeing her. Perhaps someone in her family tricked Ibrahim into meeting him, so that the brother or father could end Ibrahim's unwanted attentions forever."

Her speculation was dramatic, but I felt a qualm. Haluk had been quite contemptuous of young Ibrahim and his presumption of trying to court his daughter. I had trouble imagining the erudite and generous Haluk coming up behind the young man and smacking him over the head, but I had to admit that I barely knew Haluk at all.

I turned back to Karem. He was very tall, broad of chest, strong, a man who could easily knock a man down with a rock. Karem returned my gaze stolidly, showing only sorrow for the incident, not guilt or remorse. His dark eyes were honest, not menacing. But again, I had to acknowledge that I barely knew him.

"The lieutenant wants us gone," Karem told me. "He and his men will find the culprit and turn him over to the magistrates."

Studying the enraged stance of the lieutenant, I hoped he'd find the real culprit, and not simply someone to take the blame.

Even as I had this thought, the lieutenant shouted

down the street where his men had retreated. More shouting came back to us, and then four of the soldiers returned, carrying Ibrahim's friend between them.

The young man protested loudly, and another cuffed him to silence. The lieutenant drew his sword.

"No!" I cried. I ran at the lieutenant as quickly as my injured leg would let me and thrust myself between him and the young soldier. "He did not do it. Leave him be."

I'd moved so abruptly that I'd given no one, not even Brewster, time to stop me. The lieutenant glared at me in outrage, but I stood my ground.

"Tell him, Karem," I ordered. "He is not to touch that young man. He is innocent. I know it."

Chapter Six

Brewster came forward, rumbling with fury. "Leave it, Captain."

I remained solidly in place. "I will not stand by and watch a man be killed for another's convenience," I said hotly. "The lad obviously did not murder his friend. Look at him."

The young soldier was still weeping but at the same time regarded me in stunned amazement. He was not guiltless in trying to harm Haluk's daughter—I had not forgiven him for that—but the lieutenant had no business running him through only so he could report that he'd taken care of the problem.

My voice took on the tone I'd used with reluctant men in my command. "Karem, tell him, *now.*"

Karem was spared the anguish of obeying by Lady Mary. She strode forward, her Spanish lackey hurrying after her, and spoke to the lieutenant in strident tones.

The lieutenant looked as though he'd had enough of Lady Mary. His face was set with fury, and both Lady Mary and I were within easy reach of his deadly sword. I tried to step in front of Lady Mary to shield her from any blow, but she ignored me and halted inches from the lieutenant, her voice as loud and hard as any man's.

The lieutenant scowled at her as she went on, then he snarled something, shoved his sword into its sheath with a snap, and swung away, his boots dislodging curls of sand. He gave a curt order to his men, who released the young soldier but herded him down the lane with them.

The lieutenant glared at me and Lady Mary, then the rest of our party. He snapped something at Karem, then turned and stamped after his men.

"Well," Lady Mary said, looking pleased. "That told *him*."

"What did he say to you, Karem?" I asked the tall man.

Karem heaved another sigh. "That *I* must now explain to the authorities what we have found here. You will go away now, sir. You are foreigners, and might be blamed."

"Blamed for what?" Lady Mary bristled. "Being concerned? But I understand your caution, my good man. We might be detained unnecessarily. I suggest we withdraw to my villa and take a morning repast. Captain? Grenville?"

She glanced uncertainly at the Porters, clearly not certain what to do with them, but Porter gave her a bow. "Thank you all the same, ma'am, but we need to be off to the digging before it's too hot," he said jovially. "Good day to you."

He doffed his cap, and Mrs. Porter curtsied. Lady

Mary gave them both a gracious nod, a lady dismissing her inferiors. Porter offered his arm to his wife, and they strode off together, heading west and south through the streets.

I envied them. I longed to see sandy, ancient Egypt beyond the confines of the town, but politeness dictated that I follow Lady Mary and Grenville to whatever Lady Mary called her "villa."

I disliked also leaving Karem alone with the body. Examining it might give a clue as to who killed him, but Karem remained resolutely in front of the dead man, and finally I let Brewster steer me away.

I looked back before we left the square. Karem stood like a sentinel, his pale turban a beacon in the sunshine. That same sunshine touched the colorful red cloth of the Turkish soldier's uniform, the uncaring wind already brushing sand into his black hair.

***

Lady Mary's villa turned out to be a house a half mile outside the city walls. Built of stone, it had been erected about fifty years ago when a Frenchman decided to make a go of living in Egypt. Obviously he'd given up the endeavor, because the house had started to fall to ruin. Scaffolding now covered one entire side, indicating Lady Mary's determination to restore it.

An avenue lined with date palms led to the house, which was a two-story structure with a colonnaded front veranda. Behind the villa, the land sloped down to a marshy lake, the remnants of the ancient Lake Mareotis.

A canal had once cut from this lake around Alexandria and back to the Nile. The lake, like the canal, had stagnated with silt over nearly fifteen-hundred years, but during a recent battle had been refilled with water from Aboukir Bay when dams had been torn down. Result—a reed-filled lake that was a ghost of its former self.

"The gardens behind will also be restored," Lady Mary explained from her perch on her donkey as we approached the house. She waved her hand at an area beyond the scaffolded side of the villa. "Orange groves, rose bowers, fountains, intimate shaded walks ..." She turned her head to smile at me, and winked.

I smiled politely in return, pretending not to notice the wink.

The architecture of Lady Mary's house was reminiscent of southern France or perhaps the Italian states. Instead of the grand entrance leading straight into the house, as it might in England, the huge front door gave onto a large courtyard surrounded by the four wings of the house.

Lady Mary dismounted from her donkey here, the animal led away by a young Egyptian boy. The Spanish man remained, still holding the parasol.

An Egyptian woman, swathed from head to foot in black, emerged and took Lady Mary's shawl and the parasol that the Spanish man finally folded up. Another Egyptian man in a white galabiya hastened into the courtyard, keen to divest Grenville and me of hats, gloves, and walking sticks. I gave up everything but my walking stick, showing him that I needed it in order to remain upright.

Brewster was very reluctant to let me traipse into a house he didn't know with people he'd never seen before. He folded his arms and stood like a rock in front of the door through which Lady Mary had already vanished.

"It's all right," Grenville tried to reassure him. "Lady Mary is not dangerous—at least, not in the way you are thinking. I give you my word that Captain Lacey will not be harmed. He is married now, and therefore safe."

"Begging your pardon, Mr. Grenville." Brewster didn't move, didn't show any amusement. "But you don't know who's in that house. It's big, and there's workers everywhere. Even her ladyship herself don't know, I'd wager."

"Well, we can't leave yet," Grenville said. "It would be the height of rudeness. Remain within earshot, and if we are in danger, we'll shout like the devil."

Brewster glowered. "I hear one thing wrong, I'm coming in, don't no matter what."

"Sit in the shade at least," I told him. The sun was already warm now that we were away from the sea, and the air was bound to grow much hotter as afternoon approached. "You'll be no good to me swooning from heatstroke."

Brewster said, "Huh," at the word *swooning*, but he moved off to a bench shaded by old rose vines.

"He has the easier task," Grenville muttered as we turned to follow Miguel through the double doors where he waited. "Do not agree to accept accommodations for the night, Lacey, or we'll never be shot of her."

He spoke as though from bitter experience, his look even more pained as we ducked through the doorway into the darkness of the house.

I doubted Lady Mary would extend an offer for us to spend the night once I had a look inside. The place was a wreck.

The massive drawing room we stepped into had

once been beautiful, with painted columns, friezes, and Greek-style pediments, but now sported a gaping hole high in one wall, which let in the only light. The long, graceful windows overlooking the non-existent garden had been boarded up.

A marble staircase rose at one end of the drawing room, but it went nowhere, the top of it having crumbled and fallen away. I imagined the local people had mined it for stones, and I wondered if the villa's second floor were accessible at all.

"Not a palace, no," Lady Mary chortled as she caught my expression. "Not yet, anyway. It is not the most pleasant house in which to stay at present, but give it time. Now, Miguel, we shall have tea."

Miguel, who had not said a word so far, nodded at her and glided off into the deeper regions of the house.

"Such a dear boy," Lady Mary said as we seated ourselves on folding chairs much like those Grenville had brought from London. "I met him while traveling in Spain. He was a teacher of some kind and had just lost his wife, poor thing. He was at a loose end, so I suggested we travel together. He speaks many languages and is entertaining company. It's never good for a woman to travel alone—she needs a dragoman to help her over the rough patches. I know dragomen are usually Turks or Egyptians, but it is a term we could agree upon."

"I understand," Grenville said, sliding into his smooth, wealthy dandy persona. "I was surprised to see you here at all, Mary. I thought after the Greek isles you were giving up travel."

Lady Mary pressed her hand to her heart and turned to me. "Yes, I was most distraught. I nearly *died*, Captain Lacey," she said, widening her eyes.

"An earthquake when I was in the mountains, in Delphi—I wanted to see the Oracle. I and my horse fell down the path, and there I lay in a tangle for *hours* before they found me. My niece, such a devoted thing, had to nurse me back to health, and I vowed to give up my peripatetic life. But then she married, and I was lonely without her, so I decided to travel again."

"I read of her marriage," Grenville said, giving Lady Mary a nod. "My felicitations."

Lady Mary beamed, her dark eyes sparkling. "To a Russian count of vast wealth. A brilliant match. I am rather good at matchmaking, Captain Lacey. Now, I remember Miguel reading out to me from London newspapers that you have made a match yourself, Captain. To Lady Donata—Pembroke's daughter. Very surprising. I thought she'd enjoy widowhood forever after being married to that awful Breckenridge. It must have been a love match with you."

She gave me a sly smile that said she knew full well that my marriage with Donata was a misalliance. Donata certainly hadn't married me for money or connections; therefore it followed that she must be far gone in passion for me. It was the only explanation for her making so mad a choice.

Grenville answered for me. "It was a love match indeed. The *ton* is agog with it."

"I can imagine." Lady Mary dismissed the *ton* with a wave of her hand. "Gossipy busybodies. Is it any wonder I wander the world in search of beauty? Grenville does as well, Captain. We are birds of a feather."

The look Lady Mary shot Grenville was predatory—she obviously longed for the two birds to share a nest.

Grenville flushed and cleared his throat. "I have promised the captain I would show him every fascinating corner of Egypt. So far, we have seen old streets, barely anything left of ruins, and a death. The poor fellow."

"The Turks will clear that up," Lady Mary said, no longer interested. "Nothing to do with us. I have a boat, you know, for traveling down the Nile. I plan to have a look at Thebes."

"I imagine we'll go to Cairo," Grenville said easily. "And see the pyramids at Giza. A pity there is so little left of Alexandria and its great library."

"Indeed," Lady Mary said. "So much destroyed in antiquity. Very sad."

"One hears tales, though," Grenville said, gazing absently across the dusty stone drawing room. Outside came the sound of hammers, and Egyptians calling out to one another. "Bits and pieces found, especially by Napoleon's learned men who came to roust the land from its slumber. Books, papyri ... Not everything was carried back to the museums, I suppose."

Lady Mary gave him a roguish look. "Very clever, Grenville. Do not tell me you are after that ancient Greek papyrus the French scholar was supposed to have hidden before he left Egypt. No, do not lift your brows and play the ingenuous tourist with me. I know you too well. Fancy, the great Lucius Grenville, out to dig up Egypt in search of a lost library book."

Chapter Seven

I gave her an astonished look, as did Grenville. Lady Mary took in our expressions and laughed.

"Oh, my dear friends, everyone in Egypt is after that book. The story has been going around for years. Ah, Miguel, there you are." Lady Mary turned her pleased smile on the Spanish man as he set down a tray upon which rested a teapot and delicate Wedgwood cups. Lady Mary kept her hands in her lap and let Miguel pour the tea and pass it around.

Grenville lifted the cup Miguel gave him. "You take my breath away, Lady Mary. What do you know of this?"

Lady Mary waved her teacup, sending a dribble of tea rolling down the cup's painted side. "The lost book of the Alexandrian library, found by one of Napoleon's savants. The story goes that Monsieur Chabert, a mathematician in Napoleon's Egyptian expedition, stumbled across a papyrus scroll in

Greek, a mathematical treatise on the movement of the planets or some such thing. He found it days before we defeated the French army and Napoleon fled like a coward, leaving all his men behind."

"The French were allowed to keep their antiquities," Grenville pointed out. "With a few exceptions."

"Yes, like the stone with all the writing such a fuss is made about." Lady Mary took a calm sip of tea. "I imagine Monsieur Chabert concluded that his book would be taken away from him, so he hid it, intending to find it again one day. But he never did. So the tale goes."

"A plausible story, certainly," Grenville said, as though he had only passing interest.

"Who knows?" Lady Mary glanced at me over her teacup. "Chabert died and took the secret of the book to his grave. It might be a tale for entertainment, put about by Mr. Salt to stir up Englishmen to come and dig for treasure."

I drank my tea, which was surprisingly good, in silence. I doubted that Denis would send me to Egypt looking for this book without a chance that it existed. He was too careful for that.

Grenville cleared his throat, uncomfortable under Lady Mary's intense gaze. "I suppose a way to began searching for this lost papyrus is to speak to those who knew Monsieur Chabert."

"And you wish me to introduce you?" Lady Mary smiled broadly. "Oh, I do love having the oh-so-famous Mr. Grenville in my debt." She shot me a look that was half conspiratorial, half coquettish. "I know everybody in Egypt, Grenville, so of course I am acquainted with those who were connected with Monsieur Chabert. I will happily introduce you. Few of them believe the story, I must warn you. And then you must come and see *my* dig."

"Are you hunting for treasure too, my old friend?" Grenville asked her.

"I am, and please forbear from using the word *old* to describe me, my dear fellow. I'm younger than you are."

She wasn't younger than Grenville by much, I suspected, but I was too polite to say so. I wondered if Donata knew Lady Mary and what she'd have to say about her. I suddenly missed my wife very much.

"Agreed," Grenville was saying. "You introduce us to Chabert's cronies, and we'll see what you're unearthing. Do you wield your own spade?"

Lady Mary laughed heartily, which made her large bosom jiggle. "Isn't he a delight, Miguel? No, of course we employ the Egyptians. They love digging in the dirt and will do anything for extra coin."

After seeing that the Egyptians who lived in town had next to nothing, I well believed they needed the blunt. Whether they loved finding things for Lady Mary was another speculation.

"That is settled then," Lady Mary said, beaming at us.

The conversation moved to gossip about acquaintances common to Grenville and Lady Mary, and then to places they had both been. Grenville had encountered her often in his travels, it seemed, in Rome and Greece, in the German states and even Russia.

"He follows me about," Lady Mary told me with conviction. "My niece, when she travelled with me, would exclaim on the coincidence. But it never was, was it, dear boy?"

Grenville strove to hide an aggrieved expression. "Always a delight to see you, Lady Mary."

She laughed, pleased.

After an interminable time of more tea, poured by the always silent Miguel, served with a Turkish sweet of thin sheets of pastry wrapped around honey and almonds, Grenville and I at last took our leave.

As we walked down the palm-shaded avenue, the brown swath of Alexandria in the distance, Grenville let out a heartfelt, releasing sigh.

"That woman is the most frightening thing on seven continents," he declared to the sky.

It was unusual for Grenville to disparage a lady, from which I concluded that his feelings on this matter were profound.

"You have never mentioned her in the nearly three years I've known you," I pointed out.

Grenville shuddered as he removed his handkerchief and dabbed his brow. "No, I have not. I last heard of her settling in Russia with her niece and had hoped I'd never see her again. Very likely the count soon had enough of Mary and showed her the door."

"She is a bit overbearing," I admitted. "Full of her own importance. But I've met other such women — they seem harmless if irritating."

Grenville sent me a long-suffering look as he tucked away his handkerchief. "I am certain her company will quickly pall even on you, my friend. I first met Mary in Rome, where she was taking her niece, a pretty little thing, on her Grand Tour. Gentlemen had Grand Tours, Mary told me, so why not ladies? I made the foolish mistake of agreeing with her. From then on she latched on to me as her champion and spent all winter trying to make me propose to her niece. Turns out, her niece had not taken in several Seasons, and no wonder, with her dragon of an aunt hovering over her. Lady Mary decided that a foreign aristocrat would do for her niece instead. And barring that—me. Lady Mary forced me into so many corners, trying to make me say words that would obligate me to her niece for life that I trembled whenever I spied them."

"What about the niece?" I asked. "Did she share her aunt's wishes?"

"No, indeed. The poor thing was hideously embarrassed, but I dared not comfort her, or Mary would declare us compromised and lead us to the altar. With great relief did I read of her niece's marriage to the Russian count. I hope it was a love match and not simply a young girl trying to flee her aunt's clutches."

I hoped so too. I set my walking stick too hard into the dirt and had to pause to yank it out. "I believe Lady Mary has now set her sights on you for herself, Grenville. I'd have a care."

Brewster, who'd listened to every word, guffawed loudly.

"Yes," Grenville said darkly. "I had noted that. Thank you very much, Lacey."

Brewster bellowed another laugh, and we continued down the road to Alexandria and our lodgings.

***

Bartholomew and Matthias had done wonders in our absence. The earthen floors of our house were now covered with carpets, the shutters thrown back to let in the light.

They'd unpacked all the amenities Grenville had brought from London—cushions and rugs for the chairs, candlesticks and wax candles, tables for our books, footstools to keep our feet comfortable, extra bedding that was soft and free of bugs.

"If I'd had you two with me in the army, I'd have ridden out the war in great comfort," I remarked to the brothers as I settled into a chair in the now-inviting drawing room.

I'd never have been able to afford Matthias and Bartholomew in the army, I knew full well. I enjoyed their expertise these days because Grenville paid them high wages.

The afternoon was marching on—we'd spent much time with Lady Mary. However, I was too restless to sit for long and proposed a walk to see what the Porters were up to. Grenville declined.

"A refreshing sleep is what I had in mind for the heat of the day," Grenville said. "But tramp away and enjoy yourself."

He had not yet recovered from our voyage, I could see. Grenville was usually more robust.

I left him in care of Matthias, while I, Brewster, and Bartholomew struck off south and west toward the desert see what we could find.

While I was sorry that the great city of Alexandria was now reduced to a muddy town surrounded by farmer's fields, I took a moment to enjoy that I was there. Alexander himself might have taken this path, on his way out of his camp toward Siwa, the oasis where he was declared to be descended from the gods.

As we walked, the road turned to a mere track that wandered among the cultivated land. Egyptian men in the fields dug or hoed, or simply stretched out on the ground and slept.

Nowhere did I see sands or the remains of ancient

temples sticking out of it. I was about to confess I'd underestimated the distance out to the desert when a lad ran up to us.

He must have been about eleven or so, with curly black hair and wide brown eyes, a cut on his cheek that looked red and angry.

In beautiful French, he said, "I will take you to the monuments, sirs. You are English? I will show you what the others know nothing about."

Neither Brewster nor Bartholomew understood French, and Brewster rumbled a warning. I held up a reassuring hand and addressed the boy.

"What monuments, young man?"

"You come with me. I show you." He thrust his hand into mine.

It was the bone-thinness of the hand that won me over. He was poor and hungry and simply wanted a few coins to take home to his family.

I was also aware he could be a clever pickpocket, so I turned him loose right away and motioned him forward with my walking stick. "Very well then," I said, keeping to French. "Show us."

"What you doing, guv?" Brewster asked.

"It will do no harm to see what he wants to lead us to," I said. "I'm curious anyway. He claims he will show us ruins other diggers don't know."

"He'll tell you anyfink for a coin, Captain," Brewster said. "And could be leading you off to a gang to rob you."

"Possibly," I said. "Let us see, shall we?"

Brewster grumbled but heaved a sigh and marched on, pushing ahead of me to keep up with the boy. Bartholomew wore an interested expression as he strolled beside me.

"It's different from what I thought it would be,"

he remarked, looking around. "Egypt seems an ordinary place. It's like the fens in East Anglia more than anything else."

I'd grown up near the fens, and thought it quite different, but I understood what Bartholomew meant. "This is the delta region," I explained. "A very fertile land. The crops of Egypt fed the entire Roman empire."

I could well believe it, seeing the acres and acres of fields spreading out in all directions.

And then, as we followed the lad, the fields simply stopped. We skirted the edge of muddy ground where tall reeds grew and a few feet later, we were marching through sand.

I stared about me in some awe. I'd been to northern India and the Punjab, where the landscape could be barren, but nothing like this. Sand and rock spread to the horizon, the land rising to a ridge in the distance. I knew that far, far out in the haze, many miles distant, was an oasis, but I could scarcely believe any water would be found in all that emptiness.

"Come, come," the boy said. He trotted fearlessly into the trackless waste, and I hastened to catch up with him.

My leg ached but the warmth felt good on my bones. The sun was sliding to the west in front of us, blinding us in a cloudless sky. When night fell, it would be inky black.

The lad moved quickly, running barefoot over hot sand. Brewster jogged after him, and Bartholomew easily passed me on his way to keep an eye on both of them.

I lagged, my old injury tiring me, but at the same time, my heart beat faster with excitement. I was here in this ancient land, the blue sky soaring overhead, the fog and stink of London far behind. I loved warmth and arching skies, views stretching to all sides. I was not too worried about where the boy took us — I was good at finding my way around, even in unfamiliar places.

The lad suddenly cut to the right, off the track we'd been following. Brewster yelled, "Oi!" and the boy halted and waited for us.

Without words, the lad pointed to a slight rise in the land, which was shadowed by the rapidly setting sun. Then he sped up the small hill and halted on top of it. Brewster and Bartholomew were hard on his heels, leaving me to struggle and pant up the rise.

The boy waited for me to reach him before he pointed both forefingers down at a mound of sand. "Here," he said. "Dig here."

"He's touched," Brewster said, wiping his forehead with his sleeve. "Too much sun in these parts." The big man was breathing hard, face beaded with sweat.

The lad dropped to his hands and knees and started moving sand. I knelt next to him, pushing in my larger hands to draw the dirt away.

"Now *you're* touched," Brewster said, but he leaned over, interested, his shadow blocking the worst of the sun.

"No," I said. "I think the lad is right. There's something here."

I took my walking stick and moved caked dirt from around the top of a hard stone. The stone's lines were regular, the edge that stuck out of the earth sharp and even.

Eagerly I pulled at the sand. Down about four inches, I saw the figure of a duck scratched into the stone, identical to the symbol I'd seen on the obelisks lying in Alexandria — a hieroglyph.

"Good Lord," I said. "It might be another of the needles."

The boy shook his head. "A temple," he said. "My grandfather says they're all buried here. We dig it out for you, for the English."

My excitement grew. I had the feeling that digging down to find out what was here would be more complicated than simply hiring the local men with shovels, but I then and there determined that I would excavate it.

As these thoughts went through my head, and the boy waited eagerly for my answer, the sun slid below the horizon. The sky blazed red, the sun's rays catching in dust to turn the sky the color of blood. Beautiful, then it faded quickly to dark blue, then black.

I rose, a chill setting in. I opened my mouth to tell the boy to take us back to the city. At the same time, Brewster shouted a warning, and I knew we were not alone in the sudden dark.

Chapter Eight

Our guide ran down the ridge, ignoring Brewster's shout. The lad grunted in the darkness and disappeared, right before a curved sword blade came at me.

I blocked it with my own sword, out of its sheath the instant I'd heard Brewster call out. I'd never lost my sense of danger after the wars—if anything, living in London, a city full of predators, had heightened my reflexes.

Bartholomew tried to leap to my aid, but I shoved him aside with my shoulder, snapping at him to find the boy.

Blades clanged. Starlight flashed off a scimitar and in wild dark eyes over a black facecloth. My attacker was young, in the prime of his youth, and I was older and injured. On the other hand, I had years of experience fighting in Mysore and Spain, while I had the feeling this lad hadn't yet seen true battle.

I turned aside his sword and thrust at him,

making him jump and swing. We came in close, his breath huffing through his facecloth, I grim and silent. His blade wafted close to my face, and I shoved my elbow into his ribs, making him stumble. I threw myself against him, tangling my good leg with his to continue his fall.

The man was wiry enough to catch his balance, but he'd forgotten about Brewster.

Brewster fought not for glory but to stay alive. He was behind the soldier before the young man could recover, his arm around the soldier's neck, his thick knife at his ribs. The scimitar clattered to the ground as the soldier clawed at Brewster's choking arm.

"No!" I yelled, before Brewster could plunge the blade in. "Don't kill him. God knows what the punishment would be for you murdering a Turk."

"Wasn't aiming to tell anyone, guv," Brewster said grimly. "Lots of sand out here." His grip around the soldier's throat cut off the man's breath, and the knife was no doubt aimed at a vital organ.

"Let him go," I said in a hard voice.

"'Fraid not, Captain. He has assassination on his mind, and it's my job to keep you alive."

"Let him speak, in any case." I took a step forward and yanked the cloth from the young man's face.

I saw whom I'd expected to see, the young soldier who had attacked Haluk's daughter, whose friend had lain dead near the site of the ancient library.

"Why are you trying to kill me?" I asked the question in French, and I spoke loudly and slowly, as though that would help him understand me.

The soldier stared at me, uncomprehending. I repeated the question in English, with the same effect.

"Bartholomew," I called into the darkness. "Is the

lad all right?"

"Aye, that he is." Bartholomew strode forward, holding the boy by the arm. "I caught him running to leave us to our fate."

Bartholomew gave the lad a shake, and the boy ducked his head, ashamed.

"You brought us out here so he could attack us," I said, realizing.

The boy hung his head even more. "He gave me coin. He said he would kill you and threatened to beat me if I told you."

"Ask him why." I pointed the end of my blade to the soldier's chest. "As you have betrayed us, you may as well act as interpreter."

"I don't speak Turkish," the boy sneered, jerking his head up. "I'm not an Ottoman."

"You speak it enough to let him bribe you to bring us out here," I said, unforgiving. "Ask him."

The boy took in our uncompromising looks, swallowed, and babbled something to the soldier.

The soldier could barely answer through Brewster's grip, but Brewster refused to lessen his hold. The soldier gasped out words, and the lad translated. "You killed my friend. I saw you."

I frowned in puzzlement and answered immediately. "You saw no such thing. Your friend died in the middle of the night, and I was in my lodgings far from that spot. I assure you I was in my room, fast asleep, until dawn."

The lad hurriedly fed the words to the soldier— hopefully correctly.

The soldier tried to shake his head. His answer was more agitated, the young man not reassured by my claim of innocence.

"He says he saw you," the lad told me. "I told him

he's a liar. All the Turks are."

The boy had changed sides rather quickly. I wondered what tunes he'd have sung if the soldier had managed to overpower us.

The soldier was choking out the same words, over and over. I gave the Egyptian boy a stern look, and he shrugged. "He keeps saying he saw you."

I turned my attention to the agitated young man. "What is your name?"

The lad answered before the soldier could. "His name is Ahmed. Ahmed Sadik. Everyone knows Ahmed."

"I am Captain Gabriel Lacey," I said to the soldier. "I swear to you upon my honor that I never met your friend, or touched him, or killed him. All right?"

The boy translated. Ahmed listened in disbelief, but he ceased his struggles, his brow creased with worry.

"Let him go, Brewster," I said quietly.

"Not wise, Captain," Brewster growled.

"Keep your knife on him, certainly. But I'd like to speak to him man to man, not captor to prisoner."

Even in the faint starlight I could see Brewster's extreme annoyance with me, but he eased his big arm from around the man's neck. The knife remained at his ribs, and Brewster also kicked the fallen scimitar hard enough so that it skittered across the ground and sank into a sand drift.

"Why do you believe I killed your friend?" I asked Ahmed. "How could you see, if you were supposed to be in your barracks?"

"I followed him," Ahmed answered, the lad translating. "I thought he had gone to meet a lady, the daughter of Haluk. She is not worthy of him. I sought to stop him. I did not find him in the dark, but I saw a man—you—in the place where he was found this morning, and the glint of a knife in your hand. Then when I saw Ibrahim dead this morning, I remembered this. I know you must have killed him."

"I assure you again, I was not there. You say you never found Ibrahim—this man might have had nothing to do with it."

Even as I spoke I didn't truly believe that. Ahmet might not have witnessed the murder but he likely had seen the murderer, even if he hadn't realized it at the time.

I glanced up at the moonless sky. "It is very dark at night, in any case," I said. "How can you be certain you saw me?"

Ahmed and the lad went back and forth for a time, both of them speaking rapidly.

"Your tallness," the boy finally said. "Your build. The way you move. He thought it was you."

I shook my head. "Well, it was not. I have several people who can swear I was at home all night— Englishmen and Egyptians both. Besides, Ibrahim wasn't killed with a knife. He died from a blow to the head, probably struck with a rock."

Ahmed, after the lad finished repeating what I'd said, suddenly folded up onto the ground. Brewster hovered over Ahmed as the young man curled his arms around himself and sank his face into his knees, moaning words and rocking back and forth.

"What is he saying?" I asked the lad.

The boy looked disgusted. "That he has no honor, no friends, nothing. That you might as well run him through."

While a moment ago, Brewster had been ready to do just that, the large man now stood motionlessly, watchful but not murderous. Brewster had a sense of fairness — Ahmed at this moment had ceased to be dangerous, though Brewster would make certain he remained that way.

"Nonsense," I said briskly to Ahmed as the boy relayed my words. "You are grieving for your friend — it has nothing to do with honor. You are hotheaded and rash, and if you ever threaten a lady again, I will thrash you soundly, but there is no need to give way to melodrama and misery."

Ahmed raised a sad face to me, starlight glittering on his tears. "He was my closest friend, closer to me than a brother. When he pined after that girl, I told him he'd come to grief. My commander has arrested another soldier, a troublemaker, for the murder, but I know he did not do it. I know it was an enemy. But if not you, then who? How can we ever know?"

"I will find out," I said. The fact that the lieutenant had arbitrarily chosen another to take the blame angered me greatly. He was simply trying to appear to be doing something about the situation. "First, you will lead us back to town," I told Ahmed. "And then you will tell me everything about Ibrahim and exactly what you saw last night."

Brewster heaved an aggrieved sigh. "God's balls, you're off again, are you, Captain? Can't keep your long nose to yourself."

"Perhaps it was why I was gifted with such a nose, Brewster," I said.

***

The Egyptian servants of the household were alarmed when I turned up out of the dark with a Turkish soldier in tow. I saw a flash of shocked faces and then every single one of the servants vanished. It was left to Bartholomew to usher us into the drawing room and then run off to bring us refreshment.

Brewster insisted that Ahmed turn over his weapons — an alarming number of knives and daggers came out from under his clothes — before he'd allow the young man past the courtyard. Ahmed unwrapped the cloths that kept sand from his face, sat down on a cushion in the drawing room, and became a person.

Bartholomew had managed to procure Turkish coffee, and he set it down in front of us. Ahmed sipped it humbly.

I could not sit on the floor like the nimble Ahmed, so I took one of the low folding chairs and nodded my thanks to Bartholomew before enjoying the thick brew. I would have to learn its secret and take some back with me to England.

Grenville was notably absent. Bartholomew whispered that he'd gone out, but the servants didn't know where. Matthias apparently had accompanied him.

Bartholomew was not happy that both the Egyptian lad and Brewster were allowed to stay in Mr. Grenville's drawing room, but I could not speak to Ahmed without the boy, and Brewster would never be persuaded to leave me alone with the quick-to-violence Ahmed. I told Bartholomew to hand Brewster and the boy coffee as well, which Bartholomew did, with polite deference.

I let Ahmed drink, then I told him to tell me all about Ibrahim.

Speaking through the interpreting lad, Ahmed related his tale. His friend Ibrahim, it seemed, had been off duty at a marketplace a few months ago, when he'd caught a glimpse of Haluk's daughter.

"He saw nothing," Ahmed scoffed. "A man like Haluk would not allow his daughter to be spied in an open marketplace. She was with her mother in a closed chair, which was surrounded by servants. He saw her eyes as she glanced out the window, and Ibrahim believed himself struck with love. I told him that the daughter of Haluk was not worthy of his attentions, to wait until he returned home to Constantinople and marry a girl there. But Ibrahim was always stubborn."

Ahmed shook his head, sad that his friend had not listened to sense. "The girl and her father rejected Ibrahim's suit in the rudest way—they have no honor. Ibrahim was crazed with grief. He would not eat or drink, and in the end, he tried to run himself through. I saved him, I stayed with him and hid this deed from others so he would not be dismissed. I finally made him understand that she was not worth dying for. Then when I saw her emerge yesterday, to display herself so brazenly, without a care, while my dearest friend had nearly died because of her—I lost my senses. If she had stayed at home in the first place, Ibrahim would not have seen her and would not have been humiliated, would not have tried to kill himself. I struck out. I was not myself. I am thankful you were there to stop me. It was the will of God that you were in that place at that moment."

I agreed. I'd been in time to save a young woman from being hurt, and to save Ahmed the wrath of my vengeance or at least an ignoble death at the hands of the Turkish government.

"You must apologize to the lady and her father," I said severely. "Make it up to them. Where I come from, you could be imprisoned or hanged for trying to strike her."

Ahmed shook his head. "I was maddened. I will send my apologies to the girl, and a gift. But I will make clear the gift is for *her*. Her father, Haluk? He is unworthy. He is ..."

Here the boy turned to me with a puzzled expression. "I do not know how to translate this word. It is, I think you English say, *shit*."

"I understand," I assured him. I asked Ahmed, "Why do you despise him so? I found Haluk to be hospitable and learned."

Ahmed regarded me with imperious disdain. "They say he was sent to Alexandria because he is a traitor, spoke against the sultan. Nothing could be proved, and he had many friends in high places, so he was not instantly killed. But he was forced to come here, far from court, so that he might wither and die in this nowhere."

"Hmm," I said. "You believe the story of his betrayal?"

Ahmed shrugged. "Everyone says so."

As in the London *ton*, I thought dryly, the word of "everyone" was sufficient to condemn.

"You claim to have honor," I pointed out. "If so, you will apologize to Haluk as well. I have a daughter about the same age as his. We fathers are very protective of and frightened for our children. You hurt him as much as you tried to hurt the young lady. You will understand this when you have daughters of your own."

Ahmed gave me a dark look as though the time of fatherhood was comfortably far away. Then he sighed and nodded. "It will be as you say. I will show him that my honor is greater."

Not quite the spirit of what I meant, but at least Ahmed had agreed. If I had managed to turn his anger from Haluk and family, well and good.

"It is highly unlikely your friend Ibrahim went to

meet this young woman," I pointed out. "As you have said, she is well guarded, only goes out with attendants, and she had already rejected his suit. In that case, who else might he have been going to see?"

Ahmed's brow furrowed. He'd likely never had to ponder such a puzzle, only fight those his commander pointed him toward.

"Haluk, maybe," Ahmed said. "Yes." He became animated again. "Haluk met him to kill him!"

I held up my hand. "If Haluk had wanted to speak to Ibrahim in secret, he would have arranged to meet him in a much more private location, perhaps even had him brought quietly to his house. Haluk is a wealthy man—someone would have noted him moving through the town in the middle of the night. Besides, why would Haluk need to murder? He had already turned down Ibrahim's suit, and Ibrahim had accepted that fate. Moreover, if Ibrahim had agreed to a meeting with Haluk, I assume he would have told you of it."

Ahmed deflated. "That is true."

"Who else, then? Ibrahim might have made a liaison with a lady, as you suggest, but I don't believe that lady was Haluk's daughter. Was there another woman he liked to meet?"

Ahmed shook his head. "I do not know," he finished mournfully.

A clatter echoed in the courtyard. Ahmed scrambled to his feet, as did I, but it was only Grenville returning, a boy in the courtyard having dropped a tray when dodging out of his way.

Grenville retrieved the tray, patted the boy on the shoulder, and breezed into the house. "Lacey, I've been ... Ah."

He raised his brows to find Ahmed in his

voluminous trousers and black boots, long blue coat, and turban in a half crouch in our drawing room. Grenville watched, nonplussed, as Ahmed rose and executed a dignified bow.

"I must return to my quarters," Ahmed said, after I'd introduced them. "I will be punished if I am too late."

"By all means." I gestured for him to precede me out of the room. "Brewster will return your weapons once you are outside. Please continue to think, and if you remember anything that might help discover who killed your friend, send me word."

Ahmed gave me a bow, a bit lower than the one he'd made for Grenville, sent Brewster a frown, and stalked from the room. Brewster followed closely behind him.

The lad, finished with his task, held out a dirt-streaked hand. "I too, must return home. You pay now?"

I conceded that he'd helped a great deal, even if his first intent had been duplicitous. I fished for a silver coin and dropped it into his hand.

The boy's eyes widened, he grinned at me, then he bowed rapidly and rushed from the room.

Grenville watched him go. "Now I feel as though I would have been more entertained if I'd remained at home, waiting for you. I was better after my nap and went for a walk," he said, explaining his absence. "I have things to tell you, but apparently my adventures were not as interesting as yours."

The servants, who'd emerged again now that Ahmed and his knives had gone, entered with a great tray of food. They lowered it to the table after a moment of debate—I had already noted that most Egyptians ate on the floor.

The tray held meat, fish, and vegetables surrounding a pile of cooked grain. A pleasing scent of seasonings and spices wafted from the whole of it.

As in Haluk's home, the servants had not brought forks or spoons, but Matthias produced a box that held the silver cutlery Grenville traveled with. We also had been given no plates—we were expected to eat from the communal dish.

As we partook, spooning food into bowls Matthias likewise produced, I told Grenville how the Egyptian boy had led me to buried stones in the sand, and how Ahmed had sprung upon us.

Grenville listened to and remarked upon all I had to say, and returned to the topic of the ruins I'd found. My excitement had risen again as I told him I wanted to dig them out.

"I'm afraid they are already spoken for, my dear fellow," Grenville said apologetically. "Henry Salt holds the firman—the permission from the pasha and the local authorities—to excavate near Alexandria. The Porters are working for him. The boy was wrong to imply otherwise. Likely it was the only way he could think of to get you out to where Ahmed attacked you."

I felt a sharp twinge of disappointment. I'd grown quite eager to run out into the desert again and uncover the slabs carved with hieroglyphs.

"The lad certainly had my measure," I said, shaking my head and scooping up meat and grain onto my fork. The savory meat had been spiced with cumin and turmeric, a fine concoction.

"He knew what would please you," Grenville answered. "That is one problem with these local fellows—they will tell you stories you wish to hear but that are not necessarily the truth. They don't consider such lies evil, though—it is more hospitable to make you happy."

"Whereas I always tell the bare truth, no matter how unpleasant," I remarked.

"Not entirely. You are married now, so I am certain you engage in a small amount of lying. When your wife wears some absurd new fashion, I imagine you tell her she is stunningly beautiful in it."

"She *is* stunningly beautiful," I replied. "And Donata knows the fashions are absurd."

My heart pulled as I thought again of Donata so far away. Egypt was a beautiful and exciting land, and yet I knew that it would never be perfect without Donata's presence.

Grenville gave me a small smile. "Do not worry," he said. "I will obtain a firman when we are in Cairo, so that you can find somewhere on the Nile to dig to your heart's content."

"You are kind to try to soothe my humiliation," I said, feeling like a complete and gullible fool. "But let us end the discussion. Tell me what you were about this evening."

"Ah, that. I met a fellow, an Englishman, I knew at Oxford. He has a largish house not far from here, and he's invited us to a soiree tomorrow night—for the foreigners who have collected in Alexandria. I know you are not one for gatherings of the *haut ton*, but I accepted for one important reason. Lord Randolph claims to have actually seen the book Denis is looking for. He might be key to helping us find it."

***

"Guv."

I opened my eyes to darkness, my fist already swinging before I recognized the voice. I hit nothing—Brewster had prudently retreated a few feet from the bed.

"What is it?" I asked sleepily, heaving myself onto my elbows.

"I saw him. The man what's hunting you." Brewster was breathing hard, and I could smell his sweat. "I spied him lurking in the streets. I wager he's why Ahmed swore by all that's holy that you were the one with the dead soldier. He saw your double, Captain. I just saw him too."

Chapter Nine

I struggled up, my heart banging, the sheet sliding down my bare torso. I'd flung off my nightshirt after lying wakeful and too hot.

"Are you certain?" I asked as I snatched up my dressing gown.

"It were him," Brewster said, stoic in the dark. "I never forget a man what shot me. Easy for him to follow us about, innit? Mr. Grenville might as well travel carrying banners and having trumpeters announce him. Weren't no big secret where we was going."

I got to my feet, drawing my dressing gown around me. "What was he doing when you saw him?"

Brewster shrugged. "Walking about. Thought I'd follow him to his lodgings and give him a pummeling, but I lost him in the dark." He sounded annoyed. "Don't worry, Captain, I'll find him again."

"Have a care," I said, alarmed. "He's free with a

pistol and happy to use violence."

"So am I, guv." Brewster's statement was uninflected. "You watch *yourself.* You're apt to run off in any direction."

"Then perhaps I'll confuse him," I said with tight humor. "At least we know *where* he is. I intend to hunt him in return, catch him, and shake some answers out of him."

"If *I* catch him, guv," Brewster said slowly, "I'll kill him. He's a dangerous man, not one for talking to."

Brewster had a point—the man had meant me and my family nothing but harm from the beginning. But my unflagging curiosity wanted to know why he was pursuing me. And more importantly, *who* he was.

I'd been struck when I'd first seen him how much he resembled my father, and in Malta how much he resembled me. Was he an illegitimate son my father had gotten on one of his mistresses? Which would make him my half brother. That thought unnerved me greatly.

The question was, why had he written me letters threatening to tell the world that I was not truly Gabriel Lacey of Norfolk? Was he a madman, perhaps thinking *he* was the legitimate son, and I had usurped his place?

On the other hand, the resemblance might be coincidental, and the man playing upon that coincidence. Men who were not related could look like one another, remarkably so.

Considering my father, however, the man being a by-blow was not out of the question. My father had been a stickler for propriety and rigid behavior in his own home, but then he'd squandered what was left of our fortune on expensive courtesans in London.

In any case, I wished to speak to this man, to find out who he was and why he wished to harm me. I'd prosecute him for putting my family into danger and nearly killing Brewster, but I'd speak to him first.

"Thank you for the warning," I told Brewster. "I shall heed it."

Brewster studied me for a few moments, likely fearing I'd push past him, leap down the stairs, and go out searching for the man then and there. I admit I was tempted, but if Brewster, who was very good at his job, had lost him, I hadn't much chance of finding him again on my own.

"He won't go far," I assured Brewster. "If he's determined to hunt me, he'll remain close. We'll find him, and if he killed Ibrahim, we'll have him arrested for that. Sent back to England at the very least."

Brewster retained his stolid silence. "You're soft, Captain. I think that's what Mr. Denis don't understand about you. Soft and yet more ruthless than any man I ever clapped eyes on. You confound him."

I looked at him in surprise. I'd been trying to decide what went on in Denis's head since the day I'd met him, and now Brewster implied that Denis was trying as diligently to find out what went on in mine.

"Yes, well, confounding Mr. Denis is probably why I am alive," I said. "Good night, Brewster. Put a guard on the front gate. I'm not too soft to take precautions."

"Right." Brewster turned his back and tramped away, forgoing politeness as he usually did.

I let the dressing gown slide away, looked at the nightshirt, then gave up and settled back into bed in my skin. But I was wide awake now, and unable to sleep until daylight.

***

I spent the morning groggy and out of sorts. Brewster and I went out after breakfast, scanning the streets for our hunter, but we found no trace of him.

I returned home, disgruntled, and lay down for a mid-morning nap. Brewster, who could go without sleep for amazingly long stretches of time, returned to the search.

Grenville organized a party that afternoon to go out to the fort of Qait Bay, which stood on the site of the ancient lighthouse. I was tired and worried, but I drew on my resolve and accompanied him and his acquaintances.

I found myself in a party of gentlemen who were as well read and well traveled as Grenville—a few Englishmen, a Florentine who spoke perfect English, and a Frenchman who did not seem interested in the antiquities rivalry between the French and British. Indeed, the party was congenial, Grenville knowing how to put men of like minds together.

"It is rumored that part of the lighthouse tumbled into the sea," the man from Florence said as we approached the fort. "If we could swim deep enough, we might find it."

An intriguing thought. The fortress of golden stone towered formidably before us—it was said that the lighthouse, a beacon of the ancient world, had been five times as large as the current building.

The fortress was interesting for itself. It had been built by the Mamelukes in the fifteenth century by a sultan who'd successfully resisted the Ottomans and made treaties with them. Qait Bay had left behind his architecture not only in Alexandria but in Cairo and other cities in the Near East.

"Began life as a slave," the Florentine gentleman told me as we strolled together along the base of the outer walls. "Had several masters before he was freed, then he became one of the greatest rulers of the Arab world. Makes one think."

We went in through a low arch of a gate to a broad stretch of open ground leading to the fortress itself. Straight flanking walls of stone rose into a blue sky, and rounded crenellations stretched across the top of the walls to circular towers on either side. It was a striking place, incorporating both military severity and elegant proportionality.

"The Mamelukes all began as slaves," I remarked, recalling what I'd read in the books Grenville's friend from Malta had lent us. "And they went on to become a formidable army and build an empire. It makes one think, indeed."

Thus philosophizing, we left the courtyard and strolled around what remained of the rampart walls. We looked out at the dark blue Mediterranean, and I wondered if it indeed hid the remains of the Pharos lighthouse.

My troubles fell away as I walked. Herodotus the Greek historian had landed on this shore and had written his account of his travels, and the feet of Alexander himself had touched these very sands. I breathed the soft air, my heart squeezing with amazement that now I stood here as well.

Grenville and the rest of his friends were climbing to the top of the old walls for the view. He waved down at me, gesturing for us to follow.

We did, slowly, I less lithe than the others. The Florentine, not noticing I'd dropped behind, moved to Grenville and fell into conversation with him. I hauled myself to the top of the walls and stood leaning on my walking stick, trying to catch my breath.

And then I saw him. From the ramparts I could look down both into the fortress's courtyard and out to the narrow streets surrounding the place. The humanity of Alexandria spread before me — nearly naked workmen on the scaffolding, wealthy Turks out for a stroll, Egyptians wandering about on errands or halting for conversation with their fellows.

I caught sight of a face, a build, a way of walking that jolted me. I came alert, peering into the crowd below.

It took me some time to find him again because he wasn't wearing European dress. He'd donned a galabiya and a turban — I'd only glimpsed him because he'd looked up and straight at me.

"Brewster!" I shouted.

Brewster, who had been following within earshot, was instantly at my side.

I pointed. "There!"

We both stared down. As though feeling our gazes, the man looked up at me again, and for one instant, our eyes met. Dark hatred flared in his, then he turned his head and flowed back into the crowd, becoming one with the sea of turbans and fluttering cloth.

Brewster had no compunction about hurtling down the crumbling wall, his large form moving surprisingly fast. Grenville came to my side.

"What is it, Lacey?"

I pointed. "Bloody man who's been following us. Brewster spied him in town last night, and I've just seen him."

Grenville didn't answer. We watched Brewster

moving through the crowds, unceremoniously shouldering men out of his way. He left behind shouts, raised fists, and gestures I didn't know but could guess the meaning of. He turned a corner into the narrow streets and was lost to sight.

"We'd better go after him," I said.

Grenville nodded. I began to descend from the wall, but Grenville, always polite, turned back to take leave of his fellows. He caught up to me as I entered the lane into which Brewster had vanished, and we were soon swallowed by the mass of people moving about their daily business.

We found Brewster at the end of a street, his way blocked by a throng of angry Egyptians. He shouted at them in English, demanding them to get out of his way. They shouted back at him and didn't move.

Grenville and I waded in. Grenville began to apologize, knowing more of the native language than I did. The Egyptians calmed a bit, but Brewster was red-faced with rage.

"He ran in there, guv." Brewster pointed to a closed gate. "I tried to go in after him, but these—" He growled a word I couldn't hear. "They blocked me way, pushed me back." He balled his large fists.

"There?" Grenville gestured to the battered gate, his brows raised in astonishment. "Are you certain?"

"I *saw* him, I tell you."

Grenville set his walking stick on the hard street. "Well, well. That's where the bey, the man who administers Alexandria, lives. No wonder they wouldn't let you in."

"Why was our man going in there?" I asked, my heart beating swiftly. "A friend of the bey's, is he?"

"*If* he was the man Brewster saw darting inside," Grenville said.

Brewster's look was indignant. "Begging your pardon, Mr. Grenville, but I know how to follow a bloke. Had me eye on him all the time. He went in there." He again pointed his broad finger at the gate.

I had the feeling Brewster had only added the *begging your pardon* to keep himself from hauling Grenville up by the lapels and shouting his point into Grenville's face.

Grenville made a conciliatory gesture. "I meant no offense, Mr. Brewster. But the streets are crowded, and the men are dressed similarly."

"It were him," Brewster repeated.

"I believe you," I said quickly. "But who the devil is he, and why is he a guest in *that* house? Either that or he paid these men to block our way."

I looked at the Egyptians, tall and lean in their ankle-length garments. They turned faces toward us with interest, waiting to see what we'd do next.

When I'd been in India, the natives would often turn and flee when they saw Englishmen or make themselves as invisible as possible. Here, we were the objects of great curiosity and even entertainment. I supposed that, in India, I'd been part of an army in the habit of crushing natives, while here, we were guests, just tolerated by the pasha.

The Egyptians' interest increased when the rest of our walking party caught up to us, clearly wondering why we'd dashed down this particular street. The Florentine spoke the Arab language well and soon had the men on the street laughing.

A few of the Egyptians gestured for us to follow them. Grenville nodded and began to comply.

"Come along, Lacey," he said. "They want to make it up to us."

Brewster, of course, didn't like the idea. "You're

going to leave 'im in there, to come out and have a go at you again?"

"Not much we can do," I said. I chafed as well, wanting to lie in wait for our quarry.

But the men had surrounded Grenville and his party, urging us on, and I wasn't sure what would happen if we refused. Besides, if we befriended these men, they might be persuaded to keep a lookout for my hunter and alert me when he emerged again.

I hobbled quickly after Grenville, waving Brewster to follow. He did, grumbling.

The men took us to a cramped shop, open to the street, where we were served thick, spicy coffee. Then the proprietor and a lad that looked enough like him to be his son produced a tall, cylindrical brass tube attached to a glass bowl of water and set it on the table between Grenville and me.

The top of the elegantly curved tube held a brass bowl with a lid—smoke issued through slits in the top. Several leather cords wrapped around the contraption, each with a brass mouthpiece at the end.

Grenville thanked the man graciously as the son set more pipes on the tables of our friends. "Have you ever tried a hookah, Lacey?" Grenville asked me.

"In India," I said. I hadn't liked the experience, which had given me a raging headache, so I took up the mouthpiece in trepidation.

"It's a bit different here." Grenville lifted the cord to his mouth and inhaled in a practiced way.

I took a sip of my coffee and lifted the mouthpiece to my lips. While the crowd that had followed us watched, I sucked in the smoke, making the water bubble in the glass bowl.

The sensation was much better than what I remembered. The smoke was as pleasantly spiced as the coffee, the bite smooth rather than bitter. I did not feel lightheaded at all when I removed the mouthpiece and exhaled.

The Egyptian men watching me gave me approving looks. I also caught glances between them, as though they'd wagered that the pale Englishmen would fumble with the hookahs and perhaps topple over when the heady smoke trickled into them.

"I bought one of these last time I was out here," Grenville said after he took another pull, the water bubbling agreeably. "But a dratted porter broke it while I was disembarking in Venice. We will have to visit a market and purchase all manner of trinkets to prove we were actually here."

"Of course," I said. The act of inhaling the smoke through burbling water was soothing, though it could not erase my frustration. Brewster had wandered back down the street to watch the gate of the house, but I doubted it would do him much good.

After a long time, when the hookah was empty of tobacco and our cups drained of coffee, we departed the shop, taking leave of our new Egyptian friends.

I made it clear through the Florentine gentleman's translation that I'd be appreciative of information about the man who'd gone into the bey's house, and received a cacophony of promises that I would be informed the moment he stirred a step out of the gate. Grenville dispensed coins all around, hands thrusting out, none too proud to accept.

"I wouldn't put too much hope into it," Grenville said as we walked away. "These men might tell you any number of things for more baksheesh."

"I would not want them to be hurt, in any case," I said, beginning to regret I'd asked for their help. I didn't trust my hunter to be kind to any who got in his way. Besides, he might have promised them still more baksheesh to inform him about *me*.

Grenville's planned outing had included a visit to the local market, and he saw no reason to alter things. Resigned, I followed him around the corner and into a colorful marketplace that was buried among the narrow lanes.

Vendors lined the walls under hanging tents, wares spread out on cloths at the men's feet. All manner of things seemed to be for sale here, from rusty nails to beautiful bolts of cloth to beads to "antiquities" of dubious provenance. The smells nearly overwhelmed us—burning wood, incense, coffee, charred meat, and closely packed animals and humans.

One of the vendors pointed at a stone with markings of a beetle on it. "From the pyramids," he said in halting English.

I had no idea whether this statement held truth, but I paused to look. The vendor also had a collection of bones, and alarmingly, hidden in a box that he opened for me, a mummified hand.

"Of a queen," he assured me. "Mummy is very good for the humors."

I decided to forgo the shriveled skin and bones of the mummy's hand and take the stone. I liked it— one side was carved into the shape of a beetle, and the other side had been etched with hieroglyphs. I made out a hawk, a symbol that looked like a looped rope, a circle with a smaller circle inside, a beetle, and a u-shaped symbol.

"A seal," Grenville said as we walked away after he'd purchased a hookah pipe and quite a lot of other trinkets, including a necklace of wide plates of beaten gold. He touched the hieroglyphs. "This side was pressed into wet clay and would leave a mark. This might indeed have come from the tomb of a king." He withdrew his hand and shrugged. "Or copied last week and faked."

"No matter," I said, sliding it into my pocket. "Curiosities interest me. Be careful—I might soon have a collection to rival yours."

"I sometimes wonder why I bother with it, Lacey," Grenville said in sudden moroseness. "I have no sons to pass it all to."

I regarded him with surprise. I'd never heard him worry about such a thing before.

"You have a beautiful daughter," I reminded him. Claire was a very successful actress, and Grenville had only recently learned that he was her father.

"Yes, I do." Grenville brightened and his look turned fond. "I intend to shower her with gifts when I return." The thought seemed to cheer him, and his brief melancholia passed. "I believe this Egyptian journey will be very good for me. Even meeting Lady Mary again has made up my mind about a few things."

He had no intention of sharing what he meant, only adjusted his hat and began to whistle.

***

The soiree that evening took place at the home of Lord Randolph Carver, the third son of the Marquis of Highworth. Third sons were often shunted off to the military, a commission purchased for them to get them out from underfoot, but Lord Randolph had learned how to invest winnings from his rakehell gambling days, and made a fortune.

In his fifties now, Lord Randolph traveled restlessly around the world, enjoying the benefits of that fortune. He had taken the finest house available to foreigners in Alexandria and there he hosted the most lavish parties.

Grenville and I were admitted to find a throng already there. The house, similar to the one we let, surrounded a courtyard, but this courtyard was vast and filled with orange trees and greenery. Greek-style pillars with sculptured busts of famous men of antiquity lined the walls, and so we were greeted by Archimedes, Aristotle, Euclid, Alexander, and many others.

The guests were English, with the exception of a few Frenchmen and those from Italian cities, such as the Florentine gentleman who'd been in our walking party today. These gentlemen dressed as pristinely as they would at a gathering in Mayfair, with the exception of two who had taken to wearing Turkish-style dress. I was given to understand that those gentlemen were regarded as eccentrics.

The courtyard led into public rooms, which were whitewashed and painted with figures and landscapes meant to resemble ancient Greek art. Nothing Egyptian was anywhere in sight.

The guests were mostly gentlemen. I glimpsed few ladies in the crowd—one of them Lady Mary. I preferred the company of ladies whenever possible, and I steeled myself for an evening of male bluffness.

I had stood, a glass of claret in my hand, at such soirees often enough in India. But there was a difference here, I sensed, and not only the fact that I no longer wore my regimentals or was expected to dance attendance on a commander's wife.

In India, the ladies and gentlemen had done their utmost to pretend they were anywhere but India. It might be steamy hot and the air filled with insects, but they strove to behave as though they dined at the finest estate house in England.

The guests at this soiree were in Alexandria by choice. Whether they'd come to hunt a fortune, or for the adventure, or were on assignment by the British ministry, they acknowledged that they were surrounded by an ancient Greek city. Here the legendary men we'd read about in our schooldays had walked—Alexander, Julius Caesar, Marc Antony. We'd read Tacitus in Latin and acted out the battles.

Of Egypt itself, however, I found only talk of delving it for treasure and not much about its history. Lord Randolph's secretary, a scholar from Oxford, told me about Lord Randolph's excavation sites in Memphis and one in Thebes, and offered to guide me around them if Grenville and I journeyed that way.

I resolved then and there to encourage Grenville to obtain the firman he said he might be able to in Cairo, and find for us a place to dig through rubble ourselves.

I still felt cheated of the site I had been taken to yesterday evening. The desire to find antiquities of my own surged, the more hieroglyphs on them the better. I imagined myself triumphantly presenting my finds to the scholars working to decipher the Rosetta stone, perhaps discovering the very piece that would break the code.

As I finished speaking with the gentleman, agreeing we'd pause in our travels to watch Lord Randolph's men unearth things, I saw Lady Mary setting sail across the room to us.

Tonight she wore a silver gown covered with black netting that was unfortunately tight on her plump figure, and garish slippers that flashed with brilliant red and violet beads. Her headdress, also silver and black, sported a profusion of feathers that waved as though in a hurricane wind. Even my wife, who enjoyed the rather ridiculous at times, would have lifted her brows at this concoction.

The secretary had turned to speak to others. I avoided an encounter with Lady Mary by simply pretending I did not see her, and moved steadily across the courtyard, my walking stick tapping.

I slid into an anteroom that appeared deserted and let out a sigh of relief. A crush affected me as much in Alexandria as it did in Mayfair.

But, to my disquiet, I was not alone. A man stepped out of deep shadow on the other side of the room. He wore the dark blue uniform of a British cavalry regiment, had a head of unruly dark brown hair, a once-broken nose, and eyes the same color as mine.

He halted without surprise, and I found myself face-to-face with my double, the man who hunted me.

Chapter Ten

I did not move or speak as I looked into eyes that could have been a reflection of mine. My conviction that he was my father's by-blow increased, though I could not open my mouth to ask him whether this was so.

While I stood in silence, the man looked me up and down. "Which of us, I wonder," he said quietly, "will emerge from this room as Captain Gabriel Lacey?"

His even tones sparked my rage. My shock fell away, and I seized him by the shoulders and bore him back against a painted stone wall.

I never felt my injured knee, forgot to be afraid. I ought to have shouted for Brewster, for Grenville — for anyone — but my famous temper had taken over my senses.

"You went after my family," I snarled at him. I thumped his head into the wall, against the painted foot of a modestly clad Greek lady. "You shot my friend. I will kill you for that."

In the next instant, he'd broken my hold and shoved me away. I landed on my hurt left leg, and at last I felt pain.

We were about matched in strength and age, but his body was whole. He had *me* against the adjacent wall in no time, his face close to mine.

"I only wanted *you*," he growled, his breath hot on my face. "They put themselves in the way."

I was too enraged to remember the incidents clearly. I only saw young Peter, Donata's son, in danger of being run down, Brewster crumpling in a heap with blood pouring too quickly from his side.

"Why?" I demanded. "Who the devil are you?"

He looked me straight in the eyes, his as dark as mine. "I am Gabriel Lacey."

I stared at him for one stunned instant, than my fist came up and went for his throat. He caught my hand in a practiced grip and slammed me into the wall once more. He kicked my injured knee, and I bit down on my tongue, tasting blood.

"My father's bastard son," I said furiously. Bloody spittle came out with my words and landed on his face. "He gave you my name? Or did you take it?"

"No, you idiot—"

His words cut off as the very large gloved hands of Brewster landed on his shoulders and yanked him backward. The imposter struggled but couldn't break Brewster's tight grip.

The man snaked his hand into his coat and pulled out a glittering knife. I yelled a warning and grabbed his arm, but he twisted and cut me across the palm, ripping through my glove and leaving a streak of red.

Ignoring pain, I seized his wrist and clamped my

fingers around it, forcing his hand open. The knife clattered to the stone floor.

Brewster turned the imposter around, one giant hand holding him up while he balled up his other fist and punched the man full in the face. The imposter's head snapped back, and blood poured from his nose.

"That's for shooting me," Brewster told him, his anger clear.

The imposter's dark eyes held maddened rage above the scarlet trickle. "I wasn't aiming for you, man. I wanted *him*." He thrust his finger in my direction.

"Tell that to me wife," Brewster growled. "She was ready to put pennies on me eyes and send me to the ferryman. Then she had to wait on me like I were a baby until I got better. This is for putting her frew that."

Brewster balled his fist again. The imposter braced himself, turning his cheek to take the blow, but when Brewster let fly, his strike landed in the man's gut instead. The imposter grunted, folding in on himself.

"What the devil?" A cultured voice rang from the doorway. "Captain Lacey?" A tall gentleman with a thick head of light hair going to gray gazed in distress at Brewster and the imposter, then he pinned me with a blue-eyed stare. "And who are *you*?"

It took me a moment to realize that this man had addressed my double as *Captain Lacey* and was asking me for *my* identity.

The gentleman was Lord Randolph—I hadn't yet been introduced to him, but I'd seen him greeting other guests before I'd slipped away from the crowd. He wore a well-tailored suit and pumps made for a Mayfair drawing room, and held me with the imperious gaze of a man used to others giving way before him.

I drew myself up, wiping a trickle of blood from my lip. "I am Captain Gabriel Lacey."

The imposter heaved a laugh. He hung in Brewster's grip, the silver braid on his regimentals spattered with scarlet. "Lord Randolph already knows that *I* am the true Captain Gabriel Lacey."

"I do not understand." Lord Randolph's voice contained the cool sangfroid of Grenville's along with a note of authority that said his ancestors were bashing away at the barbaric Saxons long before my ancestors were even conceived. "You there—" He switched his glare to Brewster. "Release him at once."

Brewster didn't move, not a man who instantly obeyed.

"He is not Gabriel Lacey," I said. I pulled out a handkerchief and dabbed my mouth. "He is my father's illegitimate offspring. I suppose he is trying to use my name for his own purposes."

The imposter laughed again. Not crazed laughter, but that of a man who has heard something absurd. "I am not a bastard, you fool. I am as legitimate as you are, even more so. Your father never sired me. He was a madman. And a murderer."

I stared at him, wondering what the devil he meant by that, but just then Grenville and others poured into the room, coming to investigate the commotion.

"Grenville," Lord Randolph demanded, pointing at me. "Who is this?"

Grenville regarded us both in bewilderment. "My friend Captain Lacey, of course. I told you about him, and you invited him here tonight."

"Then who is *he*?" Lord Randolph moved his

pointing finger to the other man.

"I haven't the faintest bloody idea." Grenville's quizzing glass came out, and he fixed it on the imposter. If we had been at White's, the false Captain Lacey's social ruin would have been complete.

"I met him yesterday," Lord Randolph said, puzzled and angry. "At the home of the bey of Alexandria. He told me he was Captain Lacey. We discussed my dig at Memphis, and the legend of Alexander's tomb. He is well-informed."

"Well, I've never met him," Grenville said. He sniffed and dropped the quizzing glass back into his waistcoat pocket. "He has been following us about, attempting to assassinate my friend, the true Captain Lacey."

Lord Randolph started at the word *assassinate*, and the crowd behind Grenville murmured in shock.

The imposter only laughed again, the sound of one confident he was in the right. "You will find, Lord Randolph, that if you listen to Grenville, who has also been duped, you will back the incorrect Captain Lacey."

"He's a madman," I said, regaining my composure. "Brewster, take him out and give him to the police, for God's sake."

"Yes, indeed, Brewster," the imposter said. "Do so. I'll lead the way, shall I?"

He tried to start off, but Brewster still had hold of him, not intending to lose sight of him again. Brewster marched him from the room, the crowd pulling back as though fearing either of the two would touch them.

I followed, but I found my way to the courtyard blocked by Lord Randolph.

"Captain Lacey, I do beg your pardon," he said,

sounding anything but apologetic. "You and Grenville must explain why I spent several hours yesterday talking to a man who claimed to be you."

I longed to rush after Brewster, to shake the imposter, to make him tell me what he'd meant. *I am as legitimate as you are, even more so. Your father never sired me. He was a madman. And a murderer.*

The words rang in my head, blotting out any interest in the social niceties of the soiree.

Grenville, when I could hear again, was busy soothing our host. "I apologize for the spectacle, Dolphin. We had no idea he'd be here."

"He arrived most punctually," Lord Randolph said with a frown of disapproval. "I was surprised he did not accompany you, but as I had spoken to him before, I made nothing of it. Captain Lacey." He gave me a curt nod. "Please rest here and recover from your ordeal. I will send for refreshment."

In other words, Lord Randolph did not wish me to roam his soiree with a blood-splashed cravat while his guests stared at me. Lord Randolph might once have been a libertine himself, but his gaze told me that he did not like others disrupting his gatherings.

I nodded my acceptance. Lady Mary, who had shoved her way to the front of the crowd, now turned and shooed the guests out.

"Let the poor man rest, do. What a shock for him. So distressing." Uttering more such phrases, Lady Mary herded the others back into the courtyard.

Conversation burst into life as Lord Randolph's guests headed for the drawing room. Lady Mary turned to me before she exited to the courtyard, her eyes bright.

"You are very naughty, Captain Lacey, for not telling me of this adventure. You as well, Grenville. I shall let you make it up to me later."

She nodded to us, her feathers bobbing every which way, sent Grenville a wide smile, and finally departed. She raised her hand and her voice as she went, calling out to the Florentine gentleman who'd walked with me at the fortress.

Lord Randolph again began his stiff apologies, but Grenville cut him off. "More to the point, Dolphin, you need to tell us what he said to *you*. I want to know all about this man who has been violent toward my friends."

Lord Randolph looked me over, his blue eyes holding more intelligence than his foppish manner would suggest. "I will have my servants escort you home," he said. "I will join you there later, if I may."

I was far too agitated for polite chatting at the soiree, no matter how long I rested, so I readily agreed. Bartholomew, who had accompanied us, met me at the gate, his young face creased with distress. Grenville elected to remain, to smooth over the waters, as he put it, as he could.

"I saw Mr. Brewster taking him out," Bartholomew said as he walked beside me through the crowded streets. Though it was dark, Egyptian faces turned to me, alarm in them when they saw the blood on my clothes. "He does look remarkably like you, sir."

"And yet when I accused him of being my father's by-blow, he found this highly amusing," I said. As though I know nothing." I increased my pace, unnerved by the stares of the passersby. "I will visit whatever prison they throw him into and pry answers from him."

"If they don't torture him," Bartholomew said. "I heard that prisoners are shackled with their legs stuck out in front of them, while the soles of their feet are beaten."

I shuddered. Torture was still unfortunately common around the world. In England, we'd ceased burning people to death and had relegated the rack and the wheel to museums, but we retained the pillory, the noose, and sentencing a man to work himself to death on the moors.

"Grenville has much influence," I said as we walked on, the men Lord Randolph had sent with us watchful. "He may be able to have the fellow taken back to England to stand trial there for assault. I'm certain Sergeant Pomeroy would welcome a chance at a conviction."

Pomeroy, once a sergeant under my command, was now one of the elite Bow Street Runners, and very good at it. He gained a reward for every criminal convicted, and he'd obtained many a conviction.

We reached our lodgings. I thanked Lord Randolph's escort, who faded back into the streets, and went inside to warmth and light. I was already growing fond of this house, which Matthias and Bartholomew had managed to make quite comfortable.

My comfort did not last long. I had changed my shirt and cravat, allowing Bartholomew to sponge the blood from my skin, and was returning downstairs when Brewster came in, clearly out of temper.

"Bastards," he said feelingly. He swung his huge fist into the nearest brick pillar, and I swore the house trembled under the onslaught. "They took 'im."

"Who?" I asked. "What happened?"

Brewster shook out his hand, scowling in rage. "Bloody Turks—I don't know who they were. Came out of nowhere, surrounded me, and took him away. One tried to cuff me too. I ran him off."

"Were they police? Or the army? Maybe they wanted him for Ibrahim's death."

Brewster shook his head. "They weren't arresting him. They fawned all over him, bowing and apologizing, and escorted him off. He looked chuffed. Smug. They pushed me to the side of the street and marched away."

Bartholomew, who had come to listen, said, "Must have friends in high places."

"Apparently." My double had earlier fled inside the home of the top city official who'd made certain the local men kept us out.

Who the devil *was* this man? A brilliant confidence trickster? But why on earth would a confidence trickster have interest in pretending to be me? In taking over my life?

"He's a madman," I said decidedly. "It is the only explanation."

"A dangerous one," Brewster said. "He can turn the high and mighty to his side. He had that Lord Randolph fooled, didn't he?"

How many others had he duped? I wondered. Would I have to travel through Egypt—anywhere in the world—worrying about how this man had sullied my name? Would I be arrested for pretending to be *him*?

"*I* will grow mad if I don't find out what he wants," I said. "Keep a sharp eye out, Brewster. Who knows, he might convince his new friends to help him come after me."

The thought buoyed me more than it frightened

me. If they came for me, I would fight, and I would have answers.

I gave up for now and sat down in the drawing room, stretching out my aching leg. I tried to settle my mind, but my impatience and anger kept my thoughts whirling.

I had heaved myself to my feet again and was pacing by the time Grenville returned, Lord Randolph with him.

Lord Randolph accepted the goblet of brandy Bartholomew presented him and held it politely until Grenville and I were served ours before he sipped.

"Well, Dolphin, let's have it," Grenville said. He didn't bother waiting for Bartholomew to be out of earshot, knowing he would listen anyway. "Why did you think that man was Captain Lacey?"

Lord Randolph took another sip of brandy and responded calmly. No need for agitation, his expression said. "He presented himself at my house, said he knew he was rudely punctual but that you'd told him to go on ahead as he was so impatient to speak to me. He apologized and said his curiosity often made him brush aside niceties."

It was the sort of thing I might say if I were in a hurry to quiz someone. "Bloody cheek," I said.

"When I told you about Lacey, I said he'd been injured in the war," Grenville said. I tapped my walking stick to the boot of my left leg to illustrate the point. "But this man seems agile."

Lord Randolph gave a smooth shrug. "He leaned heavily on his walking stick and moved slowly. He looked and walked very much like you." Lord Randolph ran his gaze over me where I stood. "He is different from you, I see that now—your faces are not exact, and his nose has been flattened. But you are very alike. Who is he?"

"That is what I wish I knew," I said. "Why did he want to speak to you privately, Lord Randolph?"

Lord Randolph answered readily. "He wanted to know about this papyrus Grenville mentioned — the lost treatise from the Alexandrian library. Chabert's secret find that he reportedly hid." The man gazed at me, his haughty bearing deflating somewhat. "I am sorry, gentlemen. I am afraid I told him rather a lot."

Chapter Eleven

I sank into a chair, my weak leg no longer supporting me, and sucked in a breath as pain bit. The imposter had kicked me hard, knowing which leg had been injured and exactly where to hit it.

Grenville was the one who answered Lord Randolph. "How the devil did he know what we planned to discuss with you? Oh, damnation." He shook his head in realization. "Lady Mary knew we were after the book. I suppose she spread the tale far and wide."

"I have not heard her speak of it," Lord Randolph said. "Not that I spend much time in conversation with her if I can help it. But I said nothing, and I've heard no one else discuss it. That is not to say gossip could not have reached him. The community of British in Egypt is small, and we all know everything there is to know about one another. We know about those from the Continent as well. Chabert, for example, was carrying on openly with a lady during his stay in Egypt though his wife waited patiently for him in France."

"What lady?" Grenville asked, coming alert. "Perhaps she knows where he hid his treasure."

"I am not sure she does," Lord Randolph said. "Plenty of people have asked her, and she returns the same answer every time—Chabert did not confide to her the whereabouts of the book."

"She's still alive then?" I asked, coming out of my fog of pain.

"Yes, indeed," Lord Randolph answered. "And in Egypt. She is Signora Beatrice Faber, famous for her travels in the Near East. Which I unfortunately told your double. If, as your man says, he was rescued then he will certainly find her and speak to her. But as I say, Signora Beatrice professes to know nothing."

I leaned forward, resting both hands on my walking stick. "And where can we find this lady?"

"On the Nile." Lord Randolph spread his fingers. "I mean that quite literally. She has a lavish barge on which she lives while she sails up and down, pausing to look at whatever strikes her fancy. She has done this for many years."

"You call her 'Signora'," Grenville said. "She is Italian?"

"I heard somewhere that she is Venetian," Lord Randolph answered. "Having met her only once, and it never coming up in conversation, I haven't learned exactly where she is from."

It hardly mattered—I only knew I needed to speak to this woman. She might have told Lord Randolph she had no information about Chabert's book, but that might not be the truth. She might be protecting Chabert's memory and his wishes. Or perhaps she was searching for the book herself, either for love of Chabert or for profit.

"What else did you tell my double?" I asked Lord Randolph.

Lord Randolph heaved a sigh. "That the book exists. I've seen it. Oh, a very long time ago." He gestured with his goblet. "Chabert showed it to me. He wanted an independent opinion, and I was a scholar of the Classics, though you wouldn't know it to look at me."

Lord Randolph beamed a broad smile, which revealed how very charming he must have been as a young man. He was not handsome, in my opinion, but true charm, I had seen, can overcome what is on a man's surface.

"So you saw the book?" Grenville broke in, eyes glittering with interest. "And is it a treatise on astronomy?"

"It is indeed." Lord Randolph sat back, rolling his brandy goblet between his hands. "But no matter what information the scroll contains, the fact that it resided in Alexandria's library at all is enough to make the world agog. In my opinion, though, Chabert knew what a furor it would cause and either hid it carefully or destroyed it."

"Surely not." Grenville, the avid collector, expressed horror. "He'd be too good a scholar to burn it or otherwise get rid of it. I wager he hid the book, intending to return for it someday and use it to make his name."

Lord Randolph sighed and shook his head. "We shall never know. Chabert died, his mistress alone knew his secrets—if he told her—and the book is gone."

I pictured Chabert's lady, Signora Faber, who'd be

perhaps as old as Lord Randolph by now, floating in a great ship on the Nile, cradling the papyrus in her hands, secretly pleased.

Into my tiredness and pain came Lady Mary's words, *A woman is behind it. Mark my words, Captain. Where there is a young man in trouble, a woman causes it.*

I jolted in realization, brandy sloshing over my hand. Had my imposter already spoken to Chabert's mistress, or tried to meet with her here in Alexandria? Perhaps Ibrahim, out after hours looking for entertainment, as soldiers sometimes did, had come across the meeting and had been killed for it.

But no, the imposter hadn't spoken to Lord Randolph about Signora Faber until earlier tonight. That did not mean the imposter hadn't known about her already, of course.

"Are you all right, Lacey?" Grenville asked in concern.

I realized I was sitting quite still, sticky brandy all over my hand, my gaze fixed like a madman's. Visions and words snaked through my head, a jumble of disparate pieces of knowledge.

The imposter must have hurt me more than I'd thought. I was drifting in and out, the pain in my leg increasing.

"I believe I will retire," I said, setting aside the brandy and climbing to my feet with difficulty. "A good night's sleep will see me better."

Bartholomew, good lad, was next to me in an instant, lending me his strong arm. I bade Grenville and Lord Randolph a polite good night, and managed to leave the room while I still could stand.

"Where is Brewster?" I asked as I ascended the dark stairs, Bartholomew close behind me to steady me. I'd seen nothing of Brewster in the downstairs rooms, nor had he been lounging in the courtyard.

"He went out," Bartholomew said. "Probably trying to find a way to get to our villain."

"Bloody hell." I let out a breath of relief when we reached my bed and I could let myself collapse on it. "I do not need him to be arrested, nor do I particularly want to tell Mr. Denis that I got him killed."

"Mr. Brewster is resilient, sir," Bartholomew said with confidence. "Never met a man as strong."

"And yet, a small bullet brought him nearly to grief." I grunted as Bartholomew slid the boot from my left leg, though he did it with great care.

"True." Bartholomew set the boot aside and grasped the second. "But if he's out alone, he won't be diving in front of you to take a shot, or a stab, or a bludgeon for you. He'll only have to fight for himself."

I gave laugh of wry humor. "In other words, I put him in far more danger than he can find for himself."

Bartholomew shrugged. "If you like to put it that way. I'll keep an ear out for his return. Would you like me to send him up to you when he's come back?"

"No." I sat up and removed my coat, waistcoat, cravat, and shirt on my own, and held them out to Bartholomew. He dropped my nightshirt over my head, and I shoved off my trousers while I settled the shirt. "I'm far too tired. Tell him to remain home, though, so I can sleep and not be anxious for him."

"I will do that, sir." Bartholomew piled up my clothes in his arms, ready to rush off and work whatever spells he did to make them clean and fresh. "Good night, sir. And do not worry overmuch."

Bartholomew was probably correct that Brewster

could take care of himself, but I would feel better when he'd returned. I bade Bartholomew good night, let him douse the candles for me, and slid into uneasy slumber.

***

That night I found myself reaching for Donata in my sleep. We often shared a bed at home, though she liked to give me a wicked smile when we did so and claim we were being quite scandalous.

I came half awake to see that my hand had sunk into the pillow beside me, my heart speeding to find her gone.

But Donata was far away, resting in Oxfordshire, feasting on treats brought to her by her father's doting staff.

I missed her profoundly. The longing manifested itself as an ache in the center of my chest and a heavy feeling that my bouts of melancholia used to bring on. I tried to simply enjoy the knowledge that such an interesting and surprisingly tenderhearted woman was now in my life, but at the moment, it wasn't enough.

I needed Donata by my side, where I could touch her skin, feel her warmth, breathe her scent. I wanted to hear her low-pitched, drawling voice admonishing me. *Tell Mr. Denis that he can send someone else on his fool's errand. You are in Egypt to enjoy yourself and look about, not chase down impossible books.*

Donata, as usual, was right. Grenville had planned a long time for this journey, and I'd be damned if I'd let imposters, books that might no longer exist, and a Turkish soldier who'd likely gotten himself killed in a brawl with one of his fellows spoil our travels.

I ran a hand through my perspiration-dampened

hair. "What is wrong with me, Donata," I muttered, "that I cannot leave a puzzle unsolved?"

In my half dream, Donata smiled. *You would not be yourself, Gabriel.* She leaned forward and touched my lips.

I needed her, even if this was only a dream. I started to reach for her, when one of my shutters gave a loud *crack*.

I jumped awake. I was disoriented, expecting to be in the South Audley Street house in Donata's very feminine bedroom. For a moment, I looked about the barren room and chipped tile on the stone walls in confusion.

My thoughts caught up to me, and I remembered what I'd heard. I slid out of bed, untangling my nightshirt from around my bare legs, and padded to the window.

The shutters were tightly fastened—I'd heard Bartholomew closing them as I'd drifted to sleep. Quietly, I unlatched one and opened it a slit.

I saw nothing below. The courtyard was empty, the fountain trickling. When I ventured to open the shutter a little wider, moonlight gleamed on something metal stuck into the shutter's frame.

I drew a sharp breath when I saw that it was a knife. Whoever had thrown it had done so with precision and also force—the blade stuck deep into the wood and didn't tremble. A piece of paper had been speared on it before it had been thrown, the paper snug against the hilt.

I snaked out my arm, seized the knife, pulled it into the room, then worked off the paper and unfolded it.

The note was short and to the point. *Meet me alone, at the end of the street, and I will tell you.*

There was no need for the note to be signed. I knew bloody well who'd sent it.

I closed the shutter, cutting off the moonlight that had allowed me to read the letter. In the dark, I dressed.

I had no intention of waking Bartholomew or Grenville, or seeing whether Brewster had returned. The imposter would only disappear if he saw anyone but me, and I was determined to hear his answers.

I was not fool enough to rush outside without taking precautions, however. I struck a spark with flint to light a spill and then touched the spill to a few candles. I pulled out the box with the pistol Grenville had brought for me—he'd said we'd need arms if we went into more remote parts of the country.

I tapped powder into the pistol and loaded it, then primed the pan. Holding the pistol upright so that the ball would not fall out, I crept out of the room and down the stairs.

The house was silent. It was that hour when the world was asleep, masters and servants alike, both the late to bed and early to rise.

I unlocked the door to the courtyard and pushed it open. The cool breeze felt heavenly after the stuffy house, the moonlight shining fully on the fountain, subduing the colors of the bright flowers.

The gate to the courtyard was unlocked—no surprise, because the imposter had to have entered to throw the knife at my window. The man who had been set to guard the gate was asleep. Very much so—his long snore proclaimed it.

I stepped out to a deserted lane. The note had not indicated on which end of the street we'd meet, but I guessed. One direction held the old walls and a cluster of houses for Europeans; the other led to an arch that gave onto a main street.

I turned and headed for the main road, my pistol ready.

I waited in the deep shadow of the arch at the end until I knew the imposter was there. When I sensed him, I stepped around the corner and leveled the pistol at his head.

Chapter Twelve

The man only looked at me and the pistol, his brown eyes in shadow. His hands were empty, hanging by his sides, but I didn't trust him not to have a weapon where he could easily reach it.

"What is your name?" I asked him in a hard voice.

He returned my gaze without flinching. "I told you. It is Gabriel Lacey."

"That is nonsense." I moved the pistol closer, pressing the cold opening to his temple. "Who are you?"

The man spoke slowly and clearly. "Gabriel Marcus Roderick Lacey."

I hid my start, cold pouring through my blood. "You have one wrong," I said. "My second name is Augustus."

His eyes never flickered. "I know. I've learned everything about you."

"Then why change the second name?" My father had hung *Augustus* on me, I suppose in hopes that

I'd conquer empires and bring him the spoils.
Roderick had been his given name.

"I didn't," the man said calmly. "I was christened
Gabriel Marcus."

"By my father?"

The man barked a laugh. "Good God, man. Why
do you believe my existence and everything about
your family is focused on you? Your pride will be the
death of you."

I dug the pistol deeper, and the imposter at last
made a movement of pain. "Your reticence will be
the death of *you*," I said firmly. "Roderick is my
father's name. Why else would he give it to you?"

"It is also our grandfather's name."

I stilled. True, Roderick was a family name that
cropped up again and again down the years of
Laceys.

I said, "If you are not a by-blow, then why claim
we share a grandfather?"

"Because both instances are true." The man's
brown eyes stared straight into mine. "First, I am not
your father's by-blow. Second, we share a
grandfather."

I'd had enough. "Be plain," I said. "Or I will
march you to the soft sands of the desert and end
this. It will be a while before you are found — perhaps
never. Or I might simply beat you until you are
bloody, frighten you as you frightened my stepson. It
would be more satisfying."

I had learned from Denis that a quiet threat was
often more intimidating than bluster. I saw worry
enter the man's eyes.

"Do you not wish to know whom your father
murdered?" he asked quickly.

"My father was an unpleasant man prone to using

his fists when peevish," I said. "I never heard of him committing murder. Not even a rumor of it. In our tiny corner of Norfolk, a story like that would circulate."

"Not if he did the killing far from Norfolk, far from England," the imposter said, rage filling his voice as he spoke. "Your father murdered his own brother."

The words rang with conviction. My hand wavered as I made a slow blink. "My father had no brother."

"He had no brother by the time you were born, because he had killed him," the other Gabriel spat. "Far away in Canada. His older brother, so that your father could inherit the dung heap that is your Norfolk home. What he did not know was that his brother had already sired a child, a son, who was now the rightful Lacey heir. Thank God your father did not know, because he'd have killed that boy too."

The cool air turned chill, a breeze whipping through the street and stirring up straw, dust, and the stench of people packed together.

"You are telling me," I said when I could form words, "that my father killed his older brother—*your* father—and that you should be living in our ancestral home instead of me?"

"It was stolen from me," the man said heatedly. "My entire life was. I returned to England and found you—that bastard's son—married to an aristocrat and friends with a wealthy man who will deny you nothing. I suppose you are servicing *him* too."

Now I began to believe that this man was a Lacey, regardless of the resemblance. My father would have said something like that.

I took a step back, carefully uncocked the pistol,

and upended it. "Take it," I said, and turned to walk away.

There was a heartbeat of silence behind me, and then I heard his startled voice. "What?"

I turned back. The other Lacey was staring at me, his brows drawn in angry confusion.

"I said, take it. My life in Norfolk brought me nothing but misery. I gladly give it to you." I gestured with my pistol and then turned away again and left him.

My chest was tight, and I could barely breathe as I walked along, the pain in my knee blazing through my shock.

The story was too bizarre, could not possibly be true. If my father'd had a brother, the world would know. Parishes in Britain liked to write things down and file them away. I imagined parishes in Canada did as well, and besides, I'd never heard of my father living in Canada.

The story had to be a lie.

But it had such a ring of truth.

I glanced over my shoulder before I reached my lodgings. The arch was empty, my enemy gone.

I had just let out my breath, ready to duck back into the courtyard past the snoring guard, when a gunshot exploded into the air, shattering the silence of the street.

***

The sound woke Alexandria. Shutters banged, dogs barked, and men cried out, startled from sleep.

I swung toward the noise and slammed straight into Brewster, who was one step behind me.

"Bloody hell," I snapped. "Warn me before you do that, Brewster. What the devil is happening?"

"Someone fired a weapon," Brewster said, his

expression emotionless. "Best you go back inside, Captain."

He ought to have known I would not. Bartholomew and Matthias appeared at the gate the next moment, Grenville behind them in his dressing gown, a pistol in his hand.

Brewster said not a word, only turned and trundled away down the lane. I signaled the others to stay back and followed him.

We went to the arch at the end of the street to find chaos. Egyptian men were clumped together, shouting questions. A handful of Turks had marched in to investigate, including the lieutenant who'd arrived on the scene of Ibrahim's murder.

This time, though, we found no body, no blood. The sound of the gunshot had awakened many, but there seemed to be no victim.

Brewster, who had already learned his way around Alexandria, ducked into a side alley, and I went after him.

The streets in this area were a maze of tiny lanes and dead ends, bisecting the once wide avenues. Brewster walked in silence, and I followed as quietly as I could.

Brewster stopped in an empty lane, blank walls to either side of us, and sniffed the air.

"It was here."

I delicately inhaled and caught the dispersing odor of gunpowder. "In one of these houses?" I whispered.

Brewster shrugged. It was dark—the moon had set now and the stars, while thick and white, only gave so much light. Brewster bent over a patch in the stones that looked like a black smudge. It might be blood, or dried goat droppings, or simply dirt.

Brewster looked up and down the street, scanning it with the thoroughness a Bow Street Runner would envy. "If a chap was shot here, the bullet missed. Both men ran away, in different directions, most like. We didn't hear a second shot."

"A man can be killed in other ways," I pointed out. "The shooter might have given chase and struck with a knife. Or a sword," I added, thinking of the soldiers and their scimitars. Most of the soldiers fought with rifles these days, but as with British cavalrymen, swords were handy after the carbines were fired and empty.

"We'd have come across a dead or dying man before now," Brewster said, shaking his head. "Quarry got away, shooter made himself scarce." He looked around uneasily. "Best we get back inside."

This time, I agreed with him. When we reached the crossroads that led to our lodgings, a Turkish man I hadn't seen before, flanked by two guards, one with a torch, pointed a broad finger at me.

"You there," the Turkish man said in heavily accented English. "Who did you shoot?"

The man was thickset with a long nose and a full beard. He was dressed in clothes a little finer than the soldiers', his flowing trousers and embroidered coat reminding me of what Haluk had worn.

"*I* shot no one," I said sternly. "My pistol hasn't been fired."

He held out his hand. "Give it to me."

The others on the street were fading back, the Egyptians edging into the shadows. The Turkish lieutenant and his men looked as though they'd like to slide away as well, but they uneasily stood their ground.

I was not about to hand over Grenville's costly

pistol to a man I did not know. He might simply examine it and determine the weapon clean, the bullet still inside, or he might pocket it and walk away.

The guards behind the man, who seemed to be separate from the other soldiers, raised rifles and aimed them at me.

Heaving a sigh, I stepped forward and presented the pistol, being careful not to point it at anyone. Brewster followed right behind me.

The bearded man signaled for one of the bodyguards to take the weapon. The bodyguard inspected it, pausing to admire the etched brass facings on the handle, then he lifted the pistol over his head and fired it into the sky.

The shot blasted through the night, a puff of thick smoke and powder rolling upward. I coughed, and the bearded man pressed a gloved hand to his mouth.

"Good Lord." Grenville made his appearance again, hastily dressed this time in trousers and coat, his pistol nowhere in sight. When he reached us, he gave the bearded man a startled look then recovered himself and bowed respectfully. "Sir."

The bearded man looked Grenville over, seemed amused at his state of dishabille, and jerked his head at the bodyguard to hand the pistol back to me. The bodyguard did so with great reluctance, as though he'd hoped to keep the weapon as a prize.

I took the pistol and held it loosely, resisting the urge to examine it for damage.

"Do you have another?" the bearded man growled at me.

"No," I said in surprise. "I assure you, I did not fire that shot." I opened my coat, showing the street that I had no second weapon strapped to my chest or tucked inside my pocket.

The man's gaze switched to Brewster. Brewster, without a word, opened his coat, revealing the neat lining inside. He then spread his arms and turned around, a man used to showing that he was unarmed.

I knew full well Brewster would have knives tucked into his boots and perhaps down the back of the coat, but the Turks seemed satisfied.

"Sir, what is this all about?" Grenville asked the bearded man. "Lacey, this is Bey Mahmut, the governor of Alexandria. I mentioned him to you yesterday."

Grenville kept his face neutral, but I remembered exactly when he'd told me. My double had ducked into the house of Bey Mahmut when we'd chased him from the fortress. The bey must have given the imposter refuge and had doubtless rescued him tonight, when Brewster had been marching him to the police.

Why such a high official was roaming the streets at night, fully dressed, I could not say. Grenville, who was expert at taking things in stride, merely introduced us as though we were at a garden party.

I bowed, copying Grenville's politeness. "Pleased to meet you," I said woodenly.

Bey Mahmut nodded. He looked me over, taking his time, and I realized he was comparing my looks to that of the imposter.

Imposter, I kept calling him in my mind. The other word, *cousin,* seemed wrong to me.

Mahmut finished with me and turned to Grenville. "You must go inside. Stay there until morning."

"Of course," Grenville said. "We were awakened by the commotion. Naturally, we were curious."

"My men will see to it. Good night."

"Good night, sir," Grenville bowed again. "Lacey, shall we?"

His expression remained blank as he turned away, making a small gesture for me to follow him. Brewster kept his belligerent gaze on the bodyguards as I gave the bey a final polite nod and made to follow Grenville.

The bey and his men didn't move, and neither did the lieutenant and his soldiers. I noticed no Egyptians at all on the street as we started for our lodgings. The Turks remained motionless, colorful statues lit by the flaring torches, their black boots planted on an avenue where once the most learned men in the Mediterranean had walked.

I tried not to draw a metaphor of violence winning over knowledge as I followed Grenville into the courtyard. Brewster locked the gate firmly behind us.

***

I woke again in the morning, having fallen asleep surprisingly quickly after Bartholomew helped me back to bed. Outside, the muezzin was calling, and our servants hurried out to their prayers.

The Egyptians who worked for this house were calm and easygoing men. I wondered if stopping to pray at regular intervals every day was soothing to their spirits. Praying probably wouldn't hurt me, I reflected — I'd given up church a long time ago, when my daughter had been taken from me, and I hadn't had much use for it since.

God had been looking out for me regardless, it seemed, because I'd survived to find my daughter again. Watching the men below, I joined them in a brief prayer of thanks for the good fortune that had brought Gabriella back to me.

James Denis had actually delivered her to me, I amended as I washed my face in the hot water Bartholomew provided. Denis had searched for Gabriella, found her, and arranged for her to come to London. The Lord worked in mysterious ways indeed.

It was because of Denis's role in reuniting me with my daughter that I resolved to carry on the search for his book. While I knew he'd been motivated to help me in order to bring me under his thumb—he'd found my Achilles heel—the fact remained that he'd done it. Gabriella had been restored to my life, and when she'd been endangered, he'd turned out all his men, including Brewster, to help her.

I owed Denis more than he understood for that.

Shaved and dressed, I descended to the lower floor to find Grenville breakfasting. He looked up at me, his dark blue eyes sharp.

"The next time you race out of the house in the middle of the night to have adventures, please wake me first," he said. "You will pay for your lapse by telling me everything."

"My apologies," I said, lowering myself stiffly to a chair. "I did not want to take the chance at losing him."

"I understand," Grenville said, somewhat tersely. We had a flatbread this morning that crackled and tasted good with the goat's cheese set out next to the sweet dates. "Continue."

I poured forth as we consumed breakfast, finding it a relief to confide the troubling things the imposter had told me.

"It is absurd," I said as I finished. "My father could not have had an older brother no one knew about. And then murder him, again with no one in the world finding out."

"I can think of several scenarios," Grenville said as he calmly spread soft cheese on his bread. "If both brothers were born and raised outside of England, your father and grandfather not returning until the brother was dead, those in Norfolk might not know, especially if this brother was never spoken of. Or, your grandfather did not acknowledge his first son and abandoned him, perhaps believing him illegitimate." Grenville paused to consume a bite of bread while I sat impatiently. "Or perhaps," he went on, "your grandfather sired a son by a first wife, then left both mother and son in Canada, returned to England, married again—to your grandmother this time—and she produced your father. Perhaps your grandfather believed the first son dead as well, or perhaps he never married his first son's mother, in which case your cousin is wrong about being legitimate and the rightful heir." He set down his knife, dabbed his mouth with his napkin, and folded the napkin into a neat square. "You would be amazed at the machinations that go on in landed families to claim inheritance, Lacey. My own family has many bizarre examples."

"My father never spoke of Canada in his life," I said. "Not in my hearing, anyway, and no one told me of it. He certainly never went there, at least not after I was born. If my grandfather had been in Canada, I never heard of it either. Though I admit I tried to pay little attention to what villagers said about my father and his family—they knew what a profligate and philanderer he was. I learned to not listen. When I was eight, I was bundled off to school and spent very little time in Norfolk after that."

Grenville nodded his understanding. "In any case, your father could have been raised entirely separate from his half brother. Your father might not even have known of his existence, not at first."

"And then he runs off and murders him?" I asked, incredulous. "My father had a violent temper, yes, but he was also an inherently lazy man. I cannot imagine him scouring the earth to search for a rumored older brother."

"A lazy man can pay others to do things for him," Grenville pointed out.

"My father was tightfisted, except for what he lavished on courtesans."

Grenville eyed me shrewdly. "You told me he ran through your fortune. Paying an assassin could help deplete that fortune."

Everything Grenville said was possible, but I could not make myself grasp it. "I will have to quiz the imposter again," I said. "I am not inclined to believe him outright—he will have to provide proof."

Grenville looked thoughtful. "We must find another moniker for this man. It's unwieldy to keep calling him *the imposter*. What did you say his second name was?"

"Marcus," I said. "So he claims."

"Then we'll refer to him as Marcus. Simple and brief. I could ask the bey to let us see him. Or we might appeal to our new friend Haluk—he is some sort of official. He might be able to persuade the bey to help us."

"If Haluk is in exile, possibly not," I warned. "Ahmed the soldier was quite derisive about him."

Grenville nodded. "We can but ask. Not all Turks

in Alexandria might agree with volatile young Ahmed."

That I could well believe. I said, "What puzzles me is—who fired the shot last night, and why?"

"Yes, I've been pondering that. You and Brewster saw no one?"

"Not a sign," I said. "Bloody odd."

"Then we must discover many things today," Grenville said. He pushed back his plate and rose. "Tomorrow, we will begin our journey to the Nile."

I looked at him in surprise. "We are quitting Alexandria already?" I'd wanted to scour more of it for the Hellenistic city it had once been and continue looking into Ibrahim's murder.

"We will return. I have let this house for the duration of our journey. But the pyramids beckon. Besides, we must hunt the river's length for Monsieur Chabert's mysterious lady."

"Yes, I would very much like to speak to her," I agreed. "I do not quite believe that she knows nothing about Chabert's book. A man confides in his mistress things he will not to his wife, or even his closest male friends."

Grenville sent me an amused look. "Do you speak from experience, Lacey?"

"Hardly. I never had a mistress long enough to confide all my secrets to her."

"Well, I have," Grenville said. "And you are correct. When I was very young I told my first mistress everything. I learned to regret it, and never did it again."

He raised his brows as though daring me to ask him for further details then excused himself to get ready for the day.

I watched him go, wondering if his reticence in

speaking to mistresses extended to his current one—
Marianne Simmons—and whether that was why she
grew so frustrated with him.

I had not told Donata all my secrets. I was saving
them for the day I was certain she would not despise
me for them.

***

We visited Haluk, who professed himself happy
to see us. He offered us refreshment, which we
politely accepted, though I was still full from our
tasty breakfast.

When Grenville asked Haluk whether he could
speak to the bey for us to allow us to speak to the
man we were calling Marcus, Haluk gave us a
surprising answer.

"That man, he is gone," Haluk said. "Took ship
this morning, no one knows where."

Chapter Thirteen

Gone?" I echoed. "Why?"

I did not expect an answer. Marcus leaving suddenly was not what I had expected. Perhaps he'd taken me at my word when I'd said I'd give up my home in Norfolk to him and had rushed back to England to claim the house.

I'd let him have it. The other Lacey could worry about the sagging walls, holes in the roof, and rising damp in the cellars.

More likely, he had gone to look for the book. Lord Randolph had given him valuable information, and perhaps Marcus was hunting up Signora Beatrice to find out what she knew.

Why should he want the book? I thought in frustration. For its value? Or to simply confound me because he knew I wanted it?

Grenville asked Haluk, "How do you know this? Did the bey tell you?"

"No, no, no." Haluk shook his head vigorously.

"He tells me nothing. Karem heard of your adventures in the night, Captain, and discovered all. He learned that Bey Mahmut had an English guest in his house, one who looked very much like you and called himself Gabriel Lacey, but that the man had taken ship early this morning."

Karem, who had hovered nearby to serve us coffee, said, "I can find out where he went if you would wish it, Captain. I know many men in the harbor."

I gave him a grateful look. "I *would* wish that, Karem. Thank you."

Karem bowed, looked to Haluk for approval, and then left the room, apparently to go and ask on the moment.

While Karem was gone, we spoke about the death of Ibrahim. I told Haluk how his friend Ahmed had followed me into the desert and tried to fight me. "In truth, he is very upset about Ibrahim's death and worried about who might have killed him," I concluded.

"Young Ahmed brought us gifts," Haluk said, setting down his coffee cup. "He came to our house and prostrated himself before the gate. He made a long, flowering apology, and left a basket of grain, a length of silk, and bottle of fine oil." Haluk shook his head. "Quite a lot for a young soldier. It must have set him back a long way. My daughter's heart was softened."

He looked slightly worried, as though fearing his daughter would find the gesture romantic.

"Good," I said. Ahmed must have taken my admonition to heart. "I feel a bit sorry for him, I confess. I was once that young and impetuous."

Haluk admitted that he had been so also at that

age, and we spoke of lighter matters for a time. When the muezzin called, Haluk excused himself and went to the niche in the room that faced east, kneeling on his rug and bowing deeply. Grenville and I waited, quietly sipping coffee until he finished. Not long after that, Karem returned.

Karem had sent boys running to the harbor to ask several of his friends for news of the bey's English guest. All three boys reported similar stories, so Karem knew they were telling the truth. The English stranger had set sail on a small ship bound for Cairo.

Good. I was heading in the same direction. I'd chase him up and down the Nile if I had to.

We stayed a while longer, as it would be impolite to simply rush off. Before we left, Haluk made us a present of a coffee service, small cups and a tall coffeepot of etched silver, like the set I'd admired the first day we'd come here.

Haluk also gave me a small box made of sandalwood and urged me to open it. Inside I found a hair comb made of ebony studded with blue jewels.

"Lapis lazuli," Haluk said. "My wife gives it to your wife. Because you saved our daughter."

My heart warmed. Haluk was smiling, so happy to give me the gift.

I closed the box. "Thank you," I said sincerely. "I know my wife will like it."

On our previous visit, I'd suspected that Haluk wished to hug me instead of shake my hand. On this visit, he did precisely that.

I found myself enfolded in an embrace by the smaller man, surrounded by warm silk and the scent of tobacco and cardamom. I awkwardly patted his shoulder.

Haluk straightened up, laughed at himself, and

thrust out a hand for Grenville to shake.

"Safe journey," he said, and then ever-present Karem escorted us to the door.

***

I wanted to set off for Cairo immediately, but of course, many preparations had to be made. We could not possibly leave until the next day at the soonest.

At least we would not be taking nearly as much baggage. The furniture would remain in this house, as the house Grenville would use in Cairo belonged to a friend, an Englishman who had already furnished it.

"We will have the use of most of his servants as well," Grenville told me. "He has gone on a journey with the strongman, Belzoni, to the Red Sea, in search of the lost city of Berenice. Mad." Grenville shook his head. "I am adventurous, but walking across the desert with no knowledge of where I am going or whether I'll be able to return does not appeal to me. I do hope the old chap makes it home alive."

"I'd like to meet Mr. Belzoni," I said. "I wish them safe travels."

"He'll return," Grenville said without concern. "Belzoni has an amazing knack for finding important antiquities. He enrages his rivals, but in my opinion they should cease berating him and try to learn from him. But they are snobs. Why should a man who performed at Sadler's Wells be able to find lost tombs when the scholars of Britain and France cannot?"

"He knows how to look," I suggested, more intrigued than ever. I determined to introduce myself to the man if I were lucky enough to see him.

We spent an uneventful day, except for an encounter with Lady Mary when I returned to inspect the obelisks near the harbor. She burbled with concern about the other Gabriel Lacey attacking me last night and thought it a grand idea that I continued my travels unabated.

"I will soon see you on the Nile," she said breezily as we parted. "Tell Grenville I will host a soiree there far grander than anything Dolphin can undertake. He may look forward to it."

She held out her hand, expecting me to bow over it in an old-fashioned manner. Lady Mary bellowed out a laugh as I did so, exploding a loud *haw-haw* in my ear.

"So pleased to have met you, Captain," she said as I straightened up. "But we will not be apart for long."

Lady Mary's words rang out, then she turned and sailed back to her donkey, her faithful Miguel helping her aboard.

Of the death of Ibrahim, no progress had been made. Karem, who seemed to know when every grain of dust turned over in Alexandria, came to inform us that the soldier accused of killing Ibrahim had been released—too many men had been with him the night of the murder to convince a magistrate that he'd done it.

The magistrate concluded that a passing madman, maybe one of the defeated enemies of the empire, had killed Ibrahim then fled. Alexandria was a harbor town, with men from all over the world landing there. The question of why Ibrahim had left his billet that night was not addressed.

Irrelevant, Karem said. Young men will be young men, was his opinion.

I thanked Karem for all he'd done, and he bowed and left us. I wasn't convinced the magistrate was correct that someone off a foreign ship had seen a lone Ottoman soldier, gone mad, and bashed him over the head. But it was a convenient verdict.

I also took leave of the Porters, reflecting that I'd not had time to see anything of their digs. They told me not to worry — they'd have plenty for me to look at when I returned.

Grenville and I dined with Lord Randolph that evening, then went home to pack the last of our things. I finished quickly, as I always traveled light, then went to Grenville's chamber. I lounged in a chair to watch him instruct Matthias on exactly which of his suits were to stay and which were to come with us.

"I understand why you call Lord Randolph Dolphin," I remarked as I sipped a brandy Bartholomew brought me. "A natural play on his name. But I've only heard your friends call you *Grenville*. What was your name at school?"

Grenville flushed. "I had to work bloody hard for a long time to throw off any and all ridiculous nicknames," he said. "That is why they call me *Grenville* and that alone."

"Was it so cruel then?" I asked. I knew from experience that taunts of boys could be particularly terrible.

"Not so much cruel as direct," Grenville said. "I recall telling you when we stayed at the Sudbury School that when I was a very young chap, I was rather small, weak, and timid. They mostly called me *That Weasel-Faced Sod*, which became shortened to *Weasel* after a while." He shook his head. "By the time I was in university, though, I had thrown it off. I'd learned that a quick wit and a sharp tongue assisted when strength did not. I'd also made certain to hone my skills in boxing, swordplay, and shooting, realizing that expertise will make up for lack of height and girth." Grenville shot me a curious glance when he'd finished. "That is my tale. What did they call *you*?"

My cheeks warmed. "The Fist," I answered.

Grenville left it at that, but as I moved back to my chamber to prepare for bed, I heard him laugh heartily.

The next morning, we boarded a craft small enough to navigate Alexandria's eastern harbor, and made for the Nile. It was a fair day, the wind from the sea strong. When the ship upped anchor the sails caught readily, propelling us out of the harbor to open sea.

Grenville had already gone below, but Brewster and I and the two footmen remained on deck, watching Alexandria slip away. We rounded the point of Aboukir and headed for the opening to the river.

About twenty-five miles later, we were turning south toward a broad expanse of green crisscrossed with waterways. Those waterways resolved into one, the mighty and legendary Nile opening before me. I spread my arms as though embracing it.

***

I should have been weary of traveling, I reflected as we entered the river. In my life I'd sailed the long, hard way around the Cape to India and back again, lived a brief time in France, gone to Norway and then the Peninsula, spending years fighting a seemingly endless war against the well-trained French army.

The last four years in London, however, had made me itch to explore the world again. The new, the exotic, never failed to quicken my breath.

What I saw around me was very flat and green, green, green. Water flowed everywhere. It was the time of the Nile's annual flooding, which happened with such regularity that the entire civilization of Egypt was based upon it. The tops of palm trees poked out of the rushing water, and in places we saw only rooftops — whole villages had flooded.

Plenty of other craft surrounded our one-masted ship. Rafts made of nothing but boards lashed together were poled across the shallows. Boats of all sizes moved along the deeper water, either rowed or propelled by single sails.

I saw a larger boat with a cloth canopy built over the stern deck. Under this canopy, shaded from the endless sun, were men in European dress. As they passed us, the wind taking their sails fully, they waved at me. I lifted my hand in polite response.

Nowhere did I see desert. I knew it was out there, hovering, waiting, but as we floated through the delta region, there were green lands, black earth in the few places the river didn't cover, expanses of reeds, and wide, empty sky. In Alexandria, clouds had formed from time to time, but as we traveled south, every cloud evaporated, giving way to a huge arch of blue.

The air warmed as well. Alexandria was a Mediterranean city with a Mediterranean climate. Though I'd found it pleasantly warm, especially for late September, ocean breezes had kept it from growing too hot.

As we left the sea behind the humidity rose. Bartholomew and Matthias, English born and bred, soon sought shade and dozed off in the heat. Brewster was also English born and bred, but he remained at my side, perspiration covering his broad face under his small-brimmed hat.

"Where do you hail from, Brewster?" I asked in curiosity. I knew very little about his early life.

His look told me my lack of knowledge was to his preference. "London. Thought you could tell from my speech." He pronounced *thought* as *fawt* but I had noticed that Brewster could move in and out of his London cant as he pleased.

"London is a large city," I pointed out.

"Whitechapel, if you're going to be prying. Near Spitalfields. I learned my craft scratching a living on those streets. Had to, to survive."

I was not surprised. The streets around Spitalfields were narrow and crammed with houses of dark brick under leaden skies. Entire families lived in a few rooms in each of those houses. A greater contrast with this wide land, bright with perpetual sunshine, could not be imagined.

"Soak in the heat, then, Brewster," I said. "We'll miss it when we're home."

"If I survive to go home," Brewster said darkly. He peered into the murky waters. "Alexandria was all right, but they say there's crocs in the Nile ten feet long." He nodded at the surface below us. "And you want to run up and down on it."

I scanned the river, looking for signs of huge water creatures but finding none. "Have I discovered something you fear at last, Brewster?" I asked.

"'Tain't fear, Captain." Brewster threw me a scowl. "'Tis good common sense. Somefink of which you are sorely lacking."

I could not argue with him. I leaned on the railing again, the sun on my neck, and enjoyed the warmth.

***

The hundred miles to Cairo passed without incident. As we neared that great city the next morning, I finally saw the Egypt of my imagination.

Cairo, a city at the end of an ancient caravan road that stretched across deserts and mountains, was a sprawling metropolis, unlike the sleepy Alexandria we had just left. Spires of minarets rose into the dusty air, green fields lined the shores, and humanity teemed on the streets beyond the docks.

On the west bank, the river flowed into fields and then the green stopped. In the distance, hidden by haze, I swore I could make out the sharp peaks of great pyramids.

I peered a long time, shading my eyes, the rising sun behind me marking the desert with stark shadows. I stood so long that an Egyptian sailor, his robe tucked around his waist, nearly ran into me and gave me an irritated look.

I hoisted my bag and followed Brewster down the gangplank.

At the bottom, I was nearly swept into the mass of people, donkeys, carts. Sights, sounds, smells, engulfed me. It was early, but the humanity of Cairo was hurrying to finish errands before retreating from the heat of the day.

Grenville emerged and trudged down the gangplank after us. He was pale but did not look nearly as bad as he had after our sea journey—the river had been calmer than the tossing Atlantic and Mediterranean.

He raised his hand to a man coming along the dock to meet us, a Sicilian Grenville had said he'd asked to be our interpreter. Apparently Giorgio Vanni spoke fluent Turkish and Arabic as well as French, English, and Italian, along with several dialects of the Italian states.

Signor Vanni was in his forties, I'd say, with a few gray hairs at his temples. He had smooth skin, dark eyes, and a face that would have been handsome if it hadn't been an odd shape, somewhat oval and long, his chin sharp. He would live in our house and assist us with communication in Cairo.

"Bloody hell," Brewster muttered as we walked from the ship. "Now I have to look after *three* of you."

Grenville shot him a glance a surprise. "You aren't here to look after *me*, Mr. Brewster. Matthias and Bartholomew do that."

"Ain't I?" Brewster asked, a glitter in his eyes. "When I get home, I'm asking his nibs for a rise in wages."

"You deserve every penny," I said sincerely, but he only grunted in response.

Cairo was loud, bustling, energetic, exiting, and hot. We left the docks and made our careful way through the streets toward the lodgings of Grenville's friend.

We made an odd party—a London ruffian, two footmen, a scholar, a wealthy dandy, and a lame cavalryman. We earned plenty of stares from the Egyptians on the streets and from the Turks who stopped to watch us pass.

Grenville's friend's home in Cairo proved to be far finer than our lodgings in Alexandria. This house was more like Haluk's, with a courtyard brimming with scarlet flowers around two fountains, arched doorways, beautifully painted tile throughout, and hidden staircases that folded around corners to a spacious upper floor.

Bartholomew and his brother approved and

retreated to the servants' quarters to try to explain to the cook what sort of food a gent like Mr. Grenville expected. Brewster roamed the house, looking for places danger could hide.

We had not been in the house more than an hour or two when word came that we were summoned — immediately — to the governor of all Egypt, the pasha, Muhammad Ali.

Chapter Fourteen

While Grenville ran in the same circles as the Prince Regent of England and often had invitations to Carleton House and the Brighton Pavilion, I had never seen the inside of a palace. In the army, my commander, Colonel Brandon, and his wife, had been entertained by local princes in India, but I'd not had the rank and importance to join them.

So it was with interest that I walked through the streets with Grenville — they'd sent donkeys for us to ride, but I decided I'd look a fool astride one of the small beasts. The donkey also seemed a bit relieved I didn't climb aboard.

I took note of everything for my journal to Gabriella. The streets changed as we followed our guides, from narrow and maze-like to broader roads lined with trees. I was reminded of the avenues of Paris, and remarked upon it.

"That is to plan," Grenville answered. "The pasha is determined to make Cairo a city to be reckoned with, combining the best of Europe with the best of the East to make it a unique wonder. He summons French and English architects, doctors, and engineers to help him with this modernization. Very ambitious is the pasha."

Grenville had also refused the donkey and strolled along beside me. His friend Vanni had come along to interpret, and Brewster, of course, would not be left behind. The other two walked a few paces behind us, Brewster keeping an eye out for trouble.

"I must commend him," I said. "If the pasha can bring clean streets and better medicine to the Egyptians, that will be admirable."

"True," Grenville said. He stepped closer to me and spoke in a low voice. "But have a care with this man, Lacey. He worked his way from soldier to viceroy of Egypt in no time. He raised the tax on land to an extraordinary height so he could take it for himself when the owners couldn't pay. And I suppose you've heard what happened to the Mamelukes?"

"No," I answered. The pasha had risen to power when I'd been fighting on the Peninsula, and the politics of Egypt and the Ottomans had been of little interest to me.

"The Mamelukes tried to rebel against the Ottomans and seize power in Egypt," Grenville explained. "They nearly succeeded. Muhammad Ali realized the Mamelukes posed a great danger to him. Besides, they owned much land and had become wealthy over the centuries, as well as being a military force to be reckoned with. So he invited the prominent Mamelukes to a celebration at the palace. When they marched into a narrow passage near the palace walls—this is 700 men, Lacey—he had them all assassinated, his soldiers shooting them from above."

I stilled a pace, the horror of that seeping through me. I too easily pictured the scene—a narrow passage with walls like the sides of a canyon, riflemen firing down on soldiers unprepared to fight, men dying in the dust.

I knew from my readings of history that countries were often dragged into reformation by utterly ruthless men to become a place the world envied. I thought of the Roman emperor Octavian, later known as Augustus, who'd thought nothing of posting lists of prominent men to be killed so that he could confiscate their lands and money. Rome had risen to its pinnacle under Augustus, but that fact didn't make his actions any less coldblooded and cruel.

The avenues of stone and trees now became sinister, and I felt eyes watching me.

The palace, in a district called the Shubra, was a delicate and splendid piece of architecture. Signor Vanni, who had lived in Cairo for several years, told us that it was not finished, but I found it already quite beautiful.

The building we saw from the outside was white and square, but we stepped through its gates into paradise. The gardens were lush and green, filled with orange trees, palms, flowering plants, and walkways reaching down to the expanse of the Nile.

The garden was pleasing, but my breath was entirely taken away when we went inside an enclosed pavilion. Arched walkways surrounded a pool that reflected the open sky, but the rooms held Greek-style pillars, corbeled ceilings that could have come from Versailles, and portrait paintings as clear and precise as anything by Gainsborough or Reynolds.

We were taken to a chamber in a corner of this astonishing place. The large room was decorated with tiles and gilded pillars, and the arched ceiling had been painted with Eastern designs but also very European cameos and plaster relief.

Apparently I would not be kicking my heels in an anteroom, as I'd once speculated, while Grenville met with the ruler. In a chair on a dais at one end of the room, sat our host, Muhammad Ali, the wali of Egypt.

He was a fairly large man with a full salt-and-pepper beard that framed a hard and strong face. The eyes that regarded us were shrewd, intelligent, unyielding, and gleaming with confidence. I saw before me a man who knew what he wanted and would do anything to get it.

The pasha dressed in fairly simple Turkish clothes—a dark tunic and trousers covered with a colorfully embroidered sash. A long saber rested against the arm of his chair, a reminder that he'd been a military man for a long time.

He was surrounded by functionaries both military and civilian, their clothes subdued like his, almost European in style, as though they could have come from a shop in Paris. The pasha himself glanced at us once and away, returning to his conversation with a man who hovered next to him with a sheaf of papers.

One of the men broke from the crowd and bowed politely to us. He said in perfect English, "His eminence was pleased to hear that Mr. Grenville visits his city. He wishes to speak to you about your journey and welcome you to Egypt."

"How very kind of him," Grenville said with just

the right amount of deference. "May I present my friend and traveling companion, Captain Gabriel Lacey."

"A military man, yes," the functionary said, unsurprised. He turned to me. "His eminence will be very pleased to speak to you as well."

His eminence seemed to pay absolutely no attention to us. We were led to a round table upon which had been placed coffee and pastries, but there were no chairs. Another lackey poured the coffee for us, and we sipped, standing, wondering how long we'd be expected to wait.

An hour, it turned out. Signor Vanni had been allowed in with us, but Brewster had not, much to his anger. I fully understood—a ruler who held power tightly in his large fist would not want Brewster, an obvious man of violence, anywhere near him.

We didn't speak—I believe all three of us were too intimidated to do so. Vanni, from what little I'd seen of him so far, seemed cultured, learned, and well-mannered. He wore a dark suit that was similar to Grenville's but even I could tell that its material was nowhere near as costly nor its tailoring as fine.

Vanni must be a bit like myself, gentleman-born but with very little income. Grenville called him an old friend, but I suspected Grenville was paying Vanni to be our interpreter and pretending not to, to save the man's pride.

At long last, the pasha made a gesture with his large fingers, and the functionary led us forward.

Grenville gave the pasha a low, but still very English, bow, and I followed suit, planting my walking stick to balance myself. The pasha looked me over with his dark eyes, taking in every nuance of me, then Grenville.

He looked straight at Signor Vanni and spoke in the Turkish language, his voice rising in a question. His eyes flicked back to me.

"He asks whether you were in the army," Vanni supplied. "And if so, what rank and what branch."

"Cavalry," I answered promptly. "Captain. Went home when this happened." I tapped my walking stick to my left boot.

Vanni translated, and the pasha's eyes suddenly lit with interest. "You are a rider?" He asked through Vanni. He snapped his fingers, and two men immediately went to him and bent to listen to him.

The pasha then got out of his chair, moving more quickly and lithely than I'd imagined a man of his stature could, and strode to the door, his servants and functionaries hurrying after him. The pasha disappeared outside, and the functionary who'd greeted us beckoned us to follow him.

"His eminence wishes you to come. He has something to show you."

Grenville and I exchange an uneasy glance. Vanni did not look reassured either, but there was nothing for it. The functionary led us out into a smaller courtyard and through a gate to a walkway through the park.

Our destination proved to be the stables — very ornate stables, built along the lines of the grand palace behind us. The setup was a bit like Tattersall's in London, with a central riding court surrounded by a colonnade with horse boxes beyond that. The only difference was that the ring where the horses would be paraded or ridden was covered here, cutting off the severity of the sun.

The pasha was already sitting on a couch in a

pavilion at the end of the ring by the time we arrived. His sword again rested next to him, but he was leaning forward animatedly, interest in his eyes.

Four Turkish stablemen emerged from the stalls, each leading an exquisite beauty of a horse.

They were grays, three dappled and one so light as to be almost pure white. The horses were small but graceful and sturdy, their faces wide at the eyes and almost concave, their noses narrow. Manes and tails had been brushed to flow, and they gleamed in the shade of the ring.

I stood entranced. I loved a good bit of horseflesh, and these were the most elegant animals I'd ever seen. I'd heard of the Arab breed, the desert horses of the Bedouins, but I'd never had the pleasure of looking upon one.

"They are beautiful," I said without restraint. "Conformation perfect, amazing beasts."

The pasha looked pleased, even before Vanni translated for him. I suspected the pasha understood more English than he let on. Then again, perhaps my look of rapture said enough.

I was stunned again when one of the horses, a mare, was led aside, a saddle and bridle put on her, and the horse brought to me. The pasha gestured to me, uttering a few words.

"He's letting me ride it?" I asked Vanni incredulously. I looked to the English-speaking functionary, expecting that I was mistaken.

The functionary nodded. "Please," he said. "The groom will help you mount."

Grenville gave me a look that told me I must not refuse. Not that I wished to, but I wanted to be certain I'd been given permission to ride before I approached the horse. I had the feeling that if I did one thing wrong with this animal, the guards around the pasha would take up their rifles and shoot me dead — making certain the horse was not hurt, of course. The pasha might apologize to the British officials for the action but that would hardly console me or my family.

The pasha nodded in my direction, eyes sparkling as though he enjoyed my discomfiture.

Drawing a breath, I handed Grenville my walking stick, limped the few steps to the horse, and allowed the groom to boost me into the saddle.

The horse was small, and I was a large man, but the mare did not flinch at my weight. I easily found my balance on the saddle and started her off slowly, not wanting to press her too much. The horse's vibrancy came instantly to me through the reins, and I knew this mare was ready to show off.

I let her. I walked her around the open space, then nudged her to a trot. She sprang forward as soon as my legs touched her sides, gliding into a dainty gait that was easy to sit.

The mare's canter was even better. She loped like a dream, turning and pivoting around the ring, instantly responding to my commands.

The last horse I'd ridden in the cavalry had been much the same in temperament, though he'd been a large, long-legged charger. I'd been very fond of that horse, who'd been shot out from under me the day the Frenchmen had captured me and amused themselves torturing me. I could forgive them crushing my knee and making me walk with a stick the rest of my life, but I had never forgiven them for killing my beloved horse.

My love for riding welled up in me again as I guided this wonderful animal around the ring, the pain and misery of my injury flowing away.

I knew I could not ride her all day and into the night, nor could I put her over the low wall and dash away with her, much as I wanted to. With reluctance, I took her back to where I'd begun, patting her arched neck as I slid from her back to my unsteady feet once more.

"She is astonishing," I said to the pasha. My eyes must have been shining—my mouth ached with my wide smile. "Thank you a hundred times for allowing me to ride her. I am honored."

The pasha took my effusion with calm pleasure. He spoke directly to me, and Vanni said, "He asks whether you were a good cavalryman."

I shrugged, modest. "I did my duty."

"He was bloody good," Grenville said as he handed me my walking stick. "He came through all the battles and never lost a man. He was injured only because of trickery and deceit."

I was a bit embarrassed to hear Grenville champion me so warmly, but the pasha looked impressed.

Vanni listened to his answer then turned to me with an expression of a faint dismay. "He asks if you will come to train some of his officers in British cavalry moves. For an hour every morning."

I gave the pasha a startled glance. "I'm hardly an expert," I said. "And I do not yet know the plans for our stay in Cairo."

The functionary looked at me in alarm and said quickly, "I would not refuse, sir, were I you."

The pasha watched me. When I didn't answer, he snapped something to the functionary.

The functionary cleared his throat, more unease in his dark eyes. "His eminence asks you what you wish in return for this deed," he said. "What is your greatest desire?"

I did not need to think about my answer. "To dig for antiquities," I said promptly.

The pasha's face split into a genuine smile, his body shaking with his laughter. He waved a large hand, and the functionary said to me, with an air of relief, "It will be so. Return here at the second hour after sunrise tomorrow."

***

"You promised him *what*, guv?" Brewster demanded as we walked from the palace through the wide streets of the Shubra.

"He cleverly talked his way into receiving a firman to dig wherever he wants for anything he wants," Grenville answered for me, swinging his walking stick. "I have been busy calling in every favor from every official in Cairo, in hope of obtaining any permission at all, and Lacey simply walks in and rides a horse for five minutes."

Grenville sounded amused, not resentful. But then, he hadn't just been coerced into training the officers of a powerful man who thought nothing of murdering those who got in his way.

"You have to make them let me come with you," Brewster growled at me. "His nibs will not be happy if I let you perish inside that place." He jerked his thumb at the jewel of a palace falling behind us. "This pasha might be the ruler of all Egypt, but Mr. Denis is the ruler of *me*."

"I doubt the man wishes me harm," I said, trying to sound confident. "He is training his armies in the latest fighting methods, and I did serve under Wellington, the man who defeated Napoleon. It is meant to be an honor." And if I could ride one of those horses again, it would be a true pleasure.

"Just you make certain I can follow you," Brewster warned. "Or we'll take the next boat for home. I trussed you up and put you on a ship once — don't think I won't do it again."

"I will do what I can, Brewster," I said soothingly.

Brewster wasn't satisfied, but he said no more as we entered the narrower, busier streets and made our way back to our house.

I had hoped to see the pyramids that day, but the visit to the palace had taken much time, and the afternoon had already turned hot. Bloody hot. Though it was the end of September, the temperature soared, the sun burning as soon as we stepped out into it.

Better to visit the pyramids in the morning hours, Grenville said. The trouble with that was, the pasha had just claimed my morning hours for training.

Ah, well. I would make certain I reached the pyramids directly afterward, and I'd learn to endure the heat.

Meanwhile, Grenville and I had questions to be answered.

I found I needed to rest from my ride and our walk across the city. I settled into the house's small library to read while Grenville spent the afternoon visiting the Englishmen and Europeans in our area of Cairo — its foreign quarter much more extensive than the Alexandrian enclave. He caught up on the latest gossip and casually asked about Signora Beatrice Faber, who had been mistress to Monsieur Chabert.

Grenville discovered, he told me when he returned, that the lady had gone to Thebes many weeks ago, proposing to return to Cairo in October. Whether she would or not remained to be seen.

Brewster had also gone out, walking the streets both to learn the lay of the city and also to look for the other Gabriel Lacey, the man we'd agreed to call Marcus. Brewster said he found no sign of him, which displeased him. He'd keep looking, he said.

Grenville suggested we retire and nap, now that the sun was at its hottest. We'd rise again and go out after dark, when Cairo truly came alive.

I tried to follow his suggestion and lie down, but sleep would not come — I'd rested enough with my reading. I soon rose again and went back downstairs, the tiled wall of the enclosed staircase cool under my fingers.

"Do you wish to go out?" Vanni asked me as I made for the courtyard. It was hot, but the cool splashing fountains and shade of the flowering trees was inviting.

"I am a bit restless," I confessed. "Even if it's the same temperature as hell out there."

Vanni gave me a small smile, his dark features warming. "It is much worse in the heart of the summer, I assure you, Captain. The cool air in the mornings and evenings these days is sweet to me. If you would like to walk, I can show you a thing or two."

He seemed anxious to be quit of the house so I let him lead me out. Brewster saw us go and came after us, cursing the heat and telling me what he thought of me venturing into it.

As we moved out of the foreign quarter and into narrower streets, mud-brick buildings surrounding us, Vanni seemed to grow nervous. He shot me a quick smile when I glanced at him, but swallowed, his prominent Adam's apple moving.

He led me to the end of a street that ended in a T

and took the left direction without halting.

"Where are we going?" I asked him.

The walls narrowed in on us, the street deathly silent. The inhabitants might be sleeping inside the houses to avoid the heat, but I felt a prickle of unease, as though watchers lurked behind the closed shutters. I thought of Grenville's story of the pasha luring the Mamelukes into a choked passage and raining death down on them from above, and glanced around me in disquiet.

"It is not far," Vanni said. He spoke perfect English, but as his nervousness rose, his accent deepened.

Brewster said not a word. He only trudged behind me, scanning the closed shutters for signs of life.

The lane petered out at a dead end that formed a little courtyard, the walls around us dirty and crumbling.

Vanni halted at a high wooden door in this cul-de-sac and turned a sorrowful look to me. "My apologies, Captain. I was told to bring you here as soon as I could."

"Told by whom?" I demanded sternly.

I made to draw the sword from my walking stick, when to my surprise, Brewster stepped forward and took the stick quite forcibly out of my hand.

"You don't want to pull a weapon," Brewster said. "Not here."

Before I could ask what the devil he meant by that, the gate opened, and a tall, bulky Egyptian motioned us inside. Vanni followed him readily, and Brewster nodded for me to go after him. Having no choice, I did so.

The Egyptian silently led the way in through another courtyard to a set of rooms that were nearly as opulent as the pasha's own. Carpets piled on carpets, low couches strewn with cushions sat near tables filled with trinkets. The arches were tiled in blue and green, giving the space a cool, nautical feeling.

The man who came through the door to meet us wore a galabiya and a turban, but he was not Egyptian. He had a smooth face, graying hair that stuck out on either side of the turban, and a hard look similar to the ones Denis's ruffians always wore.

"Welcome, Captain," the man said, in a cant from the heart of London. "Mr. Denis told me to keep an eye out for you, if you came this way." He spread his hands, his smile wide, showing a few missing teeth. "And here you are."

Chapter Fifteen

I turned an astonished look on the still-nervous Vanni. "You work for James Denis?"

"Regrettably," Vanni said, his face reddening. "I owe him quite a sum of money, but he is allowing me to repay him in service."

Hence Vanni's inexpensive clothes and his faint air of desperation.

"You knew of this as well," I said accusingly to Brewster.

"Not until Mr. Vanni tipped me the wink this afternoon, Captain," Brewster said. He fixed his gaze on the man who'd greeted us. "He's not to be hurt."

"Of course not," the man said smoothly. "I mean to be of service. My name is Sharkey. Sullivan Sharkey." He looked me up and down, clearly trying to decide what I was made of.

I had concluded long ago that Denis kept agents throughout the world, men who could obtain artwork, valuable books, or antiquities for him, as well as less tangible things—favors, obligations, influence. Denis owned people. I suspected he owned Mr. Sharkey as much as he did Vanni.

Sharkey looked like the sharks I'd seen—glittering eyes, smiling mouth, oily skin. It was a good name for him.

I wondered suddenly why Denis hadn't asked Sharkey to find Chabert's book for him, since the man was already in place, but I kept my mouth closed. Denis did not always tell everyone who worked for him what he was about, and Sharkey might not know of the book. If Denis wanted this man to help me look for it, he would have instructed me to seek him out. But Denis had not even mentioned him.

Brewster had his lips firmly pressed together. He did not look overjoyed to be here, but I noted that he kept hold of my walking stick.

"Well, what can you do for me, Mr. Sharkey?" I asked. "Presumably you brought me here for a reason."

The man did not invite us to sit down or offer us refreshment. As a host, he was lacking in even the most basic manners.

"To make your acquaintance," Sharkey said, pressing his hands together. "And to tell you that if there is anything you want in Cairo, you have only to ask me and I will provide it."

He had the arrogance of the pasha and, I suspected, some of the power as well, at least in Cairo's underworld.

"That is kind of you," I said, keeping my expression neutral. "I am here to sightsee, nothing more."

"Not what I 'eard," Sharkey said. "'E wants you to

find something for him, don't 'e?" His gaze chilled. "I'm in this godforsaken hellhole because I'm good at what I do, Captain. So anything you want, *you come to me*. Understand?"

He gazed at me belligerently, a man angry that a trusted task had been given to another. I saw that he might try to make things difficult for me if I did not bring him in on the treasure hunt.

But if Denis had wanted me to ask for Sharkey's assistance, his letter would have told me to do so.

"I assure you, I have no wish to take over what you do in Egypt," I said truthfully. "As I say, I am here to look at ancient ruins, and then I will return to England. I do not work for Mr. Denis."

Sharkey skewered me with an intelligent eye. "Ain't true. Everyone knows about the cavalry captain he's taming to his hand. He'd never have let you come here without you bringing something to him in return." He tried to soften his tone, become the affable Cockney once more. "If we work together, you and me, we'll make him happy that much quicker, and split the reward. Then you can enjoy poking about the 'eathen tombs to your 'eart's content."

I straightened, keeping my weight off my bad leg. "I am afraid that must be left up to Mr. Denis."

Sharkey's gaze went flat, like that of a predator in the shadows, waiting to strike. "You don't want to make an enemy of me, Captain. You're a long way from England. You need friends in Egypt."

"I have plenty of friends, Mr. Sharkey," I answered, letting my tone harden. "I thank you for your concern."

Sharkey paused, his brows coming together as he reassessed me. I saw him realize he'd taken the wrong tack, assuming me to be another Vanni. He'd come at me like a bully, but as I'd indicated to Grenville when I'd told him my nickname at school, I too had quite a lot of bully in me.

Sharkey stepped closer. Vanni had retreated to a discreet distance, but Brewster was right beside me, his sharp eye on the man and the large Egyptian behind him.

"You've made a mistake, Captain," Sharkey said, his voice smooth. "You'll want to watch yourself on the streets. 'Tain't like Alexandria around here. Cairo's full of thieves and men with knives."

I studied him as intently as he studied me. Was it Sharkey's ambition to take over the Egyptian branch of Denis's empire, the same way the pasha itched to take Egypt from the Ottomans?

I decided I was being fanciful, but my idea might be close to the mark.

"I will keep it in mind," I said, and gave him a small bow. "Good day, Mr. Sharkey. It is too bad we cannot come to an agreement—an ally here would have been helpful."

Sharkey lost all pretense of politeness. "Get out, Captain, before I have my men throw you to the pavement."

I had no wish to linger. Brewster silently handed me back my walking stick, giving me a warning look, but I was not foolish enough to draw my sword here among Sharkey's guards. I used the stick to prop me as I stepped into the courtyard and moved to the gate, though my anger kept me upright more than anything else.

Once outside the gate, I strode forward, not bothering to look about. The cul-de-sac where Sharkey lived was well-chosen—no one could approach this house without his knowledge.

Vanni had come out before me, but I got ahead of him and lost my way. Vanni had to catch up to me and steer me to the correct street.

Sharkey had been right about the dangers of Cairo. Even in the heat of the day, sharp eyes watched me from doorways. I was aware that I was out of place, a foreigner, in a section of town where I was not wanted.

"You like to stir up trouble, don't you, Captain?" Brewster asked when we'd reached the busier, wider streets around the foreign quarter.

I had not climbed down from my anger. "If Mr. Denis did not inform Mr. Sharkey of my task, he must have had a reason. I was not going to fall at the man's feet and beg him to help me keep Denis appeased."

"I didn't say you should," Brewster said. "It's the way you go about things, guv. Like poking a bear with a stick. Sharkey can make things hard for you."

"Things are difficult enough already—I'm sure I won't notice the difference," I said with grim humor. "How did he become Denis's agent? I'd think Denis would want someone with more finesse."

"Sharkey used to be no different from me," Brewster said. "A pugilist, and a good one. Mr. Denis raised him up, because Sharkey got results. Always. Never missed. But he's gotten above himself, I'm thinking."

"It is clear he has," I said. "But if you think I will tell Grenville we should pack up and flee Cairo because of him, you are wrong."

"'Swhat I'm afraid of, guv," Brewster said darkly.

***

The next morning, a contingent of Turkish guards

arrived at our door to convey me to the palace. Whether the half dozen men were meant to ensure I did not forget my appointment or to protect me on the streets, I did not know, but men, carts, and beasts scrambled out of the way as we walked.

Vanni was allowed to accompany me, but Brewster was not, which put him in a bad temper. Brewster did concede that I'd be well protected with six fully armed Turkish bodyguards, but he pointed out that I'd not be able to protect myself from *them*.

Grenville said that he and Brewster would scour the town for knowledge of Chabert's book and the whereabouts of the other Lacey. The man had not surfaced yet, but that did not mean he'd given up trying to eliminate me from the family tree.

After meeting Sharkey, I'd been tempted to let the quest for Denis's book go to the devil. Denis had not warned me of Sharkey, which annoyed me greatly. I could forget about the task, ride the pasha's horses, dig in the dirt, and buy gifts for my family back home. An idyllic holiday.

By the time I reached the palace, I knew I'd do nothing of the sort. The possible existence of a book from the Alexandrian library intrigued me. I'd never be able to leave Egypt without first doing my damnedest to find it. If it existed, what a prize it would be.

Denis knew me well, blast the man.

At the palace, I again had the privilege of riding the mare. Four Turkish cavalry officers listened to me explain, through Vanni, the things I had done in the campaigns of Talavera, Salamanca, Vitoria. Mostly I had ridden at enemy lines, swinging my saber, hoping that artillery and infantry didn't blast me out of my saddle, but I didn't elaborate on that.

I showed them how to feint and turn, and demonstrated the intimidating factor of yelling at the top of one's voice when one charged.

I thoroughly enjoyed myself. Drilling did not heat my blood to the fever pitch of true battle, but I could relive my younger days, when I'd been unstoppable on horseback.

My knee reminded me, when I at last dismounted, that my antics of ten years ago took more toll on me now. A groom helped me to the pavilion at the end of the ring where a spread of food and drink had been laid out for us. The pasha himself was not there, but he'd assigned plenty of guards to watch us.

The cavalry officers and I sat on cushions, drank fragrant coffee, and ate everything in sight. The four were fine men, open and talkative, impressed with my riding and wanting to hear all about fighting against Napoleon's crack generals.

By the time the meal was finished, I realized I'd made new friends, even if we didn't speak a word of each other's language. They wished me well and looked forward to more lessons tomorrow.

I returned home, buoyed, able to put my unpleasant encounter with Sharkey yesterday afternoon out of mind.

More pleasure was to be had when I arrived at home. Grenville had arranged for us to make a journey to the pyramids, and we set off at once.

***

The most difficult part of our journey proved to be getting ourselves across the Nile to Giza. A profusion of boats ran from the banks, from fishermen's tiny craft to the barges of the wealthy, but there was teeming confusion and a great crowd. The river itself was congested, this being the largest city in Egypt and the destination for many travelers coming south from the Mediterranean.

Grenville had been granted leave to borrow the craft of another Englishman, but when we arrived, the boat was not there, and no one seemed to know where it had gone. Grenville and Vanni walked up and down, offering to pay to be ferried across, but the Egyptians were strangely reluctant to take us. I wondered if Sharkey had spread the word to withhold help.

At long last, Grenville did manage to find a small raft piloted by an Egyptian man who had at some point in his life lost an eye. The socket had scarred over, but it was still a concave mess.

We crowded onto the craft, the river lapping a few inches from my boots. The man poled us forward, then hoisted a sail when we reached deeper water. Because the raft was so small, we were all recruited to help turn and move the sail to catch the wind. Grenville made no complaint as he closed his expensive gloves over the rough ropes, his dark eyes sparkling as though he vastly enjoyed himself.

The breeze from the water cooled us somewhat, but by the time we climbed from the river on the other side—and Grenville dropped many coins into our ferryman's eager hand—the day had turned scorchingly hot.

I glanced with envy at the light-colored, simple galabiyas of the Egyptians and the loose clothing of the Turks. I vowed then and there to obtain Turkish or Egyptian dress, with a turban to keep the sun from my head. Brewster might disdain me, but I saw no reason to suffer in clothes made for climates that were cool and damp.

As I'd observed in Alexandria, the sands began at

the edge of the cultivated fields, an abrupt transition from rich black soil to crumbling pale sand. Behind us was green among the high water of the river; ahead of us, bone-dry earth.

We'd hired donkeys at the water's edge, not to convey us but the baggage Grenville had brought. We'd need refreshment, he'd explained, and shade. Not confident we'd find any on this side of the river, he'd brought it with us. It took some time to load the donkeys, and then we were off.

The sun had reached its zenith. The sky was a blank, light blue, tinged with dust. The pale tan color of the desert floor was the same in every direction, unchanging from where we stood all the way to the horizon, which was swallowed in haze.

The first thing we beheld was the Sphinx, its head thrusting up from the sand beside the narrow trail. I looked at the rounded rectangular shape meant to be the neck up to the well-carved face. Despite the shattered nose, the eyes, ears, and hood of the king were rendered in great detail. I wondered if the rest of it had been as detailed before the sand and wind had taken its toll.

The Sphinx, while remarkable, was dwarfed by the enormous pyramids that rose a little way behind it.

Astonishing. I could think of no other adjective to describe the Great Pyramid, which was the first we reached, except *colossal*. The base was a perfect, enormous square, while the sides rose and rose to a peak, the exposed stones like stair-steps for giants.

I ignored the others, the Egyptians and foreigners who were either milling about between the pyramids or digging trenches or pits, the Egyptian men's voices raised in song.

I forgot the heat, the pain in my leg, the dry dust caked around my lips, the sun beating on my head through my hat. I walked to the bottom of the Great Pyramid and looked straight upward, my neck aching as I tilted it back and back and back.

Blocks had been stacked together to form a "step" a little higher than my chest. There was nothing for it but that I found another smaller slab of stone, climbed upon it, and pulled myself up to the first block of the pyramid. There were many, many more blocks above me, but I was seized with the need to climb all the way to the top.

I had clambered up to the next step when I heard Grenville calling below.

"Ahoy, there, Lacey! Have a care. If you fall, I am the unfortunate man who will have to explain to your wife."

I waved down at him. "I'll not go far." I turned and heaved myself up to the step above that.

My knee began to hurt, but the pain was swept away on a tide of fevered excitement. I'd never felt such a thing before, the frenzied need to stand on this very ancient monument, to touch it and become part of its past.

Herodotus had stood where I did now—indeed, we knew the name of the king who built it— Cheops—because of him and other Greek historians. Ancient Romans had come to look upon this place, some even leaving their names marked in the stone. The Arabs who'd conquered this world must have looked upon it in awe. The pyramid might have been built by an ancient king, but now it belonged to the world.

At this moment, it belonged to me.

I heard huffing behind me, and Brewster heaved

himself up to sit on the stone below. He drew out a handkerchief and mopped his face.

"Looking after you will be the death of me, guv."

"Grenville has raised his pavilion." I pointed at the open tent where Bartholomew and Matthias were setting out folding chairs. "You can wait there out of the sun."

Brewster ignored this offer. "You ain't going all the way to the top, are you?" he asked wearily.

"A few more steps," I said. "Here — boost me up, and I'll pull you after me."

Brewster climbed to his feet with a grunt. He didn't argue, merely heaved me to the next step, his strength unnerving.

I turned around and helped him climb up beside me. Step by step we ascended about five more blocks, then we halted, both of us out of breath.

I turned to view the plain that spread under us. The Sphinx waited patiently, its face to the tourists as they approached the pyramids. A second pyramid, this one with white stone smoothing part of its sides, stood nearby, and another still smaller pyramid peeked from behind that one.

These were houses of the dead, tombs of kings and queens. So why did I feel so alive standing here?

I decided at once that I'd return to Egypt as soon as I could, next year perhaps, and bring Donata and Gabriella with me. Grenville could ensure that they traveled comfortably — he was experienced at it. Both Donata and Gabriella had a keen curiosity and resilience, and I would show this world to them.

Grenville had seated himself at the edge of the pavilion, in the shade, with his sketchbook. He took up a pencil from the box next to him and began to draw.

As I scanned the view of the second pyramid again, I started and lifted my eyes to shade them from the merciless sun.

"What is it?" Brewster was on his feet beside me, peering into the glaring brightness.

"Is that Marcus?" I pointed to the man I'd seen striding into the desert away from the second pyramid. He had the height, the build, the gait.

"Why don't we find out?"

Brewster, without hesitation, began climbing down, helping me descend, and we struck out into the desert after him.

Chapter Sixteen

I strode quickly across the hot ground, the heat penetrating the soles of my boots.

Grenville looked up from his sketching as we hastened by, his pencil aloft. "Where the devil are you going?" he called.

"To ask someone a question," I answered in a hard voice.

Grenville dropped the sketchbook and pencil to the table, snatched up his walking stick, and joined us.

The wind had risen. As I'd climbed the Great Pyramid, the air had been still as death, but now that we hurried across the open ground, gusts blew from the desert, stirring the sand.

Fewer people gathered around the second pyramid, with much of its limestone facing still intact, fewer still around the third. We passed trenches dug along the bases of the pyramids where men were searching for something, I knew not what.

They look up and stared curiously at the three mad Englishmen heading into the open desert.

I'd seen the man called Marcus, most definitely, and so had Brewster. Brewster led the way, moving nimbly over rocks and sand with the silent speed I'd observed in him before.

The desert beyond the pyramids was wide and featureless. I knew that at Sakkara, to the south, more tombs and pyramids awaited, but I could see nothing of those places in the emptiness of earth and sky.

I could not see our quarry either. I slowed, breathing hard, wondering where the devil he'd gone. Grenville fell in beside me, holding his hat in place with a gloved hand, his fine suit coated with a layer of pale dust.

Brewster continued at the same rapid pace. I saw him pause on a slight rise, and then he simply dropped out of sight.

I ran forward in alarm, Grenville hard on my heels. My walking stick sank into sand, barely supporting me.

I slipped and slid as I climbed the low hill Brewster had ascended, then I stopped at the top in surprise.

Below me spread a maze of steep-walled riverbeds, all dry, hidden from the plain behind me by the rising ground. The Spanish called such places *arroyos*, dry riverbeds that filled during floods, though I guessed this one hadn't flooded in centuries.

Brewster was running along the bottom of the riverbed, his battered hat firmly on his head as he gave chase to our man, who was some way in front of him. I climbed down to join him, sliding badly on the earth and landing heavily, barely keeping to my feet. The top of the wash rose above my head, its sides sheer.

Grenville started to follow, but I held up a hand. "Wait. We might need someone to pull us out of here."

Grenville studied the drop, let his gaze follow Brewster, and nodded. "Brewster's gone left about twenty feet ahead of you. I can't see the other fellow anymore."

I lifted my walking stick to him in thanks and hurried off down the cut.

Grenville walked above me, shading his eyes and calling out the directions I was to go. Wind whipped his clothes, but down here in the cut the air was still, though plenty hot.

I heard shouting in the distance and made for it. My hat tumbled off, caught by a chance gust that blew through the cut, and I left it in my haste.

I rounded a sharp corner and found Brewster with his hands around Gabriel Marcus Lacey's throat.

Marcus was again in Egyptian dress, one end of his turban dragging down his back. He had a knife in his hand, which was poised against Brewster's ribs.

I caught the hand with the knife and twisted it. Brewster, lips curling in fury, let go of Marcus's throat only to punch him in the face.

Marcus's head rocked back, and he started to laugh, a crazed sound. "Out to make certain I never get your ruins in Norfolk?"

Blood ran from the cut Brewster's blow had opened on Marcus's cheek. Marcus screwed up his eyes and kept laughing.

"What is the matter with you?" I demanded. "And why are you out here in the middle of nowhere?"

"Do we have to share everything now?" Marcus asked. He spat blood, and Brewster closed his hand around his throat again. "A grandfather, a tumbledown estate, a face, our plans?"

"Speak plainly," I said. "Tell me what you meant—how is it possible that my father had a brother no one ever knew of? Are you saying my father went in search of yours to murder him? It is absurd, even for my horror of a parent."

"Call off your man," Marcus said, his voice hoarse. "I'll tell you."

"Let him go, Brewster," I said quietly.

Brewster threw me a look of anger, but he deliberately lifted his hand and stepped back.

Marcus rubbed his neck, red from the imprint of Brewster's fingers. His skin was tanned deeply from the sun and coated with dust.

"My father was born of our grandfather's first wife," he said, his voice filled with anger that ran deep. "The marriage was perfectly legal, but she was half-caste—her father French, her mother a native of the people called Mississauga. My father was raised by his mother and her people when our grandfather abandoned them to return to England. My grandmother died of grief—our grandfather married again, as you know, this time to a tame Englishwoman of Norfolk, who dutifully gave him a son, fully English this time, one Roderick Lacey."

My father. I'd never met my grandmother, who had died long before I'd been born. My grandfather had passed away when I'd been a young child. If I remembered him at all it was as an enfeebled man my father had been very impatient with. But both my grandfather and grandmother had been from Norfolk, well known to the village of Parson's Point.

The wind rose above us, dust filling the air. I heard Grenville call out, but I was too fixed on Marcus and his words to pay attention.

"I still cannot understand how no one knew of this," I said. "If the marriage was legal, there will be a record."

"Oh, there is a record." Marcus gave me a dark look. "And I know where. Grandfather Lacey lived with a French family in what is now the town of Kingston, on Lake Ontario. My father grew up there with his Indian relations, joining the British colony when they pushed out the French. His marriage to an Englishwoman was legal as well—my mother died in the having of me. My father was murdered when I was all of two, by your father's hand. The family who raised me, friends of my mother, told me all, showed me proofs."

I listened, dumbfounded. Grenville had postulated that my grandfather could have left his first wife and returned to England, possibly denying he'd ever married her.

I had tried to fathom a reason a man would do this, but if his first wife had been half-caste, our grandfather might have been convinced he'd made a mistake, that the marriage would never be considered legal. Or perhaps he was simply embarrassed by her. I'd known men in India who'd taken wives among the native women, and then not known what to do when their fellows derided them for it.

I looked for signs of the Mississauga woman in Marcus, but could see none. The Lacey blood had erased it. Considering how aggressive Lacey men could be, I was not surprised.

"Why not come to me?" I asked him, my anger

not assuaged. "Why not simply present yourself and explain who you were instead of trying to kill me and hurt my family?"

Marcus's jaw firmed. "I have told you again and again, I meant to hurt no one but you. *They* are as much victims of the Lacey cruelty as I am."

"That does not undo the fact that they were hurt!" I shouted. "Nor am I entirely convinced of your tale. You could be anyone following me about with a story of being rightful heir to the Lacey estate. Why you'd want it, God knows."

"Because it is *mine*." Marcus slammed his palms to his chest. "I am a gentleman's son, an Englishman of the bloody landed classes. I grew up working my hands to the bone helping the man who'd adopted me, lifting and carrying loads bigger than me while you went off to your schools and were waited on hand and foot."

I burst into laughter as wild as his had been. "Then you know nothing about English schools and life with my father. I'd have been glad to work like a drudge instead of being caned every day because I could not respect the shallow-minded fools who tried to teach me."

"You had everything I should have had," Marcus said stubbornly. "Even when I was in the army, I sweated in malarial swamps while you rode to glory on the Peninsula. You, the son of a murderer, stole my life."

"If all this is true, prove it," I returned. "Go through the courts, produce the records. If all is as you say, you may take over the house in Norfolk and I will wish you happy. My wife will be relieved not to have to spend the money to repair the roof."

I could hear Donata's cool tones in the back of my

mind, pictured her holding my gaze with a warning look. *Do not be so hasty, Gabriel. Calmly wait for evidence before you give away all you have.*

Marcus had stirred fury in me I hadn't known in a long time. All he said might be true, but he had stalked me, threatened me, terrorized my stepson, and nearly killed my friend. I would not embrace him readily even if he proved to be a long lost cousin. He needed to make amends.

Marcus shook his head, spattering blood to the sand. "Proving it takes money, and you know it. I've labored for every penny I have."

"Obviously you could afford to travel to England and then to Egypt. You have a friend in the governor of Alexandria."

"I *worked* for him." Marcus's eyes flashed with anger. "I taught English to his sons. He kept me nearly a prisoner. I had to escape him to come to the Nile to ..."

He trailed off as though realizing he'd been about to confess what he was doing out here. He hadn't come down the Nile to follow me. He'd departed Alexandria before I had.

"To what?" I asked him. "What are you looking for? Not me—not today."

Marcus went silent, averting his gaze. Not in submission. His mouth had the stubborn set I recognized in myself.

Brewster took a step forward, silently offering his services to beat the truth out of him.

Just then, we heard Grenville call again. "Lacey! There's—"

His words were lost in a shriek of wind. I looked up to see a wall of sand rushing at us down the arroyo, obliterating sky, walls, and very soon, us.

Chapter Seventeen

I turned my back to the wind, but my mouth and nose quickly filled with sand. I jerked my coat loose and covered the lower half of my face, straining to see Brewster in the sudden storm.

I was completely alone in a whirl of sand, which was dense like the thickest fog London ever produced. But while London fog surrounded one with clammy fingers, the Egyptian sand threatened to burn my skin from my bones.

I dropped to my hands and knees, groping my way to the wall of the arroyo. My hand found a boot, one thick enough and wide enough to belong to Brewster.

The boot was upside down, my touch landing on its sole. I found Brewster stretched out facedown, and my hand fell on a warm stickiness in his hair.

I tore my coat from my mouth to call his name. "Brewster!" I shook him.

To my immense relief, Brewster stirred and

coughed.

I jammed my coat back over my nose and mouth and crouched against the rock wall. An overhang jutted out a foot or so, which kept the rain of sand from my face somewhat. I helped drag Brewster to a sitting position, hearing his groans even over the howl of the wind.

The sky darkened, the cloud turning an opaque gold color. All the sand in Egypt, it seemed, was rushing down this arroyo. Brewster and I sat shoulder to shoulder, the two of us huddling behind my spread coat. Brewster breathed heavily, his body sagging against mine.

"Are you all right?" I tried to ask, but sand grated in my throat and my words barely sounded.

He must have understood, because he nodded. "Didn't hit me," he croaked. "Were a rock."

I had to wonder, though, if the rock had been wielded by Marcus's hand.

Of Marcus, there was no sign. I don't know if he'd been able to flee, or whether he crouched in the wash not far from us. I wondered what had become of Grenville as well. We were somewhat sheltered down here—Grenville had been exposed at the top.

I worried about him but we could not leave to look. Sand crept in around us. Would we be found hundreds of years from now, bones buried in the dust? We had rushed out here with no water. I had heard that sandstorms in the Egyptian desert could last for days; my morbid thought was not so farfetched.

I reflected that running out here after Marcus had probably been one of the most foolish things I'd done in my life, and I'd done many a damn fool thing. I wanted to apologize to Brewster, but I knew I needed to keep my mouth closed so it wouldn't dry out. If we survived, I'd apologize profusely.

We sat, immobilized, hot, and thirsty. Time dragged on. I pulled out my watch, which hung from a fine fob Donata had given me, and brushed sand from it. It told me that it was four in the afternoon, but as I studied it, the ticking slowed then ceased.

I let out a breath and tucked the watch away. The sand rendered the sky a dark yellow, light fading as the sun was swallowed.

We waited while the wind pounded and sand flowed around us. Brewster and I pushed the drifts away with our boots, but they swirled back to us. I knew now how the monuments of the ancients had become buried as the years had gone by. No matter how carefully and cunningly men had built their temples and tombs, the relentless sand had swallowed all.

Sunset flared, the sand becoming blood red for a moment or two, then blackness descended. My tongue was stuck to the top of my mouth, my lips glued together. My limbs were so stiff I couldn't move.

Brewster slumped against me, asleep or awake, I could not tell. I fought against drifting off, fearing the sand would simply cover us, but in the end, my body took over, and I slept.

I woke to Brewster shaking me. I moved my coat, sand cascading down my body and into my boots. It was dark, but when I drew a breath, the air was almost sweet.

"Wind died," Brewster said, his voice a bare rasp. "Sand stopped."

I could see that, and I let out a breath of relief. Brewster helped me to my feet. I unfolded painfully, sand in my boots, my trousers, my shirt. My knee had frozen in place, and I cried out as I straightened my leg.

Brewster steadied me without comment. It was too dark to see the seriousness of his head wound, but he seemed unwavering. He led me out into the arroyo, the steep sides cutting off the desert above.

The clouds of dust and sand had faded, and the dark night sky unrolled above us in all its splendor. The moon, a thin crescent, hung high in the sky against a glittering backdrop of stars.

I had not seen the stars this clearly in a long time. We occasionally had fine nights in London, but usually the smoke, soot, and glare from the gaslights blotted out the stars.

I had certainly never seen the sky like *this*. The entire bowl of the heavens opened over us, the smudge of the Milky Way blazing a trail through the constellations. The sky was rendered more beautiful, perhaps, because I was alive to see it.

I had to clear my throat several times before I could speak. "Can we get out?"

Brewster led me along the arroyo to a place the walls weren't quite so high. Without a word, he leaned down and boosted me up, pushing me as I scrambled and slithered to the top. Footholds were scarce, and the last pieces of my gloves shredded on the rocks I clung to, but at last, I gained the top. Brewster tossed my walking stick to me, which landed with a clatter beside me.

I dropped to my stomach and reached into the gulch to help Brewster ascend. He slipped three times back down the side, but on the fourth try, I was able to grab him firmly and haul him upward.

He heaved a long sigh as he flopped over onto his

back at the top. "Most definitely a rise in wages," he said breathlessly.

It seemed a hundred years since I'd so eagerly leapt up the blocks of the Great Pyramid. The night was still, the heat gone, the breeze now that we were out of the cut, sharp.

We'd seen nothing of Marcus as we'd made our way down the arroyo. I spied no huddled figure of Grenville out here, either. I hoped he'd been able to return to his pavilion before the storm had become too fierce, but I could not suppress my fears that we'd find his body lying on the ground between the arroyo and the pyramids.

I assumed Matthias and Bartholomew would have rushed out to look for Grenville the minute he went missing, helping him to safety. They might be looking for us as well.

The only trouble was, I had no idea where the pyramids lay from here. I wasn't certain exactly where the arroyo was in relation to them. I saw no silhouette of pyramids against the stars, in any case, and no lights anywhere.

"We should make for the river," I said.

"We should stay here," Brewster countered. "Mr. Grenville and your footmen will be looking for us. They're partial to you."

"And if they cannot find us?" I rested my weight on my walking stick and looked around. "I'd rather not wait to die of thirst, or be bitten by a snake or torn apart by jackals while Grenville tries to search for us. We know that the river lies to the east—it will be hard to miss. If we cannot find someone to take us across this late, we can rest on the shore until morning."

"Oh yes?" Brewster said skeptically. "How do we

find east then?"

I pointed my walking stick skyward. "The stars are a map, Brewster. They show the way even better than a compass."

Brewster eyed me dubiously. "If you say so, guv."

"Look." I tried to wet my lips with my dry tongue. "There is the plough, plain as day. If you follow a line from the last star of the plough itself, you get the pole star. That is due north, or mostly so." I pointed high overhead. "The W is Cassiopeia. At this time of year, at this time of night, she is in the east, Hercules to the west of her. We head that way." I brought my arm and stick down and pointed due east.

Brewster watched and listened but with none of the fascination I'd had when an old farmer had told me this under the empty skies of Norfolk.

"Maybe in England it's that way," he suggested.

"The stars are the same the world over, Brewster." I began walking—hobbling, rather. "We can see a few different ones this far south, but the constellations themselves don't change. No matter what happens on this earth, the stars are forever. Makes our troubles seem a bit petty, does it not?"

"Mmm," Brewster rumbled. "Lost in the middle of the desert. No water. Head aching. Following a madman." His boots crunched on rock as he moved ahead of me. "*Petty* is not the word in me mind, guv."

"I will make it up to you with plenty of ale," I said. "The Egyptians invented ale, did you know?"

"If they did, I haven't seen enough of it this journey," Brewster said over his shoulder. "I'll take a few barrels, please."

"You shall have them," I promised lavishly.

We fell silent, picking our way slowly across the

desert. Neither of us wanted to trip, fall into a hole or down a gully, or step on a snake who'd take objection to being trodden upon.

The air was indeed cooler — in fact, it was growing bloody cold. The afternoon had roasted us, and now the night tried to freeze us to death.

Brewster insisted on walking in front of me, checking for danger as we went. I came behind, hunkered in the coat that had kept me from choking on sand, my walking stick testing the ground before my feet.

After an hour of this, I judged — my watch was still not ticking — Brewster pulled up.

"'Struth. It worked." He pointed ahead of us. Starlight gleamed on the surface of the river, its ripples reflecting the riot of stars overhead.

"Simple navigation," I said modestly, though in truth, my heart was banging in relief.

We moved forward cautiously, though I know both of us wanted to run gladly to the water. But we had marshland to navigate, with mud that might suck us down, not to mention more snakes and possibly crocodiles on the banks.

Eventually, we trudged through muddy fields, the Nile's inundation rendering the farms one shallow, spreading lake. Crocodiles could lurk here too, not a pleasant thought.

At last we reached a few mud houses on fairly dry land, right on the river's edge. The village, what there was of it, had been built on a small rise, which was now an island.

No one was there, however. The inhabitants must have fled the spreading waters, to wait elsewhere until the river receded.

"We'll have shelter anyway," I said.

Brewster only grunted. We were too thirsty and exhausted to care much anymore.

I looked inside the first mud house, but there was no light. I smelled the lingering odor of goat but no one had been here in a while, I could tell. I'd hoped they'd left a water jar—the Egyptian servants placed large jars of water into niches in our house in Cairo in attempt to cool the air. I could see nothing, unfortunately.

"Guv." Brewster's hoarse cry had me backing out of the house. I found him waving his arms at a boat that was sliding silently along the river, heading south.

It was more barge than boat, with flat decks, lit windows, and an ornate sail. I'd seen a similar barge as we'd floated toward Cairo, the one with the European gentlemen on it.

I cupped my hands around my mouth and shouted, waving my walking stick. Brewster's cries joined mine, his big arms moving in the air.

The night was so still that I heard Lady Mary's voice quite clearly from the deck of the ship: "Good Lord. Is that you, Captain Lacey?"

Chapter Eighteen

I had no breath left to answer. I'd not thought much of Lady Mary in Alexandria, but at the moment, I wanted to fall at her feet and kiss her gaudy slippers.

Brewster shouted back. "The captain's here, your ladyship. Can you help us? We're nobbled."

Lady Mary was calling to whoever piloted the barge. "Stop I say, man. Put in here. We must rescue my friend."

A loud argument in Egyptian ensued, Lady Mary switching to that language to harangue her captain. The sail furled and dropped, then the barge slowed and swung ponderously around.

The pilot was not foolish enough to run himself aground, no matter what Lady Mary urged. An anchor dropped, and then two small boats lowered from the barge's side and headed for us.

Brewster and I waded out to meet them. In the boat I reached first I found Miguel, Lady Mary's

Spanish assistant. His strong hand came out, and he helped me onto the tiny boat. In the other, small Egyptian men were struggling to accommodate the bulk of Brewster.

Finally we were settled and taken out to the barge. I nearly collapsed trying to climb onboard from the small boat, but Miguel assisted me, and at last I made it.

I was a shivering, pathetic, and very thirsty wreck when I landed on the deck near Lady Mary's feet. She was not, in fact, wearing her garish beaded slippers, but sensible half boots.

"Dear, oh, dear," she bleated. "Miguel, take them to the cabin. Tea, I think, not coffee."

"Water," I said, my voice barely a scratch. "We've had none."

"Of course, my dear Captain. Come along, Miguel. And *you*." She pointed her imperious finger at an unfortunate Egyptian and babbled demands at him.

Not long later, I found myself seated on a low cushioned bench that lined a wall of the stern cabin. This seemed to be Lady Mary's private drawing room—hangings, cushions, carpets, and books were everywhere, along with little trinkets and small paintings. The pasha's palace was only slightly more lush.

But then, Lady Mary, daughter of a duke and widow of a marquis, was a wealthy woman indeed. Her widow's portion, it was said, had been immense, and her father had left plenty in trust for her. She traveled the world, going where she pleased, apparently in great comfort.

She welcomed Brewster into her cabin as well and said not a word about the state of our sandy clothes and muddy boots. She only watched as servants brought in ewers and poured water into large goblets with a soothing, liquid sound.

Both goblet and the water within looked clean, though I knew I wouldn't have cared if it had been mostly sand. I poured the water into my mouth, Brewster doing the same, willing my throat to work to swallow it down.

Brewster wiped his mouth on his sleeve and held out the goblet for more. I was ready to simply seize the ewer the servant held and imbibe its entire contents, but I forbore and let the man refill my glass.

Once the ewers were empty, the servants departed and returned with tea served in dainty porcelain cups. The cup Brewster lifted disappeared in his big hand, but he drank the tea with as much relish as he had the water.

"Now, good heavens, you must tell me what happened," Lady Mary said. "What were you doing on the shore of the Nile in the middle of the night? On the west bank, no less? You do know that the west bank holds the cities of the dead, while the east is for the living."

Brewster snorted. "Thought *we'd* be one of the dead—that's a fact, your ladyship."

"We were caught in a sandstorm," I began, and then told Lady Mary our adventure. I left out everything concerning Marcus, letting her believe we'd simply been exploring when we'd been cut off by the storm.

"What about Grenville?" Lady Mary asked worriedly. "Where is he?"

"I hope he is safely at home."

"Oh." Color left her cheeks, leaving patches of deep pink. She had used the rouge pot this evening.

"Dear me."

"We saw no sign of him as we walked," I said. "His footmen look after him well. Mother him, I would say. I imagine he is all right."

I spoke with a conviction I did not feel, but Lady Mary looked to be on the verge of swooning.

"Well," she said, with the air of a person trying to be brave. "Then we must see you to your lodgings and make certain. If not, then I will sail this barge back across the river and find him."

Determination filled her words. I admired her resolve, even though I uncharitably wondered if she meant to make Grenville so grateful to her, he'd unbend and propose.

Nevertheless, I agreed we should return to Cairo at once and discover what had become of him and the rest of our party. I would not forgive myself if Grenville had perished in that storm—I'd not discouraged him from following me into the desert, and then I'd ordered him to remain at the top of the arroyo. He'd have had more shelter if he'd climbed down with us.

"Captain?"

Lady Mary's worried voice came from far away. In spite of my agitation about Grenville's welfare, the bench seemed to slide out from under me in my exhaustion. I landed on the carpeted floor, which was soft and flat, the boat's gentle rocking like a hammock on a summer's day.

Someone laid a blanket on my back and slid a small pillow beneath my head. Before I drifted off to sleep, I thought I recognized the tanned hands of Miguel, but I could not open my mouth to thank him.

***

I could barely move from the gangplank of the

boat to the wheeled conveyance Lady Mary had commanded be brought for her when we landed. The cart looked like a miniature version of a landau, pulled by two donkeys. I tried to laugh, though nothing emerged but a croak.

I was piled into the cart, and Lady Mary, without worry of scandal, climbed in beside me. Brewster had recovered more than I had, and marched along beside us, but slowly, not his usual robust self.

The streets were thronged, the night cool here but lacking the sharpness of the open desert. The shops and cafes were still open, Egyptian men sipping coffee or gently sucking smoke from hookahs in lighted doorways. We moved through the crowd with difficulty, though Miguel ran in front of us, opening a way.

When we reached the house, I tumbled out of the cart at the courtyard's gate. Brewster caught me, as did Bartholomew, who had sprinted out of the house as soon as the cart halted.

"Grenville?" I tried to say, but only a thin wheeze escaped my lips.

"Now, don't you fret yourself, sir." Bartholomew had a strong arm around me, half lifting me. I had no idea what had become of my walking stick—my hand closed on empty air.

I noticed quite a number of people in the courtyard. Bundles lay at their feet, and one man was lighting the lanterns the others held.

Matthias raced out from the drawing room. "Is he here?" He stared at me then turned around and yelled back into the house. "He's here! Sir! He's come back!"

More footsteps sounded, and Grenville himself darted into the courtyard faster than I'd ever seen him move. He advanced upon me, halting a foot from me, and his hands landed on my shoulders.

"Good Lord, Lacey," he said.

He squeezed my shoulders, pressing them as hard as a man might embrace another. But even now, when everything told me Grenville rejoiced that I was alive and whole—he was keeping himself from embarrassing me.

"Lacey, I have to say that I am damned glad to see you." Grenville squeezed me again, ran his hands down my arms, then let me go. "Bartholomew, Matthias, help him. Can I get you anything, my dear fellow?"

"My bed," I mumbled. "Now that I know you aren't dead in the desert, I have no more reason to remain awake."

Bartholomew caught me as I sagged. He and Matthias carried me between them up the stairs and into my small bedchamber. I still had no idea what had become of my walking stick.

Grenville's voice came through the window that overlooked the courtyard, his words holding trepidation. "Lady Mary?"

I fell asleep before the chuckle left my mouth.

***

In the morning, I could barely move. I climbed from bed, my limbs painfully cramped, my knee aching more than it had in a long while.

I had a shock when I dragged myself to the washstand and looked into the mirror. My face was bright red with windburn and studded with pinpricks of dried blood where the sand had pitted my skin.

My hands were raw, my gloves having torn completely away as I'd climbed from the arroyo.

Though I'd assuaged the worst of my thirst on Lady Mary's barge, my mouth was parched and swollen, my lips cracked.

Bartholomew entered with a silver pitcher of water, the mist gathered on it telling me the water was cool. He poured a glass and handed it to me.

I downed the water in a few swallows, and Bartholomew refilled the glass, letting me drink until I could breathe again.

After that, he sat me down, shook out a towel, hung it around my neck, and proceeded to wash and shave me as he did every morning.

I flinched as Bartholomew brought the razor down to my lathered face, certain the blade would hurt my burned skin. But the soap he'd used cooled me, and Bartholomew handled the razor so deftly I never felt its touch.

Grenville let himself in after a polite tap on the door. He was dressed in his light suit for warm climes, his face shaved, his hair combed. He came to stand in front of me while Bartholomew leaned over me from behind, quickly scraping my face.

"What became of you?" I asked, ignoring Bartholomew's frown when my jaw moved. "I was very certain I'd gotten you killed."

"And I was certain I'd seen the last of *you*," Grenville said at once. "The answer to how I escaped the storm was that I turned and ran like the devil was after me. The storm caught me quickly, but I had fixed on my destination and kept to it no matter what. The great bloody pyramids stuck out nicely, even in that hellacious dust. My pavilion was rendered useless, of course, but Matthias and Bartholomew found me and pulled me to safety. We rode out the storm inside the Great Pyramid itself."

"Inside the pyramid?" I asked, envy edging my voice.

"Not as exciting as you might think," Grenville said. "Our light didn't last long, so there we were in the pitch dark and the heat. I spent the entire time fearing for you rather than marveling that I was in the tomb of a great king of old." His brows rose as he took in my disappointment. "Do not worry, my friend, I will arrange for you to go into the pyramid. When you have recovered, of course. I imagine that today, you will remain quiet."

He gave me a severe look but I shook my head, which made Bartholomew again lift the razor away in irritation. "I must return to the palace for the riding lessons."

Grenville gave me a severe look. "Good God, Lacey, you will kill yourself. I will send word that you are ill. No one can expect you to ride around in a mock cavalry battle the day after you were scoured by a sandstorm."

"I made a promise," I said firmly. I had the feeling that the pasha, with his cold eyes and hard stare, would not take nearly dying in the desert as an excuse for missing an appointment. He'd withdraw his approval for my firman in a trice. "I can instruct without riding myself. I only need an interpreter."

"Well, you will have to choose a different one than Signor Vanni," Grenville said with some heat. "Apparently he made it back here perfectly safely, but he was not here when we arrived home, and no one has seen him since yesterday afternoon. I am much provoked. I certainly could have used his help when I was putting together the search party, trying to explain what I needed them to do."

"Vanni might be Sharkey's man," I suggested.

"He led me to him readily enough."

"Bloody cheek. I was doing him a favor."

"Vanni seemed very worried," I said. "We don't know what he has done to be in Denis's obligation— perhaps he is in Sharkey's power as well. Not a comfortable place, I imagine."

"Still, I am not happy with him for not telling me he worked for Mr. Denis," Grenville said decidedly. "How many friends must I keep from that man's clutches?"

"Denis is very good at bringing others under his command," I said, then changed the subject. "I hope you were kind to Lady Mary last evening. She did rescue me, after all."

Grenville held up a hand. "Do not worry, I was politeness itself."

Bartholomew gave my chin a last swipe with the razor, wrapped my face in a warm towel, and moved away to clean the shaving things and finish preparing my clothes. He'd rubbed balm on my skin to calm it, and I basked in the coolness of it for a few minutes before I unwound the towel.

"The fact that Lady Mary happened to be floating along the Nile in time to rescue me makes me suspicious," I said as I came to my feet.

Grenville gave me a wry look. "It is no coincidence. She is searching for the wretched Greek book as well, she told me. Our hunt made her decide, why not? I have the feeling she wishes to find it to present it to me in an attempt to seduce me with it. She offered to take us to visit Chabert's mistress when she lands again in Cairo. Apparently they are acquaintances."

"She did not tell us this in Alexandria," I said as Bartholomew returned with my riding coat.

"No, she said she was saving it as a treat. She wanted to surprise us and present Signor Beatrice, fait accompli, but coming upon you last night changed things."

I slid on the coat and let Bartholomew settle it on my shoulders. The procedure reminded me of something. "Procure one of those galabiyas for me, will you, Bartholomew?" I told him. "And a turban. I lost my hat in the wretched sandstorm. If I am to grub around the desert, Egyptian dress will be better, I think."

Bartholomew looked dismayed. "Sir, I'm not certain a gentleman should—"

"Humor him, Bartholomew," Grenville cut him off. "Captain Lacey will rush to a market and buy one for himself if you do not, and heaven knows what one of the natives will sell him."

"Quite," I said dryly. "You might have to try them on, Bartholomew. If the garment is a bit too small for you, it will likely fit me."

"Sir." Bartholomew said, his face unmoving.

"He is teasing you," Grenville said. "Do not become too stiff, Bartholomew, or we all will rag you something awful. Now, I wonder, did this Marcus fellow perish in the sandstorm? Or did someone come along and fetch him as well?"

"I saw no sign of him after the sand hit." I stilled while Bartholomew brushed off my coat, the young man not amused by our banter. "I intend to scour the city for him, and then the countryside if I cannot find him here. What I wonder is what he was looking for. He'd not been following me and Brewster; we followed *him*."

"We shall have to go back out there and see." Grenville's eyes sparkled with interest.

Bartholomew looked to be at his wits' end with both of us. I took pity on him and said no more. I checked in on Brewster, who had recovered more quickly than I had and was eating a hearty breakfast, then I departed the house for my appointment with the pasha's cavalry officers.

The Turkish guards had not come for me yet, but I started off on my own, working my sore leg, certain I'd meet them on the way. I moved through the city, the residents swarming on early morning errands, taking the remembered route through the maze of streets.

At one turning, I found my way blocked by Egyptians in robes that were none too clean, their faces hard from poverty and desperation.

I recognized ruffians when I saw them. No matter what their nationality or dress, men who beat and robbed people for a living had the same look the world over.

I turned to make my way to different street but five more toughs had closed in behind me. I drew the sword on my walking stick, which Bartholomew had brought from Lady Mary's boat last night. I was in no condition to fight, but the sight of the blade made a few of them step back.

Not for long. The entire gang closed in on me, sticks raised, ready to beat me down.

Chapter Nineteen

I fought hard, my sword finding flesh. Men grunted in pain, but I knew I'd not be able to keep it up. In my tired state, weakened by my ordeal in the desert, I lost strength quickly.

My sword was ripped from my hands, cudgels coming at my ribs, my face.

I thought I would die here in this back street, having arrogantly assumed I could navigate them alone. Last night, I had not been as certain of death as I was now.

"Donata," I whispered. "Look after Gabriella ..."

I heard shouting, the ringing of swords, men crying out, the scrambling of feet as my attackers fled. I looked up into the hard eyes of Turkish soldiers, swords drawn, some of the blades bloody. The Egyptians had gone but for the few who lay groaning on the pavement.

I was not certain whether my situation had improved. One man sheathed his sword and waved his hand, causing two more soldiers to lift me by the arms and set me on my feet.

As my vision cleared, I recognized the palace guard. These soldiers wore more colorful uniforms than the typical soldiers—they were awash in reds and deep blues, and clean whites that glared in the sun.

Their commander spoke to me in rapid Turkish, then seemed very annoyed when I didn't understand. He drew a long breath and then said curtly in French, "You. Come."

The soldiers closed around me. Nothing for it that I went with them.

They took me to the palace. When I went through the walkways to the pavilion and the ring, the cavalrymen were already there and waiting.

The functionary I'd met on my last visit hurried forward, took in my bruised face in dismay, and spoke to the commander in cursory tones. Then he turned to me with a look of profound apology.

"Captain Lacey, I humbly beg forgiveness for the trouble you found in our city. Those men will be dealt with."

I tried to make light of it. "It is nothing that wouldn't happen in London or Paris. A tourist walking alone, not paying attention to where he is going, can become fair game."

The functionary shook his head. "You are a guest of the pasha. He will not be pleased."

"No harm done," I said quickly. While I fully realized the Egyptians had been intent in killing or at least maiming me, I knew justice here could be swift and final.

"Whenever you come to the palace you will always be escorted by the guard," the functionary said, nodding at the soldiers. "You must be patient and not set off without them. Now, are you well enough to instruct?"

I was, and a bit embarrassed by all the attention as well.

As I greeted the cavalrymen, who were also distressed about what had happened, I wondered why I had been waylaid. Had Marcus sent toughs to kill me? Or had Mr. Sharkey? The latter, more likely. Sharkey had been most put out that I did not wish to take him into my confidence about my errand for Denis.

We proceeded with the lesson. I did not ride, but I could direct from the ground and critique through the functionary, who served as my interpreter today.

The men rode well—fearlessly. One had the finesse that made a good cavalryman; the other three were brave but a bit reckless, apt to not look around and see when someone was riding straight for him.

I gave them guidance on when to observe everything and when to simply look forward in the charge, to hell with anything that came at you.

I wondered where the pasha would take these men when they were finished with their training. I did not like to think of them dying on the battlefields in the deeper desert, their blood staining the ground as savages surged around them.

But for now, they were wild on horseback and affable when we took coffee, telling me of their families, wives, children. They were especially proud of their children, but I had difficulty with the concept that one of the officers had three wives.

"Why on earth would you want three wives?" I asked him in astonishment. "It is difficult enough for me to keep pace with one."

All four cavalrymen laughed uproariously when this was translated, and the functionary laughed as well.

"I am not often home," said the officer with three wives, and they all roared with laughter again.

I did, technically, have two wives. Though my first wife and I were now divorced under the laws of England, in the view of some in the world, Carlotta and I would always be married—*let no man put asunder*. Carlotta herself had become Collette Auberge, now married to the French major for whom she'd deserted me many years ago. She'd already given him several children. Such are the complications of married life.

We had more jovial conversation, the men congratulating me on my upcoming child. They expressed their deep wishes for the child to be a boy; and were taken aback when I said I hoped for another daughter.

The palace guard escorted me through the streets when I returned to our house. I noted that the Egyptians faded back from us as we passed, and even the other Turks gave us a wide berth. Everyone recognized the pasha's men.

When I thanked my escort politely and walked into the coolness of the house, Grenville was waiting for me.

He took in my battered state in shock. Though I'd managed to shield my face from most of the blows the ruffians had gotten in, I was still abraded.

I told him what had happened but forestalled his wish to rush to the magistrates. "The palace guard made their point," I said. "Sharkey's hired thugs might think twice before trying again."

Grenville didn't quite agree, but he continued. "Brewster is still out, with Matthias. We have been looking everywhere for Marcus, asking if anyone was found after the storm on the west bank. There were a few unfortunates who did not survive it, I'm sorry to say, but none of them fit the description of our man."

I felt sadness for those who'd died—it made me realize how lucky Brewster and I had been.

"I wonder if Marcus will return to the riverbed," Grenville said. "Looking for whatever he was after."

"Whatever the devil it was," I said. Much of my strength had been restored—activity, coffee, and friendly conversation had helped. "Most men are digging near the pyramids, searching for more burials and treasure. Why was Marcus out in the arroyos? He can't believe the book is there, can he?"

"Perhaps we should have a look." Grenville tried to speak casually, but I saw his nose twitching and his eyes sparkling in eagerness.

We prepared for another trek to the pyramids, this time being more thorough about it. We'd each carry water wherever we went, and Grenville made certain we'd have better supplies, like ropes and things, in case we were stranded out in the desert.

In spite of yesterday's sandstorm, the sky was soft blue, the air completely still. The pyramids rose in their grandeur, so many men milling about their bases that I fancied I'd gone back in time, to when the ancient Egyptians labored to raise the house of stone for their king.

Grenville had hired a team of men to set up his pavilion for him. He left them to it, supervised by Matthias and Bartholomew, and strolled with me and Brewster out into the desert, to seek out the wash we'd tumbled into.

It took us a long time to find it. I thought we'd followed Marcus due south when we'd seen him yesterday, but it turned out we'd gone farther west than I'd imagined.

We'd walked about a mile when Brewster, who'd gone a few paces ahead, stopped suddenly, his arms going out to fight a fall. Grenville and I sprang to him and pulled him back from the drop down the steep-sided bank.

I gazed around us, taking in the land. I was certain this was the same canyon we'd reached yesterday, but we'd come to it in a different spot—at least, I thought so. I was not familiar enough with the area to be certain.

Brewster heaved out a breath. "Nothing for it, I s'pose." He sat down, grabbed handholds in the rocks, and slid down to the wash's sandy bottom.

Grenville immediately scrambled down after him, Brewster turning to help with his big hands. "I'll not be left at the top this time," Grenville said. "If we get lost down here, I at least will know where you are."

I didn't argue. I let Brewster help me down, then I turned and piled stones in a pattern at the bottom of the bank. We'd know that at this spot, we could climb out.

I led the way as we explored, though Brewster was a step behind me, his footfalls vibrating the ground at my heels.

"What exactly are we looking for?" Grenville asked as he brought up the rear.

"I don't know," I answered. "Any signs of digging. Marcus's dead body. I have no idea."

"Right." Grenville sounded more interested than resigned.

We trudged along, peering down side passages, slots that tapered into nothing. Nowhere did we see any sign of disturbance, of earth having been turned over.

Or perhaps, I thought morosely, we found nothing because the sandstorm yesterday had covered what Marcus had been doing.

We found no sign of Marcus, either. I could only suppose he'd managed to climb out of the arroyo somewhere else and reach safety. I was very angry with the man, but I couldn't help but feel some worry for him as well. If he truly was a member of my family, I had cause to pity him.

The canyon walls rose above our heads, cutting off the view of anything but our sandy trail and sky. Great cascades of water must have flowed through here once upon a time, but I saw no sign any had done so in recent years. There was no vegetation, not even weeds—nothing.

It was Brewster who brought us to an abrupt halt.

"Guv." He pointed a thick finger to a side channel and what looked like a round hole in the base of the wall. "There."

I braced myself on my walking stick and crouched down. "An animal? Snake?" A very large one if so. We were too far from the river for a crocodile—I hoped.

"Snakes don't use chisels," Brewster said. He pointed to very regular marks around the hard edges of the hole.

I cautiously put my hand down and moved sand away from the hole's base. The opening became an oval, and a breath of cool air rose from it.

"A shaft," I said, trying to stem my excitement. It could still be a snake hole that Marcus had decided to enlarge. I began scraping away sand with both hands.

"Would this help?" Grenville had opened the

small pack he carried with him and extracted a trowel and a garden fork.

I mutely accepted the trowel and began digging in earnest. Grenville crouched next to me, scraping away earth with the fork, while Brewster moved aside the sand we dislodged with his large hands.

After about thirty minutes of this, we uncovered a square hole roughly two feet on a side. The walls inside the hole were hard-packed, the air cool. The floor slanted downward into the earth, not very much, but enough to make me wonder if we'd uncovered a tunnel.

"Do you think ancient Egyptians made this?" Grenville asked, his voice tinged with awe.

"Ancient thieves," Brewster rumbled. "Looks like what a bloke might cut toward a cache in a strongroom, say, or the cellar of a rich gent's estate."

"Could be," I agreed. Nowhere did I see the precision or decoration that the workmen of old had put into the pyramids or the obelisk I'd studied in Alexandria. This had been crudely, if efficiently, dug.

"Remind me to shore up the cellars of my country house," Grenville said, looking pained. "I wonder what the thieves were so anxious to find way out here."

"If the tombs were guarded, they were trying to find another way in," I speculated. I glanced at Grenville's pack. "You don't happen to have a candle in there, do you?"

"Better than that." Grenville pulled out a candle and then a small lantern to set it in. He opened a tinderbox and struck a spark to light the candle with a practiced touch.

I glanced into his bag to see more small digging tools, a flask, additional candles, a knife in a sheath, a packet that gave off the odor of coffee, and a tin cup.

"How did you think to bring all that?" I asked.

"Experience," Grenville said modestly. "I've been caught in the wild more than once. A cup to boil water for survival, and a flask of brandy to make you forget you're worried."

Brewster barked a laugh. "You're a gent what knows what's important, Mr. Grenville."

"Thank you, Mr. Brewster. I only lack a bit of hardtack, but I am optimistic it won't come to us needing that."

I examined the sides of the tunnel, which seemed solid. "It's a tight fit for any of us."

"I might have a go," Grenville said. "I'm smaller than either of you — they called me *Weasel* for reasons other than my pointed face."

I was not certain I wanted to see Grenville crawl into that tiny hole that might be full of any number of vermin, but he had already removed his coat and neckcloth and set aside his pack.

Without waiting for our approval, he took the lantern from me, set it into the hole, lay on his stomach, and wriggled himself inside.

Grenville squirmed and fought his way into the hole, while Brewster and I remained poised behind him, ready to seize him by the boots and drag him out if need be.

Grenville inched his way forward, saying nothing, the only sound a scraping as he pushed the lantern forward.

He made it all the way inside so that only his heels stuck out. Then we heard a muffled "Good Lord," and his boots rushed forward, disappearing from sight.

Chapter Twenty

G renville!" I called frantically.
 I heard nothing. I grabbed the trowel and began to strike at the sides of the hole, trying to widen it, while Brewster, in alarm, scraped away earth.

"Mr. Grenville!" Brewster bellowed into the hole.

A muffled yelp came back to us. Brewster and I both called his name, and then we heard coughing.

"Cease shouting," came the hollow words. "Pass me a bit of rope."

Grenville hadn't brought any in his pack, but Brewster had two coils of differing lengths. Brewster also carried a brace of pistols and a small box of gunpowder. He was taking no chances.

Brewster uncoiled one of the ropes, knotted an end, then passed it into the hole. After what seemed a very long time, the rope went taut.

A small amount of gravel rained down from the top of the tunnel, but Grenville came with it, backing out by bracing himself on the rope in Brewster's strong hold. He dragged the lantern with him, then sat up and took a long breath. His face and shirt were streaked with grime and also a white substance that smelled grievously foul.

Grenville, ever prepared, drew out a large linen handkerchief and mopped his face. "Bats," he said.

Brewster flinched and peered into the dark opening in trepidation. "They ain't coming out after you, are they?"

"I very much doubt it, Mr. Brewster. Too bright and hot up here." Grenville wiped his face again. "It was a bit like crawling back into the womb at first, but the tunnel widens out quite suddenly. There's a shaft that must lead to a nest of bats, I conclude from the smell and the fact that their shit is everywhere."

"Why bother digging a hole to find bats?" I asked. "Unless one is a student of natural history."

"Bats love the ancient tombs, my dear fellow," Grenville said. "They're all over the pyramids. Natural places for them to stay—darkness, rock walls, plenty of ledges to cling to. I'm certain many generations of bats have been grateful to proud humans for constructing homes for them."

Brewster barked a laugh, but I peered into the hole with new interest. "You think there's a tomb down there?" I asked.

"Or the entrance to one farther away." Grenville brushed off his sleeves, but the shirt would need extensive washing, if it could be saved at all. "Excavations are showing that many tombs had false entrances to deter thieves; the ancients seem to have put the true burial chambers under the ground and some distance from the tomb. It didn't deter many robbers, apparently. Chambers are being found not only stripped of riches, but the bodies themselves."

Brewster looked skeptical. "Then why bother with it? If the gold's already gone. And, begging your pardon, Mr. Grenville, seems to me you already have plenty of gold."

"It's not the value of the treasure that's the point," Grenville said. "It's the uniqueness of the discovery. Imagine finding a crown worn by a king, an armlet worn by an ancient queen. What a remarkable thing that would be. The history of the objects are most of their worth."

Brewster did not look convinced, but he didn't argue.

"Remarkable indeed," I said. I would love to pull out of the earth a beautiful armband of gold and emerald and present it to a grateful museum. "However, I am supposed to be looking for a book and a man who is likely looking for it as well."

"If Marcus found the scroll here, he took it away with him," Grenville said. "But I'm willing to wager he did no such thing. He did not enlarge the hole, and I am certain that I am the only human being who has been down that tunnel in eons." He gave me an even look. "The odds of finding the book are very long, Lacey. If we locate a new tomb, however, anything we find there might reconcile Mr. Denis for the absence of his papyrus."

At the moment I did not care about an old Greek scroll, never mind it came from the Alexandrian marvel of the library. The hint that we might have discovered a tomb no one else had sent me into a fever of curiosity.

"If we can find where the tunnel comes out ..." I began.

"Not back through the hole," Grenville said.

"There's a sheer drop. But we can extrapolate where another entrance is."

Brewster broke in. "Measure over the top, you mean?"

"Exactly."

Brewster nodded without question. I wondered how many thieves' tunnels he'd helped dig in the past, how often he'd calculated the distance from a hole to his quarry.

He and Grenville soon became a smoothly working survey team. Brewster and I boosted Grenville out of the arroyo, and Brewster passed him the rope. After carefully marking where he stood, Grenville began moving in the direction the tunnel had, counting off paces.

I joined Grenville up top, helping him tie off the rope where he said the tunnel sloped abruptly downward. I peered into the distance, but the flat plain looked the same in all directions. On the other hand, I hadn't been able to see the arroyo until I'd been right on top of it.

We helped Brewster out and continued our search. Southward, the land dipped slightly. We continued measuring with rope until it ran out, then I marked the spot with a square pile of stones.

"We'll have to claim it," Grenville said. "Make sure we have permission to dig in this exact spot. So that if anyone else, including Marcus, decides to try his luck, we'll still have the right to anything inside."

"Thief wouldn't care," Brewster rumbled.

"Good point." Grenville nodded at him. "I suppose we could camp here and bring in men to begin in the morning."

"And dig where?" Brewster asked. "You could hunt for days."

"Years," I said, less optimistic. "I share your interest, Grenville, but perhaps we should narrow down the spot first."

"I have done these things before, you know," Grenville said, giving me a patient look. "It's uncanny how the first instance usually proves to be correct. On the other hand, you are right that it won't do to let others in on the secret too soon. Let us make certain we have the firman for this area, and then move here and begin."

Brewster looked relieved. While he was not adverse to the thought of finding treasure, I knew he was uncomfortable in the open desert, especially after our experience last evening.

Grenville drew out his sketchbook. He proceeded to make several quick drawings of the area, identifying landmarks so we could find the place again. Not that there were many. The pyramids rose in the distance, the only true marker—we could not see even the gleam of river from this depression in the ground.

The sun was heading westward, another guide for Grenville to mark directions. He drew a rough map on another page, closed the book, and tucked it back into his bag.

We made for the pyramids again. I looked back as we walked, already unable to discern where we'd been.

Grenville said not a word about our discovery—he cautioned me that rumor of a find traveled around here with the speed and ferocity of the sandstorms. Brewster, an expert at keeping secrets, was as blank-faced and passive as ever.

I was the one who had to struggle to keep the excitement from my countenance. I wore my emotions openly, and the prospect of finding a tomb fired my imagination.

We were so flushed and tired from our walk, however, that Matthias and Bartholomew only gave us cool water, expressed disapprobation at the state of our clothes, and helped pack up to return to Cairo.

We arrived home well after dark to find that a message had arrived in our absence. Lady Mary expressed her wishes for us to join her on her barge for a small gathering the next evening. Fancy dress.

I disliked fancy dress balls in the extreme and nearly declined until Grenville read out from the letter that Signora Beatrice Faber would be there, the lady who had been friends with Monsieur Chabert of the library book.

***

I slept heavily that night, dreaming of sand rising up to bury me alive. I jumped awake when the muezzin called the Egyptians to their morning prayer, my heart beating thickly, my mind in a fog.

An hour later, the palace guard arrived almost at the doorstep to escort me to the training. Whoever had sent the thugs to waylay me the day before—I still strongly suspected Sharkey—was out of luck this morning.

The training went without incident, and I felt well enough to ride. Afterward we were served the usual coffee and pastries, and I and the cavalrymen talked more about life in the army, sharing stories of harrowing battles and unexpected survival.

When I returned home, I found Brewster there with his eye blackened and his cheek cut.

He explained that he'd continued looking for Marcus, without success. He'd encountered a few men he'd seen at Sharkey's house, who'd tried to waylay him. Brewster had bested them, but one had landed a lucky blow.

"His nibs won't be pleased," Brewster said. "That is, if I live to tell him. They meant to hurt me more, but I got away."

My temper mounted. "Mr. Sharkey needs to mind his own bloody business. I or Grenville will report him to the local magistrates."

"Don't bother, guv," Brewster said. "From what happened to you, and now me, he probably has 'em in his pocket. Foreigners attacked in the street? He made sure it could happen."

As Brewster spoke, I knew he was right. Denis wouldn't rely on a man like Sharkey unless he was resourceful and knew how to make the authorities turn a blind eye.

Grenville had gone out, Brewster told me, but well guarded. He was chatting up the excavators to discover who was digging where and what they'd found, and also to make certain the firman was granted to me.

I left that to Grenville. He knew the right people to speak to, and how to ensure that the pasha's promise that I could treasure hunt where I liked be honored.

Grenville did not return until late, and so there was no chance to go out to the desert. He was flushed with triumph, however. The British and French gentlemen who led teams of diggers were interested in only the pyramids, certain that they would find the best artifacts and mummies in and around them. If the eccentric Captain Lacey wanted to poke about farther west and south, they had no interest.

I hoped they were wrong. I would have the fun of

looking, even if I found nothing.

The sun set in a sky tinged brilliant red, and night fell quickly. Grenville and I dressed and walked down to the harbor — guarded by Brewster and trusted servants — to Lady Mary's barge.

Chinese paper lanterns had been strung up and down the deck. The barge glittered with light, a striking picture from afar, but once onboard, we had to duck the swinging lanterns, heated by the candles within them.

The stern cabin doors had been folded back, making an open room, into which the fetid air of the marshy bank poured.

Lady Mary had dressed herself like an ancient Egyptian woman from tomb paintings — much more modestly, fortunately. The paintings I'd seen of ancient ladies often showed them bare-breasted, in accurate detail.

Lady Mary's white muslin gown wound around her person from her silver lamé slippers to her jewel-bedecked neck. She bulged alarmingly here and there, causing gaps in the muslin, but I saw she'd prudently worn an underdress of the same color.

She'd crowned this costume with a wide pectoral of gold and lapis lazuli that lay heavily on her chest — a true Egyptian artifact. Her entire dress, I realized, had been made to highlight this beautiful treasure.

My concession to fancy dress was to wear the galabiya Bartholomew had procured for me. I'd had to have one of the Egyptian servants wind the turban around my head, much to the delight of the man and his friends. I walked onboard feeling light, cool, and comfortable. My bruised and sand-blasted face had healed somewhat, but I still drew odd looks from the company.

Brewster had come with us, but positioned himself on the dock to keep a watchful eye on who came and went. He'd been disparaging about fancy dress and kept to his own sturdy clothes.

"When my Em worked the bawdy houses, some of the gents liked to wear costumes," he said. "Made her laugh, the things they'd put on."

Instead of growing offended, Grenville merely chuckled and told him his wife was a woman of good sense.

Lady Mary ran her gaze over Grenville's costume as she greeted us, disappointment in her eyes. I suppose she'd hoped Grenville would dress as an ancient Egyptian male—in a short kilt, perhaps, with jewels resting on his chest.

As well as she claimed to know him, she ought to have realized that Grenville, in spite of the very public liaisons he conducted, was a modest man. Tonight he'd chosen to emulate a wealthy Turk in wide scarlet trousers and black boots, and a white silken shirt covered by a fancily embroidered waistcoat. He finished the whole thing with a flowing coat of deepest blue and a very large white turban that billowed over his head.

I'd never seen an actual Turk wear such a thing since we'd been in Egypt—the men seemed subdued in their dress—but Grenville's suit was greeted with compliments and laughter.

The guests were those I expected—the wealthy dilettantes and aristocrats exploring the ancient world or funding digs for the British Museum. A smattering of Frenchmen were there, but the rivalry for finds was becoming so great, I had heard, that arguments over who was allowed to dig where nearly came to blows, and so Lady Mary had kept the guests mostly British. Corruption, trickery, bribery, and outright theft were growing common, apparently. The French excavators would pay the Egyptian diggers hired by the British to not show up to work or turn and work for the French. The British would do the same. Cutthroat, Grenville said.

I was not interested in any of their machinations. I wanted to meet Signora Beatrice Faber. I scanned the crowd impatiently, seeing that the few ladies present were wives of the gentlemen here.

Lady Mary, knowing she dangled something we wanted, had us at her mercy. We'd have to dance attendance on her, I saw.

Grenville proved himself made of steel. Instead of avoiding Lady Mary, he squared his shoulders and walked into the lion's den.

Lady Mary had arranged for prizes to be given for costumes — Grenville won for most colorful — for musicians to play Turkish music, and as the finishing touch, she'd brought in a woman to perform a Turkish harem dance.

The lady did not look Turkish to me, but European, Italian perhaps. She wore billowing silk trousers that were caught around her ankles with bands glittering with beads. A tight-fitting red silk jacket covered her bodice, the garment embroidered as fantastically as Grenville's waistcoat. A red silk turban bore a feather that stuck straight up, as though it grew from the lady's forehead.

A musician picked up a narrow-headed drum, its curved body etched silver. He placed the drum under his arm and began to beat it with his fingers and palms. Another man lifted a wide, shallow drum, holding it by a wooden frame fitted behind its head, and tapped it with the fingers of his other hand.

The lady raised her arms and began to move in time with their slow, sensuous rhythm. She had tiny cymbals on her fingers that rang now and then in counterpoint with the drums.

While the lady was fully covered, her feet moving in patterns not much more complex than that of a waltz, there was no doubt that this was meant to be an erotic dance.

The woman's hips wove in slow undulations beneath the loose silk of the trousers, her hands and arms glided in sinuous patterns, and the *cling-cling* of the cymbals punctuated her change in moves.

Every gaze was fixed on her, the ladies' as well as the gentlemen's. I suspected Lady Mary was deliberately trying to shock us, but the young woman's movements were so beautiful, it was like watching a work of art.

Her fingers dipped and bent in graceful curves, the clothes flowed over her body like rippling water, her hips moved in long sweeps, while her feet made a minimum of movements. The dance was performed with incredible skill and yet seemed so effortless that it was breathtaking.

When the drumbeats escalated, the lady began to whirl, her arms flying outward into a graceful spiral. I preferred the slow movements, but I could not deny she performed with great skill.

The woman spun to a stop, collapsing in on herself, and ended with a bow over curled legs to the floor.

We stood in rapt appreciation for a moment, then burst into wild applause.

Lady Mary looked vastly pleased with herself. She

latched her fingers around Grenville's arm and pulled him away with her, and Grenville dutifully went.

I could not stop myself approaching the lady the in harem costume as she unfolded from the carpet.

"You were splendid," I said, giving her a hand to help her to her feet. "How on earth did you learn to do that?"

The lady looked startled, then she answered in English, her accent heavy. "I love to dance. The Egyptian women taught me. I live in Egypt with my mistress."

"And who is your mistress?" I asked.

"You are the captain," the young woman answered, to my surprise. "My mistress, she must meet you."

So saying, the lady put very strong fingers around my wrist and pulled me with her out of the salon and down a short flight of stairs to the private cabins below.

Chapter Twenty-One

I knew the moment I walked into the large cabin that I was in Lady Mary's boudoir. A wide bed rested on the end wall under a row of windows, its coverlets deep maroon velvet, which matched the draperies around the bed. A chaise rested on the wall adjacent the bed, also covered in maroon velvet. Rugs similar to those in our Cairo house covered the floor, overlapping as was common. A low wooden table near the chaise held a coffee service.

The woman who rose from her seat on the edge of the bed had gray hair wrapped in a colorful bandeau and wore a simple gown of light blue with a dark blue, long-sleeved bodice. A collar turned up in back and framed her neck with lace.

The lady's face was narrow, her dark eyes sparkling and lively. Her gray hair suggested she was well into her fifties or perhaps even beyond sixty, but her skin was firm, her movements holding the litheness of a younger woman.

The dancer curtsied to her then gracefully seated herself on the floor next to the table and began to fill small cups with Turkish coffee.

"Captain Lacey, I am Signora Beatrice Faber," the older woman said, holding out a hand. She wore one ring—a wide band of beaten gold studded with a large sapphire.

I took her hand and bowed over it. "I am honored to meet you."

Beatrice gave me a warm look and motioned for me to sit on the chaise. "Lady Mary explained that you are searching for Milo Chabert's book."

Beatrice had resumed her perch on the bed, and I seated myself, the dancer's flowing harem clothes inches from my boots.

"I have been hearing much of you, Captain," Beatrice went on as the dancer offered a tiny cup to me in her delicate hands. The young lady had rid herself of the cymbals but the little bells sewn into her costume jingled. "The great friend of the famous Mr. Grenville, who saved a life in Alexandria and tamed the man who'd tried to commit the deed. Who becomes admired by the pasha and defies a dangerous Cairo criminal."

"You are knowledgeable." I sipped the coffee, which was the best I'd tasted since I'd arrived in Egypt.

"I have lived most of my life on the Nile." Beatrice took the coffee her dancer handed her, but only held it in her elegant fingers. "I travel between Alexandria, Cairo, and Thebes, occasionally taking in the sights farther south. I know every European who comes into and out of Egypt, why they are here, and who they are connected with. I came here at Milo Chabert's invitation at the end of the last century and loved it so much, I had no desire to leave. When Chabert died, I gave him back to his wife to bury him, but I remained here."

"Egypt is a fascinating place," I agreed. "I intend to return."

"Yes, one either loathes it, or becomes enchanted and stays forever." She lifted her fingers toward the window as though indicating all of Egypt outside. "I have accompanied about a dozen gentlemen in total up and down the river, until I was no longer interesting, then I purchased a barge and traveled on my own. I used to dance, as Celia does, but my limbs are sore now, and Celia does the entertaining for me." Beatrice smiled, as though she knew how entranced I'd been by the young woman's performance.

"I have difficulty believing any gentleman would no longer find you interesting," I said. She had an attractiveness that would always gain attention, no matter what her age, a way of speaking and moving that was a delight to the observer.

Beatrice's smile deepened. "You are kind. I would cynically say you are trying to flatter me for information, but I believe you truly mean what you say. You are different than I thought you would be. I have never met Mr. Grenville, but I know he can be plagued by hangers-on. From what I have heard and seen, you are your own man and a true friend."

I gave her a brief bow. "I would like to think so."

The lines around her eyes crinkled. "Modest as well. In my younger days, Captain, I might have wished to accompany *you* on your travels."

"In my younger days I had no money at all," I said. "I was an impatient soldier, and then I was injured. I believe you would not have found *me* very entertaining."

"On the contrary, Captain, I believe you would have made a diverting treat. Unfortunately, I did have to make certain the gentlemen I danced for had plenty of, as you English say, blunt."

Which she must have prudently stashed away if she was now able to travel on her own boat and employ dancers for her male guests.

Signora Beatrice was a courtesan of the highest elegance, I could see, who knew how to speak to men, what to offer them in exchange for wealth or good conversation, or whatever she liked.

If she'd heard much about me, she'd know I would not take a dalliance with her or her dancer, that I would always be loyal to my wife. All the same, Signora Beatrice made certain that Celia was at my feet, her arms wrapped around her knees, ready to refill my coffee.

"Lady Mary told me that you are hunting for the Greek scroll Monsieur Chabert found. Milo." Beatrice said his given name fondly. "May I ask why?"

"A … collector wants it," I answered. "He gave me instructions to find it."

"And he pays you?"

"No," I answered swiftly. "I am not a procurer. I am doing it as a favor to him."

Not precisely a favor, I knew, but the belief that I'd readily scour the country for an artifact at another's direction made me uncomfortable. I was not a professional treasure hunter.

"Mmm," Beatrice looked slightly displeased. "I had hoped you wanted the book for yourself. For its own sake."

"I have not said I would give the book to this collector," I answered evenly. "I will do so only when I am certain he will treasure it and not promptly turn and sell it to the next man."

"Good." She gave me a nod of approval. "Milo hid it because he knew it would be fought over and maybe even torn apart by collectors, museums, and entire governments. He meant to copy it out when he had the chance and give its contents to scholars while preserving the original."

"But he died too soon," I finished for her.

Beatrice's dark eyes took on vast sadness. "He did, poor man. But your speculation—and Lord Randolph Carver's and Lady Mary's—that I once knew the whereabouts of the book, is correct. I do know. I've had it all along."

My heartbeat quickened and I leaned forward. "You have it? Are you certain it is the correct one?" I braced myself for her to say she could not read it, she didn't know, or to produce a forged copy that had never seen ancient Alexandria.

Beatrice looked amused. "Of course the book is the correct one, Captain. A treatise by Aristarchus. I read it myself—Milo and I perused it together. I can read many languages."

I imagined them, twenty years ago, a younger Beatrice and an excited scholar, heads together, poring over one of the greatest finds of the age.

"And you've kept it all this time?" I asked her.

"I did indeed. Milo entrusted me with it. I would not break his trust."

"But you've told others you didn't know where it was."

She lifted a slim finger. "I told them Milo did not confide its whereabouts to me. Which he did not—he hid it away even from me while he was alive. After his death, a messenger came to me when I was in

Alexandria and handed me a bundle. It contained the book and a letter from Milo, instructing me to keep it safe for him. Which I did. His entire estate and money went to his family in France, but the book came to me. It was his legacy. I honored his wishes."

"You must know how valuable it is." My hands closed around my empty coffee cup. "To collectors and to scholars both. You might have bought a fleet of ships with the price of it."

"I do know." Beatrice inclined her head. "You wish to understand why a woman who has already told you she chose her companions for their wealth would hold on to a book worth far more than anything they could give her. The answer is simple, Captain. I loved Milo. I would have done anything for him, and he for me."

Her eyes softened, touched by tears. In them I saw a woman who'd remained strong after loss but who would stay loyal to her love forever.

"I understand," I said. I too felt things as deeply. "Why then, offer it to me?"

"I waited." Beatrice drew a breath, as though willing her tears to pass. "I waited for someone worthy of the find. When I heard you were looking for it, I did my best to learn all about you. Milo would have approved of you, would know the book was in good hands." Her eyes crinkled. "Even if you are English."

Before I could respond to this generosity, another servant opened the door, and Grenville entered. His costume was a bit disarrayed from the wind on the river, but he pulled off his turban and bowed.

"Signora," he said. "I am honored. Please forgive me looking like a complete fool at present."

"She has it," I said, without waiting for

politenesses to be exchanged. "Signora Faber has the book."

"I *had* the book," Beatrice amended as Grenville opened his mouth to express his delight. "I was prepared to give it to you, if you promised to do well by it. But last night, it was stolen from me."

We both stared at her, stunned. A numbing coldness washed over me, followed quickly by hot anger.

"Stolen?" Grenville repeated, his gaze fixed. Celia's bells whispered as she adjusted her position on the floor.

Beatrice nodded sadly. "I kept it well hidden. The book was there yesterday evening. This morning, it was gone."

Celia looked up at me, her kohl-lined eyes holding sorrow. She nodded in confirmation of her mistress's story.

I wet my dry lips, disappointment hitting me sharply. "Then why bring me here? Why tell me you had it at all?"

Beatrice's dark eyes snapped. "So you will recover it for me. You are a man of integrity, so every Englishman who has ever spoken about you insists. I believe you will find it—for the right reasons."

I let out a breath. So close. I had been so close. To have the book snatched from my grasp was difficult to bear.

"Tell me about the hiding place," I said. "And who went near it. Everyone who *could* have gone near it."

"A good number of people, unfortunately," Beatrice said. "I keep it in my chamber, wherever I go, locked in a strongbox. I put into Cairo yesterday. Lady Mary called on me, as did several gentlemen—

old friends, all. But they have servants, some of whom are hired as soon as that person arrives in Cairo. One might have been paid to search my boat and rob me. My own servants have been with me for years, and I trust them all."

"It was not me," Celia said, giving first me then Grenville a defiant look. "I would not do such a thing to my mistress."

"I know it was not you, *cara*," Beatrice said, her look fond. "Why do you not dance for us now? The gentlemen are unhappy and need soothing."

I was about to say we would impose ourselves no longer, but Grenville gave me a slight shake of his head. He came to sit next to me on the chaise, the only seat in the room besides the bed.

Celia rose without complaint, lifted her arms, let her head drop back, and began her slow and elegant movements.

This dance, if anything, was more erotic than what she'd done in the salon. But now Celia performed in private for two gentlemen and not to amuse a gathering of ladies and their husbands. The jerk of her hips, accompanied by the jingle of bells, and the slow glide of her breasts was meant to entrance and arouse.

Watching her was soothing. There was something about Celia's flowing movements and precise placements of feet and hands that pleased the tangled knot of emotions that always roiled inside me.

It had nothing to do with carnality in my case, though I could see how she could stir a man to rush off with her to bed. I simply enjoyed watching her body move. Grenville, who had a good eye for art, regarded her with evident enjoyment. We applauded and praised Celia when she finished, and she flushed, pleased.

"Bloody hell," Grenville said as we departed the chamber twenty minutes later. He jammed the turban on his head again, squaring his shoulders to face more inanity on deck. "At least we know the book exists. Now all we have to do is search Cairo — maybe all of Egypt — for the thief."

***

Grenville undressed in his bedchamber after the soiree by wresting each piece of clothing from his body and hurtling it away from him. Matthias deftly caught the garments and folded them aside, saying nothing.

"I suppose that Sharkey took it," Grenville snarled. "He could arrange for a man to slip aboard and rifle Signora Faber's belongings."

"I never told him what I was looking for," I reminded Grenville. "It struck me odd that Denis wouldn't simply hire him to find the book, so I said nothing."

Grenville gave me an impatient look. "He could easily discover our purpose, Lacey. We have been asking about it. And my cronies are prone to gossip. A man like Sharkey will have spies everywhere."

"Likewise Marcus knows." I lounged in a chair, my booted feet crossed on a padded stool. I hadn't taken off my galabiya, being perfectly comfortable inside it. Bartholomew, however, had said that if I wanted to look as though I rushed about in a nightshirt, to please tell no one he dressed me. "He could as easily have hired a thief to search for it, and we know he is rather slippery himself."

Grenville sighed. He quieted and allowed Matthias to wrap him in a dressing gown. Matthias took away the Turkish garments and left us alone.

"If Marcus wants the book, why dig holes out in the desert?" Grenville asked. He poured a measure of brandy into two goblets and handed one to me. "Dolphin more or less told him that Chabert's mistress was the key."

"He might have been amusing himself waiting for her to return from Thebes." I sipped the brandy, letting it warm me. "His search in the desert could be about something else entirely."

"Agreed, but I think Sharkey is a better possibility," Grenville said. "Perhaps he wants to present the book to Denis before you can. To discredit you and rise again in Denis's eyes. I have the feeling he has fallen from grace — or is falling."

"What about Lady Mary?" I broke in. "She went to visit Signora Beatrice, and then the book was gone."

"But if Lady Mary has the book, why arrange for us to meet Beatrice? Even mention she knew her? What would Lady Mary want the book for, in any case?" Grenville waved an expansive hand. "Mary is vastly wealthy and cares nothing for scholarship. Or much for the rivalry between the museums. She is a bit disenchanted with her home nation, else she'd not stay away so long. She'd never steal the book for the honor of the British Museum."

I took a larger sip of brandy and rested the goblet on my thigh. "She wants it because of you," I said with certainty. "If Lady Mary had the book, she could put you in her debt — what price might she extract?"

"Oh, good Lord." Grenville blenched. "You mean she'd try to force me into a marriage for that bloody scroll?"

"Or perhaps not marriage, but at least a liaison."

Grenville's face was stark white. "I know you find this amusing, Lacey, but she is a very determined woman. I have no interest in pursuing any sort of affair with her. She would have me before a bishop saying the vows before I knew what happened." He rubbed a hand through his already rumpled dark hair. "However, we must regard this logically. Lady Mary would have a fine opportunity to search Beatrice's chamber. Or, she might leave it to that traveling companion of hers—the Spaniard. Miguel. She could distract Beatrice on deck while Miguel slipped below."

"We will ask her, of course," I said. "Though I cannot imagine Miguel walking into and out of Beatrice's private chamber without question. No, I believe the speculation that an Egyptian servant performed the theft is a correct one."

"But whose servant?" Grenville asked. He sank to another chair and drained his glass of brandy in one swallow. "That is what we must ascertain. Perhaps your friends in the palace guard could burst into Sharkey's house and make him confess."

"They do not follow my orders," I said. "But when I task Sharkey with this, I will remember to bring a bodyguard of my own."

We continued to muse, reaching no conclusion, then parted ways and went to bed.

I went to the palace the next morning without mishap and returned again, the palace guard accompanying me. As they turned around to march back home I hoped they were earning extra coin for protecting me from the denizens of Cairo.

Grenville and I spent the remainder of the day out in the desert. To Bartholomew's despair, I wore the turban, though not the galabiya. The turban kept the sun from my face and head wonderfully, and I highly recommended it to Brewster and Grenville. Brewster ignored me, but Grenville said he would consider it.

With Bartholomew and Matthias to help, we continued to measure the distance from the hole Grenville had explored to where we thought an entrance to the tomb might be. We walked a long way, searching a wide area before I suggested a rough patch of ground at the base of a bluff.

All five of us took up spades and began.

It was hard work, but my eagerness drove me on. I had a firman and I was searching for antiquities, just as I'd longed to do when I'd looked at the buried temple outside Alexandria.

The afternoon waned, the sun lowered, and we'd found nothing. I hoped I wouldn't have to admit we'd simply been digging in the dirt only to uncover more dirt.

As the disk of the sun slipped below the horizon, I drove my spade in one more time, and swore I struck solid stone.

"Here!" I yelled, my words ringing in the sudden twilight.

The others gathered, propelled by my excitement, but darkness gathered, and we could see nothing. I could feel what I thought was stone, but realized, in frustration, that we couldn't investigate it properly until morning.

We covered up our work the best we could to hide it and trudged back to the pyramids to find our ferryman to take us home. My thoughts were at the digging site all the way—I chafed that I'd have to wait to discovered whether I'd found anything at all.

That night as Grenville and I dined, Brewster marched into the room unannounced and without asking leave. He simply halted beside my chair and thrust a piece of paper at me.

"One of the coves what gave me a thumping brought this," he said. "You've been summoned."

I took the paper, a plain folded sheet, and opened it. Inside was a note whose brevity was worthy of Mr. Denis, though with none of Denis's eloquence.

I have your twin. For his life, bring me the Greek book. Tonight.

Chapter Twenty-Two

Sharkey hadn't signed the note, but I knew he'd written it.

I handed it to Grenville. He read the words, eyes widening.

"That is enough, Lacey," Grenville said, flinging the paper to the tablecloth. "Send for the magistrates."

"Not if he has them in his pocket, as Brewster speculates." I calmly ate another bite of rice and stew, though my muscles tightened, my anger stirring. "Sharkey does not have the book, obviously."

Grenville stared at me. "You seem to be taking this well. Are you going to leave Marcus to his fate then?"

"No." Burning rage was rising inside me, and also joy, because I could focus that rage on a target. "I do not have the book, so I cannot bargain for Marcus's life. I could fake the book, I suppose, but that would take time and resources. If Marcus has it, he hid it somewhere Sharkey can't find it. Perhaps Marcus told him I could put my hands on it."

"Why would he?" Grenville asked. "He must know you don't have it."

"Unless they're working together," Brewster said. "In league, sort of thing."

"We won't know until we ask him." I laid down my fork and wiped my lips with my napkin. "We will not be keeping Sharkey's appointment, gentlemen."

"No?" Grenville gave me an astonished look. "What about Marcus?"

"We will rescue him, instead," I said, and took a sip of Grenville's fine wine.

***

I suppose Sharkey meant me to turn up, fearful and trembling, on his doorstep, the Greek scroll in hand.

Even if I'd had the thing, I knew a man like Sharkey wouldn't simply take it and docilely release Marcus. He'd have his men surround and waylay us, killing us in some quiet street, making it look as though we'd died at the hands of robbers. The pasha would have some Egyptians rounded up and executed to prove he could keep the peace and the incident would be forgotten.

To my surprise, my friends didn't argue about rescuing Marcus. At least Grenville did not. Brewster only took me aside while Grenville was upstairs changing his clothes and pointed out a few facts.

"You know, guv, if you let Sharkey kill this Marcus bloke, there'll be no dispute about who inherited your land."

I gave Brewster an impatient look. "I care nothing

for my inheritance at this moment."

Donata's father would be horrified, as would Grenville. Every English gentleman was proud of his lineage. But perhaps Donata would understand. She had a canny perception about my opinions on the matter.

Marcus was a Lacey. I knew it from his looks, his temperament, his rashness, his determination. I'd be damned if I'd let someone like Sharkey murder him. If anyone would kill Marcus, it would be me.

The note said nothing about when Sharkey expected us tonight. Likely he reasoned we'd rush over immediately.

Therefore I took my time. Make him worry a bit.

I certainly worried. I was perspiring as we made our plans in the courtyard, trying to cool ourselves in the evening air.

I recalled how Sharkey's house lay at the end of a narrow lane, only one way in and out. Brewster, as he'd tramped about Cairo these past few days, had found the streets that backed the house. Leave it to a professional thief to scout the many routes into a building.

"A bakery is behind it," Brewster told us. "Top floor of that building is for storage, which backs onto the women's quarters of Sharkey's house."

"The women's quarters?" Grenville repeated. "Do not tell me Sharkey keeps a harem."

Brewster huffed a laugh. "Never saw a woman coming in or out. Not even peeking through the lattice. He probably don't trust any woman enough to let them stay. I wager the rooms are empty, or he's stashed the other Mr. Lacey there."

"Are you willing to lead the way?" I asked.

Brewster nodded without hesitation. "Only makes

sense, don't it?"

I'd briefly considered asking my Turkish cavalry friends to join me in the raid, but let the thought go. Though they'd be handy in a fight, I did not wish them to come to harm from men with no honor. And, if they did kill Englishmen, the pasha might not be happy with them. Better to involve no one but ourselves.

I was no stranger to fighting and neither were Grenville and Brewster. We were armed with pistols and knives, plus I had the sword in my walking stick.

Just before midnight, Brewster led us through the streets, skirting the more crowded areas. Bartholomew and Matthias broke off from us — they would watch the front of the house and summon help if necessary.

The lanes behind Sharkey's house were quiet. The people here worked hard and likely slept every moment they could.

The bakery was closed, but I could smell the banked fires, the lingering odor of cooked flatbread and pastries. My stomach, even knotted with nerves, rumbled.

We reached the top of the house by climbing the crumbling side of the adjacent building, our way tucked into deep shadow. Brewster led us swiftly and confidently, surefooted in the dark, and pulled me up without comment.

He opened a shutter that moved silently, and motioned us to step down into the room inside.

The wooden floor was gritty with sand and gravel. I steadied Grenville as he came in after me, and he gave my arm a squeeze to tell me he was all right. We couldn't see each other — or anything else —

in the absolute darkness.

"Put your hand on my shoulder," Brewster whispered to me. "And Mr. Grenville on yours. Don't step nowhere but where I do."

I wondered if some of the boards on which we trod were rotten. Brewster led us in a straight line— obviously, he'd scouted the route.

Another shuttered window, again opening noiselessly, led us to a narrow ledge between this house and the one behind it. The space allowed us to walk along a few feet of wall to windows that opened to Sharkey's top floor.

These windows were shuttered, and behind them were finely latticed screens. The ladies who'd lived here wouldn't have had much to look at outside their prison, but the openings would at least let air into the rooms.

We heard nothing from inside. Brewster withdrew a small chisel from his pocket, inserted it into the crack between shutter and wall, and pried the shutter loose. He then worked off the lattice, the dryness of old wood making his task easier.

Brewster then moved quietly into the room and signaled us to follow. I stepped down, part of me curious to see the inside of a harem.

The first chamber was deserted. I could discern little from what moonlight filtered in behind us, but the floors and walls were bare, any comforts for its inhabitants long gone. Sharkey certainly wasn't keeping any female company here.

Brewster tested the door, which proved to be unlocked. It opened into yet another lattice-windowed room, this one in the front of the house. More moonlight trickled inside, showing that this chamber was as plain as the one behind it. In this poorer section of town, the women must have lived in cramped misery.

Another door yielded to a tiny hall with a staircase. We went slowly down these stairs, letting Brewster test each step before we trod upon it.

We reached the next floor down, the third from the ground in this building. Brewster pressed his hand to my chest, halting me. A flicker of candlelight showed under the door nearest the staircase.

Brewster stepped to that door, bending to listen to the muffled voices inside.

Brewster suddenly straightened up and shoved me back to the staircase. "Mr. Lacey is in there," he whispered. "But there's a problem."

"He has guards?" I asked.

Brewster's mouth brushed my ear. "Sharkey's wiv' 'im."

"We wait then," I said, my heart beating swiftly.

I passed this information to Grenville, who nodded. We retreated into the staircase, pressing ourselves into the shadows.

Voices rose from inside the room.

"Your brother ain't coming," Sharkey snapped. "Stop pretending you're addled-pated and tell me where you hid the book."

"He isn't my brother, you ignorant dolt." Marcus's cool voice rang out. "He won't care whether you shoot me or not. And I told you, I don't have the bloody book."

"You hid it," Sharkey growled. "He'll find it for me, and I'll consider letting you go. Though you've given me a powerful lot of trouble already, so maybe I won't."

"If I had the damned book, I'd have fled Cairo at once, not walked tamely around waiting for you to nab me," Marcus said, no meekness in him. "You've had me here two days, and he's not come beating down your door. Get it through *your* pate that he's not rushing to save me."

"Family changes everything." Sharkey gave a grating laugh. "Trust me. I've seen it time and again. A man can be hard as nails until someone in their family is under threat. He'll come. I think I'll shoot him, just to show him he should respect me."

"He can't learn a lesson if he's dead," Marcus pointed out. "You know, Mr. Sharkey, I've hated him all my life, but at the moment, I think I like him much better than I do you."

There was the sound of a fist hitting flesh and a grunt and moan. I started forward before I could stop myself, to be caught by the slim but very strong hand of Grenville. I subsided, seething rage and impatience.

After a time, we heard another groan, then a long breath. "He's not stupid enough to come here for my sake." Marcus's voice was weaker but no less defiant. "I hope he has the book and is rushing back to England with it, far out of your reach."

"If he is, you're a dead man."

"You're going to kill me anyway," Marcus said with finality. "You might as well get it over with."

Sharkey's voice filled with iron coldness. "You're right, guv. On your knees."

"The hell I'll kneel to the likes of you."

Another grunt, and the fall of a body. "I'm weary of hearing your voice," Sharkey said. "Pick him up."

A third person was in the room with them. Marcus cursed as the other man jerked him, and I heard the precise sound of a pistol being cocked.

I was past Brewster even before I realized he was

also making for the closed door. I landed on it with all my weight, breaking it open.

Sharkey snapped his head around, his pistol ready. He turned it from Marcus, aimed it straight at me, and opened fire.

Chapter Twenty-Three

The pistol's ball went nowhere near me. Grenville, with an athleticism his languid dandy persona hid, spun me out of the way and onto the floor. The bullet thunked into the wall and stayed there.

Brewster, with a bellow of rage, went for Sharkey.

The third man in the room, one of Sharkey's thugs, met Brewster with his fists. Brewster shoved him out of the way, but not before the man brought up a knife and slashed down at Brewster.

Two flickering lamps—greasy rags in candle holders—were knocked over in the fight. One hit the floor and extinguished. The other fell to the bare bunk and caught in the straw mattress.

I climbed off the floor in time to tackle Sharkey, who was heading for the door. We both went down, Sharkey's spent pistol coming up to toward my temple.

A broad, tanned hand yanked the gun from

Sharkey's grip before it touched me. By the light of the bed, which was fully ablaze now, I saw Marcus, ropes stretched between his wrists, lift the pistol and bring its butt down at Sharkey's head.

Sharkey twisted away, avoiding the blow. He kicked my knee as he got to his feet, sending fiery pain through my leg. Brewster was still fighting the other thug, and more men pounded up the stairs. The room filled with pungent, choking smoke.

Grenville had already darted out the door—where he was going, I had no idea. I hoped he prudently had decided to quit the place before it burned to the ground.

Marcus pulled me to my feet. He stared at me a brief moment, amazement mixed with anger, then we both had to turn and fight Sharkey and the men who'd come to help him.

Sharkey rained rapid blows down on me. Brewster had told me Sharkey had been a pugilist, and while his punches lacked the elegance they might have had in a boxing exhibition, they were effective. I raised my fists to fend him off, while the room burned merrily around us.

Marcus was kicking and fighting in grand style, but his hands were still bound, and he couldn't make much headway. More men were coming. They'd trap us in the burning room.

I coughed, air squeezing from my lungs. Marcus fell. Brewster, a giant lit by the halo of fire, barreled into me, his bulk propelling me through the two men in the doorway and out into the hall.

"Marcus," I croaked. "Don't leave him."

Brewster's look told me what he thought of my sanity, but he turned and disappeared back into the inferno.

That left me to fight Sharkey's men on the stairs by myself. Sharkey was leaping for the upper floor — he must know of the escape route through the bakery, or perhaps he meant to take to the rooftops.

I wrested myself from the thugs and followed him. Below me, I heard Grenville calling my name, but I continued after Sharkey.

I caught up to Sharkey in the second of the harem rooms, before he could leap from the window Brewster had opened. I seized the man around his waist and hauled him back inside.

Like Brewster, Sharkey carried many weapons about his person. He had a slim knife in his hand, swinging it at me. But I had prepared as well, and a curved dagger Grenville had bought at the market in Alexandria helped me fend off the strike.

Sharkey got in a few slashes, cutting my coat and opening a gash on my cheek. He'd nearly hit my eye — he was skilled with a knife.

Why I didn't simply let him run off into the streets and be rid of him, I didn't know. My anger at him for waylaying me and having me beaten, then kidnapping Marcus in order to coerce me into a confrontation had risen to red fury. I slashed at him, trying to stay out of his reach, and punched him in the face when I had the opportunity.

Sharkey came back at me with his knife, plunging it straight at my heart. I danced out of the way, and he spun after me, catching me with a punch on the ribs and one in the head. My legs collapsed as he kicked my knee again, and I fell heavily to the floor.

"Damn you," I yelled at him, blood spattering with my words.

He came at me, knife held low, ready to kill me with efficiency, but he halted when a pistol appeared next to his head, pointed at his eye.

"Say your prayers, Sharkey," Marcus Lacey said.

He pulled the trigger, but Sharkey had already ducked with the reflexes of long experience. The bullet struck the lattice Brewster had leaned against the wall, splinters of dry wood exploding from it. Sharkey slammed himself out the window and scrambled up onto the roof opposite.

Marcus held the smoking pistol at his side and thrust out a hand to me. Somewhere, he'd gotten rid of the rope that had bound him, raw marks around his wrists.

I took his hand and let him haul me to my feet. I had no idea whether Marcus meant to kill me as well, but I didn't waste breath asking.

"The lower floors are ablaze," he told me. "No way out down the stairs."

"Then follow me," I said.

I darted a brief glance out the window Sharkey had used for his exit, but found no sign of him. He must have decided to take to his heels instead of lying in wait to finish us off.

I led Marcus through the open window, across the ledge, and into to the storage room of the bakery. People filled the street below, the fire having attracted attention. The baker and his family poured out of the ground floor of their house.

Brewster had climbed the walls deftly when he'd brought us up. With my injuries and hurried pace, I descended not nearly as skillfully, though Marcus kept up with ease. Amid the growing chaos in the street, no one noticed us.

When we reached the packed earth of the lane below, Marcus made to duck into a side street through the crowd, but I seized him by the arm.

"No you don't," I growled. "We have more to discuss."

Marcus could easily have fought me and gotten away. Instead, he glared at me with eyes like my father's, then gave me a nod. I towed him through the maze of streets toward Sharkey's house.

***

By the time we found our way again to the cul-de-sac that ended in Sharkey's lodgings, the entire house was engulfed in flames. Men and well-wrapped women streamed from the buildings around it, children in mothers' arms. Shouting and wailing joined the roar of the fire. A bucket line had formed in some attempt to keep the blaze from spreading, and men had come with poles to try to pull down the burning house.

I saw the very blond heads of Matthias and Bartholomew among the black of the Egyptians' as they helped haul buckets of water. Brewster had joined those with the poles, his bulk framed against the glare of fire.

I pushed my way to Brewster. "Where's Grenville?" I bellowed at him.

Brewster's coat was gashed and stained with blood, his hair singed. He peered at me from worried eyes in a sweat-streaked face. "Don't know, guv. I barely got out."

I scanned the crammed street and found no sign of Grenville, then I looked at the burning house in horror.

I imagined Grenville inside, trapped, trying to keep his sangfroid even then. "Ah well," he'd say. "I suppose it is time to lay down my cards."

"Bloody hell," I said under my breath.

I pushed past Brewster and moved at a dead run

toward the house.

Brewster couldn't stop me. It was Marcus who pulled me up short before I plunged through the burning doorway.

"What the devil are you doing?" he shouted at me.

I shook him off and kept going. There was a time for explaining what a friend meant to one and a time to run into a burning house to save him.

I'd taken three steps inside, my breath stolen by the heat, when a man stumbled out of the flames, eyes wide, hair nearly burned off. I recognized Vanni, our sometime interpreter.

Right behind him, urging him onward, was Grenville. His face had been blackened by smoke and soot, and the back of his coat was on fire.

I shoved Vanni toward Marcus, grabbed Grenville by both arms, and hauled him out into the street. Two heartbeats later, the entire house collapsed.

I slammed Grenville onto the ground, ripping his coat from him as he fell. I slapped sparks from Grenville's back then beat the coat against the ground until the flames were out. His waistcoat and shirt were covered with black pockmarks, but they hadn't caught.

Grenville sat up, breathing heavily. "Damn it all," he managed, voice rasping. "I had that coat made in Milan."

"What the bloody hell were you still doing in there?" I roared at him.

Grenville blinked. "Trying to find my way out, of course. Stumbled upon my old friend Vanni holed up in a back room. Thought I'd rescue the ungrateful sod."

"Damn you." I had my hands on my knees, my

breath labored. "I was imagining the worst."

"I hadn't given up yet." Grenville gave me a nod, dignified in spite of his red eyes, streaming face, and ragged hair. "It was kind of you to try to find me." He scowled. "But bloody stupid."

"Completely mad." Marcus had left Vanni to stand over us. "You'd have both died."

"I thought your object was to kill me," I said to Marcus, straightening up. "Pushing me into the flames would have accomplished that."

"Perhaps I've changed my mind," Marcus growled.

"He kept you alive because he wants something," Grenville concluded. "If you help me up, Lacey, I suggest we adjourn to our own house and find out what."

***

We made our slow and painful way home. The fire burned behind us, and we kept a careful lookout for Sharkey or any of his men as we went, but we did not see them.

I did not think Sharkey would give up on me because his house had burned. In fact, I imagined he'd become more dangerous than ever.

Matthias and Bartholomew had stayed behind to help. Brewster, on the other hand, stuck to his first mission, protecting me, and hobbled home with us.

Our servants were distressed to see us return beaten and burned, and rallied around to supply food and drink. One man presented us with salves he swore would have us cured by morning.

The worst of us was Brewster, who'd taken the brunt of the fighting, but he refused to go to bed while Marcus stood in our drawing room. He at least conceded to sit down, as did Grenville. Grenville had removed his ruined clothes and donned a loose shirt and trousers, throwing a flowing banyan over it all.

I faced Marcus in the middle of the room, gazing at him in silence. I had no idea what to say to the man. All my anger, my questions, my shock, had dried up with the fire, leaving me wordless.

Marcus only stared back at me, his brows drawn. He'd been burned on one side of his face, a streak of angry red marring his sunbaked skin.

It was Grenville who broke the tension. "Well," he said. "We know that Sharkey didn't have the book. What about you, Mr. Lacey?"

Marcus turned his hard stare to Grenville. "Do you think I'd have argued with the man if I'd known where it was?"

"Yes, I do," Grenville returned calmly. "I doubt you'd have told a man like Sharkey where a priceless Alexandrian book was, no matter how much he threatened you. More important that you keep it to lord it over Lacey—our Captain Lacey, that is."

"You're a bloody fool then," Marcus snapped. "If I had the book, I'd already be on a ship bound for England, to present it to the Regent or Wellington or someone else prominent in return for helping me prove who I am."

"I don't think you would, actually," Grenville said with shrewd assessment. "You could easily hire a solicitor to assist with that—no need for a grand gesture. Long lost relatives are fairly common in England, as a matter of fact. The world is full of perils. The question is, where is the book?"

"I tell you, I don't know." The edge in Marcus's voice made me believe him. "I meant to search the boat of Chabert's mistress, but that fellow Sharkey nabbed me. His men dragged me to his house, thinking I was you." Marcus turned to regard me with deep anger. "Imagine Sharkey's delight when he thought he could use me as bait to catch you."

I cleared my throat, which was still raw from smoke. "I heard you tell him I'd never come for you."

"And why should you?" Marcus looked me up and down. "If Sharkey killed me, that would be the end of your problem."

"Interesting that everyone has said that but me," I returned in a mild tone.

"Why would you not want me dead?" Marcus demanded. "I have done nothing but hurt you since I went to England in search of you."

"Because, Mr. Sharkey, of all people, was right about one thing," I said. "Family. If you truly are my cousin—son of an uncle I never knew I had—then that means something to me. I do not leave my family to die at the hands of a ruffian, no matter what they've done. I have so little family, I must cling to every fragment I find."

"You're a fool then," Marcus said, voice hard.

"So you have said. I'm inclined to believe you don't have the book, though you have been searching for it. What did you hope to find out in the desert the afternoon we saw you?"

Color flooded Marcus's face, making the burn mark look more raw. "That has nothing to do with you or your bloody book."

"Entrance to a tomb?" I asked. "Why did you think it was there?"

"Why I poke about in the sand is my business," Marcus said with swift anger. "That day, you were hunting *me*."

"Of course I was," I said. "I wanted to shake

answers out of you. You found a hole, a tunnel. Is it the way into a tomb? Or a shaft back to something else? A monument no one else has found?"

Marcus's eyes shone with rage. "Can you leave me anything at all? You cheated me out of my inheritance by being born and then not dying in all the battles you fought. Will nothing kill you?"

"I'm simply good at not being where bullets and sword blades are," I answered calmly. "I'll have you know, I obtained permission to dig in that area. Would you like to know what we've found?"

"Nothing." Marcus faced me, as though forgetting there were others in the room. "I know you found nothing. The tale I heard was that thieves used the tunnels to burrow through the earth to the burial chambers of the pyramids, but I realized that the hole is too far away. It's a rumor, nothing more, but damn it all, it was *my* rumor. Will you take everything from me?"

Chapter Twenty-Four

I stepped to him, the two of us the same height, my heart beating rapidly. "I told you, if you want that wreck of a house in Norfolk, you are welcome to it. If you slam the front door too hard, the entire edifice might fall down. If you wish to know what we found at your tunnel, I was about to offer to show you. But perhaps I should give you to the magistrates for repeatedly trying to kill me instead."

"Can you blame me?" Marcus's eyes were on level with mine. "You go on about family, but yours took *everything* from me, starting with my own father. I was raised by a dour Protestant who thought hard work and spartan living was the way to virtue. I had to work doubly hard, he told me, because I was tainted by my grandmother's Indian blood. He wanted to save my soul for my father's sake. I'd rather have had my father, thank you. But yours took him away from me."

"My father was a horrible, cruel, and petty bastard," I returned. "I was punished every day of my life for simply being alive. I think I've paid the price you wanted me to pay, long ago."

"That does not give my father back to me," Marcus said, voice harsh.

"Neither does it make what *my* father did to me easier to bear."

We glared at each other, the rest of the room silent. I was breathing hard, leaning toward Marcus, and his breath was as loud as mine.

I coughed, breaking off to turn apologetically to Grenville. "I beg your pardon," I said stiffly. "I did not mean for you to listen to our grievances."

"Not at all." Grenville had leaned back, fingertips touching. "I am enjoying myself. It is like watching a man in a mirror. But if we are to go back out to the desert tomorrow, I suggest we rest. Mr. Lacey, will you accept our hospitality and give us your word you will stay quietly? Or shall we lock you in a bedroom, as Mr. Sharkey did, and let you out again in the morning?"

***

Marcus agreed to stay, to my surprise. I supposed he thought it the best way to discover what we had found.

The next morning, as I waited for the guards to escort me to the palace, I was approached by a lone Turkish soldier who bowed to me with great civility and handed me a note.

In a fine hand, in perfect English, the letter told me that it was no longer necessary for me to instruct the pasha's cavalrymen. The lessons were at an end.

I read this with great disappointment. Had the pasha heard about my involvement in last night's fire and decided it more diplomatic that I stayed away? Or perhaps he simply felt that I had taught his officers all I could and my visits were no longer necessary.

I was saddened. I'd enjoyed riding and talking with the cavalrymen, one of the finest things about this sojourn.

Matthias and Bartholomew had returned home earlier this morning, exhausted but relieved. The fire had consumed five houses in the lane but hadn't spread to the rest of the city. They collapsed into bed, and we let them sleep while we headed out for the desert.

My canceled lessons at least allowed us to leave in the cool of the morning, which meant we'd have more time to explore before the heat of the day. Marcus walked skeptically with us to the river, our one-eyed ferryman in his tiny raft taking us across. On the other side, we continued on foot.

Grenville set up his pavilion near the pyramids as he had done every day, and we refreshed ourselves with food and coffee before we strolled out into the desert, pretending we were simply taking in the sights.

Brewster seemed none the worse for wear from the night before, though he wore a bandage on his shoulder beneath his coat. He shrugged off his hurts, stating that the only thing that had laid him low in recent years had been a shot in the gut. He pinned Marcus with a hard gaze as he said this, and Marcus frowned back at him.

I had worn my turban against the sun, finding it very efficient for keeping my head cool. Marcus's clothes had been ruined, and he hadn't had time to send for his things, so he'd chosen to wear the galabiya that had been made for me. He strode with swift ease as he walked beside me.

We moved down the arroyo and up the other bank as we'd done before, at last finding the place where we'd dug the evening before last. I had been worried that I'd not find the square opening I'd uncovered at the base of the hill, but I had marked it well.

Brewster carried a pack with more tools than we'd brought before, and soon he and I were digging away the dirt we'd filled in. I tapped the stone when we found it with the end of my spade.

"It's manmade, I'm certain of it," I said, my excitement mounting. "Something more than a thieves' tunnel, perhaps."

Marcus crouched down, his darkened skin and galabiya making him look very Egyptian. "Perhaps." He did not sound convinced. "Many of these tunnels go nowhere—have been blocked by cave-ins, or else the thieves gave up digging before they reached anything."

Brewster brushed sand aside with a gloved hand. "Nothing for it but Captain Lacey will want to see," he said, sounding more resigned than exasperated. "And then he'll dutifully hand over all the treasure he does find. It's the sort of bloke he is."

I gave him a disparaging look. "It's the finding of the things that is the fascinating part. Not the keeping of them."

"Huh. So you say."

Brewster continued to brush away the sand, his movements brisk, eyes alight. He was interested too, though he'd never admit it.

Grenville was not as reticent. "Well, let us get in there and see what we can see. I did not wriggle my way into that other foul hole to turn back now. I want to find something besides bats."

"That is why I've brought Marcus," I said. "I want to hear these rumors you were told. What made you look where you did?"

Marcus heaved a sigh. "I purchased a map." He drew it now, with his finger in the sand. It included the tunnel Grenville had found, which dropped away to a large chamber—where the bats had been. Two more tunnels ran parallel to the first, both leading to a square chamber below and to the right of the cave.

Marcus pointed to one of the tunnels. "This opening might be to this shaft here. But as I say, there is probably nothing in it. The Egyptian in Alexandria who told me the tale might have been exaggerating. He certainly made a show of being secretive, but I am certain he was only trying to pique my interest."

I studied Marcus's drawing, which Grenville then copied into his sketchbook. Real or not, it seemed a reasonable guess at the layout of a tomb and tunnels to reach it. The antiquities sold all over Cairo had to come from somewhere.

Today Grenville had brought with him a roll of canvas and folding wooden poles, which he and Brewster set up to give us a bit of shade. The temperature rose as we continued to dig, clearing the hole.

I pushed the debris we took from it into a careful pile to one side, planning to look through it later. Who knew what a thief might have dropped when he'd run away several thousand years ago?

We dug for hours. Grenville, who'd designated himself as our timekeeper, stopped us for water, food, and rest throughout the day, but other than that, we simply worked.

The task kept us silent. Whatever would happen with Marcus I did not know—my choices were either embracing him and conceding all he claimed or prosecuting him for attempted murder and his assault on Brewster.

Such considerations fell away in the face of our task. Brewster worked side-by-side with Marcus without a word.

We cleared away plenty of rubble by sundown to reveal a square opening at the base of the five-foot-high bluff.

Grenville had his lantern ready and passed it into the hole. I caught my breath as the light picked out the uniform beauty of hieroglyphs. I reached forward and touched one, marveling that someone had cut this thousands of years ago.

"Pity we can't read them," Grenville said. "It might be a thieves' code for *dead end ahead.*"

"No," I said with certainty. "These were carved with care. A thief would scratch an X or some such. They likely couldn't read the hieroglyphs any more than we can."

"Agreed," Brewster said. "Thieves leave marks no one knows but men in their own gang. They'd not make a sign for the rest of the world."

"Of course it's a tomb entrance," Marcus said, examining the hieroglyphs, sounding as excited as I was. "Why else would it be decorated? But it might simply lead to tomb that has already been excavated or robbed. I understood that before I began my search. But I was curious."

Avid curiosity was another Lacey failing. I hardly cared whether this tomb had already been found, and apparently Marcus did not either.

I ran my hands over the hieroglyphs again, as though touching them could convey their meaning. The beetle was used often, as was the hawk, and what looked like the seated form of a girl.

Gathering twilight was our enemy once more. In a few moments, I could no longer make out the symbols.

"We should cover it up again," Grenville said. "Too dangerous to try to explore more in dark. We'll return tomorrow with more men and dig through."

"Better camp here," Marcus advised. "Tomb robbers still abound, and excavators can play dirty tricks on one another. Word is that Drovetti will pay thieves to cut into tombs and take things out, damn who has the firman."

"I agree," Grenville said. "I'll go back to Cairo and return with camping gear and Bartholomew and Matthias, who would be incensed to miss this."

Marcus said nothing. He sat down in the dirt and drank water, wiping the droplets from his mouth.

We agreed that Grenville should go while Brewster, Marcus, and I remained at the site. The three of us sat under the pavilion and ate a small meal while we waited. We didn't speak, perhaps each of us knowing that any conversation we began we likely spark a violent argument.

I wasn't much interested in quarrels at the moment. I had an ancient monument at my fingertips. Whether it proved to have treasure in it or to have already been emptied didn't matter. The thrill of the hunt, of the finding, had fired my blood.

Marcus slept, or seemed to, his arm over his eyes. Brewster and I remained awake, keeping our eye on Marcus, though I was tempted to drift off in the heat.

Grenville returned in a few hours, the footmen

following with large packs on their strong backs. Bartholomew and Matthias set up our camp, and we prepared to sleep under the stars.

We settled down, Grenville quickly dropping into the sleep of the just. I lay awake, uneasy. I expected Sharkey to come upon us and try to stab or shoot us in the dark. We'd destroyed his house, injured him and his men, and the fire that had demolished five houses had likely brought the notice of the pasha on him.

Grenville had reported, before he fell asleep, that there was no word of Sharkey in town. Bartholomew, who had learned to communicate with our Egyptian servants, said that there had been much talk throughout Cairo of the fire, but no news of the foreigners who'd lived in the house. No bodies found in the smoking rubble either.

If Sharkey had escaped, he did not search the desert for us that night. We saw nothing but a few snakes and scorpions, who gave our small fire a wide berth. A beetle once poked its head above the sand and then withdrew with a snap. I wondered how such creatures moved about underground and reflected that their skill would be handy in our coming excavation.

Day dawned, and we went early to work.

With Matthias and Bartholomew to lend their strength, we cleared away a great deal of rubble inside the tunnel, finding larger chunks of stone deeper inside rather than only sand and gravel.

At the peak of the afternoon's heat, we broke through the last of the rocks that had filled the tunnel, and found a straight, square-sided shaft.

Brewster wanted to be first inside, to make sure all was well, but Grenville forestalled him.

"Let Lacey," he said. "He's been waiting for this moment for years."

I had indeed. Since the night Grenville had first invited me into his private sitting room in Grosvenor Street, and I'd asked where he'd obtained the beautiful antiquities, I'd longed to see the places from which they'd come.

Brewster seemed to understand. He let out a muted grunt but turned aside and waved me forward. I crawled into the darkness, one of Grenville's lanterns lighting my way.

I found wonders. The low walls of the tunnel were covered in hieroglyphs, and farther along, paintings—beautiful paintings in bright reds, yellows, greens, golds. The large men walking were done in the odd style of the ancient Egyptians, everyone sideways and out of proportion, but the wildlife—birds, snakes, crocodiles, hippopotami— were so real, every feather and scale reproduced exactly, that they might come to life and fly past me to the light.

"Come," I called back. "It's beautiful."

No one had been here for eons—I somehow knew this. The paintings were undisturbed. I was the first human eye to see them for centuries. The thought made me shiver in awe, but also humbled me.

I would have artists come and copy them exactly before wind and dust and people crawling through ruined them. Or perhaps they could be removed intact by chiseling out the walls themselves.

That was a difficulty for another day. I continued along the passage, coming upon nothing but more paintings—no heaps of gold or caches of emeralds had been conveniently piled before me.

But it didn't matter. The artist of however many

thousands of years ago had reached forward in time, touched my eyes, and enchanted me.

The others crowded inside the tunnel as I moved on. I heard exclamations as they reached the paintings, and Grenville's sketchbook rustle as he sought to copy at least a little.

The tunnel continued onward, and I followed it until it began to slope. A faint smell came from the bottom, and I recognized the pungent odor of bat.

"We need rope," Brewster said. "No telling when that's going to drop off."

Bartholomew had thoughtfully brought in two coils. He passed one up to us.

Matthias said, "I ought to go back and keep watch, sir. In case anyone has followed."

He looked above him worriedly, as though the dark, closed-in space unnerved him. Grenville seemed to understand and waved him off. Bartholomew went with him. Truth to tell, I felt better knowing the brothers would be outside and on guard.

The four of us went on, Marcus readily helping as we tied the rope around our waists and the lantern to one end of it. I pushed the lantern ahead of me—it would be the first to fall if the tunnel indeed dropped.

It did not. The downward slope became steep, but we picked our way along, holding on to the side walls or the ceiling to keep from slipping. I kept smelling bat dung—the stench became quite thick—but we had yet to see any of the animals.

The tunnel ended abruptly in a square opening that emitted a faint draft. I groped inside with my hands but touched only empty air.

I carefully lowered the lantern through the hole,

measuring off how many feet I released. After six feet, the lantern struck stone.

I lay on my belly and peered through the opening, hoping the lamp had not simply landed on a rock ledge. I saw the lantern balanced evenly on a floor, the light showing me regularly shaped stone blocks in a chamber of about ten feet on each side.

In the thick dust on the other side of the chamber, something glittered.

I untied myself from Brewster and swung into the hole, ignoring his startled shout. I held on to the tunnel's ledge to lower myself the six feet, landing easily on my feet.

Without waiting for the others, I snatched up the lantern, strode across the chamber, and flashed the light on what I had seen.

In the middle of a pile of sandy gravel the glimmer of gold, bright blue of lapis, and the blood-red fire of rubies winked up at me.

Chapter Twenty-Five

L ord love a duck," Brewster breathed. He stood just behind me with the others, lifting another lantern. "Tell me you ain't tamely handing those over to a bloody museum, guv."

He reached forward, ready to reverently lift a handful of the jewels that spread themselves before us.

I grabbed his wrist. "Wait. Grenville," I called to him. "Draw it. As precisely as you can."

Grenville darted forward, turning to a clean page in his book, pencil ready. He crouched down on his heels, peering at the jewels, and then began to sketch.

"What for?" Brewster asked. "We can lay 'em out on the table at home and draw them there."

"Because," Marcus answered for me. "Whatever string or wires held everything together will have deteriorated long ago. This way, we'll know what they are supposed to look like when we try to put them back together."

"Looks like a jumble to me," Brewster said. "Like someone dropped 'em. Or threw them in the corner."

"Why on earth would they?" Grenville asked as his pencil moved. "They're beautiful."

"The rest of this room is empty," I observed.

The floor was blank, except for one solid bench-like piece of stone along the opposite wall. It was the size and shape of a bed for one, or the resting place for a coffin, I realized. The walls and even the ceiling held more paintings, but large bits of them had been gouged out or fallen away long ago.

"I am guessing that thieves did find it this place," I said. "Whatever treasure was here, they took, including the body of whoever rested there. Perhaps their hands were so full they dropped the jewelry. Or they'd found so many more valuable things that these didn't signify."

Marcus let out his breath. "What it must have been like then, eh? Full of glorious things."

"Sorry, Lacey," Grenville said. He bent to examine the cache then adjusted a detail on his drawing. "I know you wanted to find a mummy cloaked in gold surrounded by a treasure of the ages."

"This will do nicely," I told him. "Rubies will look lovely in my wife's hair."

"And mine," Brewster said. "I want something for my trouble following you about."

Marcus's eyes flashed in the lamplight. "A find like this? You're going to decorate your wives with it?"

Grenville continued to draw. "I can think of no better end for them. These were obviously jewels made for a princess. Look at the pictures. The men dominate, but over and over, I see a woman, a very young one, and a man handing her gold, jewels, animals. Her father perhaps? Or a young husband? Poor woman couldn't have been very old."

I studied the paintings around us and decided he was right. The jewels had been placed here in memory of the young woman. A pang of pity touched my heart, though she had been dead and dust centuries before I'd been born.

"We'll display them and honor her, whoever she was," I said.

Marcus snorted. "No one will let you keep a bit of them. Trust me, I have tried treasure hunting before."

"Is that why were you after the Greek book?" I asked as we waited for Grenville to finish. "More treasure hunting?"

Marcus shook his head. "I wanted to find it because you wanted it," he said. "And I was interested for its own sake. A scroll from the Alexandrian library? I would be celebrated."

"Mr. Denis wants that scroll," Brewster rumbled warningly. "'S my job to see he gets it."

"I don't think it exists," Marcus said. "Your man sent you on a wild goose chase, along with his tame dog."

Brewster gave him an unfriendly eye. "You watch your mouth. I'm still displeased with you for shooting me."

"Gentlemen." Grenville closed the notebook and rose. "We are in a burial chamber. Have a bit of respect. Now, we need to pick up the pieces very carefully and find a way to carry them out."

We settled on simply folding the pieces in our handkerchiefs and transporting them in our pockets. The four of us gathered on the floor as Grenville, with slim, deft fingers, divided up the pieces of ruby, lapis, gold wire, and the carnelian we found underneath, along with beads that proved to be made of beaten gold.

I declared we should each have an equal share of the find, and that Matthias and Bartholomew should get a bit of it too. Grenville agreed and divided the stash exactly four ways.

Marcus shot a glance at Brewster as Grenville laid a ruby, then a gold bead, on Brewster's large handkerchief.

"You'd trust a thief with this?" he asked, not in anger but in curiosity. "Why will he not simply kill us all and flee with the lot?"

Brewster scowled, but I held up a calming hand before he could speak. "Brewster answers to a higher authority," I said. "His employer would not be pleased, and he knows it."

Brewster turned on me with a look of hurt. "You fink that's the only reason? I'd never rob you, guv. I'm grieved you'd say so. I truly am."

I raised my brows, nonplussed. I'd come to think of Tommy Brewster as a friend—he'd taken me to his home, introduced me to his wife, and had come to my aid many times, at a cost to himself.

But I'd had no idea he might think of me as friend in return. I'd believed Brewster viewed me only as the troublesome captain Mr. Denis expected him to look after.

Brewster looked away, still scowling. I'd have to make it up to him, explain I'd only been trying to assuage Marcus. I had the feeling I'd be standing him ale for a while before he forgave me.

There was nothing else to do in the chamber. The four walls were solid, the paintings damaged, the entire place robbed except for the jewels, which fit into our pockets. We'd found all there was to find.

Brewster insisted on going ahead of us, so we boosted him up into the tunnel. He pulled us up in turn, each of us climbing out with the aid of rope and Brewster's strong arm.

We crawled back to the brilliant paintings that greeted us with their vibrant beauty. I was struck anew with how the pictures depicted cheerful, happy scenes, incongruous with a tomb, but I supposed whoever created them did so to comfort the princess who'd lain here.

Ahead of us, Brewster stopped abruptly.

I coughed at the dust that filled the passage and muffled the lantern light. Had another sandstorm begun above?

"Guv," Brewster said, his voice was strangely subdued.

He lifted his lantern. Instead of more dark tunnel sloping upward before us, his light fell on rubble that blocked the passage from floor to ceiling, cutting into the middle of the exquisite paintings. Sand trickled around our knees, and the air became heavy.

Our way out had been completely sealed off.

***

After we stared, stunned, at the solid rubble, Brewster reached out a fist and pounded on it. "Oi!" he shouted. "We're still in 'ere!"

"Not a natural collapse?" Grenville asked, his face pale in the flickering lantern light.

"We would have heard a collapse or felt an earthquake," I said tightly. "Someone did this deliberately."

Brewster yelled again, louder. *"Oi!"*

Very faintly, we heard an answering shout. "I'll send word to Mr. Denis you're indisposed."

And then, nothing.

"Douse the lights," I said abruptly. "All but one. Save the candles."

"Bloody hell." Brewster obeyed, blowing out his light as I blew out mine. "If I get out of here, Mr. Sharkey is a dead man." His eyes glittered with terrible rage, and I knew he'd follow through on his threat.

"We dug our way in," I said, trying to sound calm in spite of the watery fear pouring through my veins. "We can dig our way out again."

"Our tools are outside," Marcus pointed out. "What about your footmen? Why weren't they on guard?"

"They were," Grenville said, voice grim. His lantern alone remained lit, pale light flickering over his sharp face. "That worries me very much."

"I'm more worried about getting us out of here," Brewster said. He put large hands on the rubble and began to pull.

The pile shuddered then rocks rattled toward us, billowing a cloud of dust through the passage.

"Stop!" Grenville cried. "Before you bring it down on us. I'm certain Mr. Sharkey means to bury us alive."

"Which is why he's a dead man," Brewster said.

However, he ceased tugging the rocks until the pebbles stopped sliding and the air cleared a bit.

Marcus asked the question we were all thinking. "What do we do now?"

"Go back to the burial chamber," I said. "The air was better in there."

There was not much point in debate. We turned and inched our way back down the tunnel.

The paintings seemed a bit more sinister now.

They depicted life under the open sky, with sunshine, birds, animals playing in the river. Reminding the dead what it was to be alive.

At the end of the tunnel, Brewster again lowered us into the chamber then climbed in after us. There was nowhere else to go after that. The tomb had a solid roof and floor and four walls without a crease.

"If Matthias and Bartholomew are all right, they'll go for help," I said. "They'll dig us out."

"If Sharkey didn't kill them," Marcus said, echoing my fear.

Grenville answered. "Those lads are resourceful. Bloody clever. They'll find a way."

"They're servants," Marcus said. "Why would they risk themselves for a man of your class?"

Grenville raised disdainful brows at him. "I don't think much of your upbringing. Loyalty and friendship has nothing to do with a man's place in life."

"I'll wager Sharkey took care of them," Brewster said unhappily. "A pity—they're good lads." He wiped his brow. "I don't fancy starving to death down here, and that's the truth. A mate of mine told me his mum stuck him in a cellar and forgot about him when he was a lad. Drank herself to death upstairs. They found him just afore he were gone. Said it was the worst pain he'd ever felt in his life."

"We have our pistols," Grenville said quietly. "If it comes to that."

Brewster looked at Marcus, who had come weaponless. "Don't worry," he rumbled. "I'll do you quick."

I broke into the morbid discussion. "Gentlemen, let us not be so quick to give up hope. I've had to face—"

"Oh, God's balls," Brewster cut in. "He's going to give us another of his travelers' tales. Been in a tighter spot than this, have you guv? In India, maybe?"

"Spain, if you must know," I said, ignoring his derision. "French soldiers beat me senseless then strung me up by my ankles and left me to die. Yes, thus far, that was a tighter spot than this."

"Good Lord." Marcus gave me a look of shock. "What the devil had you done to them?"

I shrugged. "Nothing. I was simply a lone British officer riding by at the wrong time. That is not to say I didn't put up a hell of a fight." I had been wandering the countryside in the first place because another man thought I'd coveted his wife, but I did not wish to share this with Marcus or Brewster at the moment.

Grenville, who knew the entire story, said nothing, but Brewster's belligerence to me softened a bit. "True, we are upright and breathing."

"Yes, we are." I waved my hand at the walls. "The air isn't fetid. Smells strongly of bat leavings, but it's not stuffy — in fact, it's cool and pleasant. There must be another shaft somewhere letting in the breeze."

The others looked cheered at the thought. "But where?" Grenville asked, flashing his lantern around the ceiling. "It could be a tiny opening in a corner. We might bring the hill down on top of us if we try to dig that way."

"It does not hurt us to look."

In Donata's library this summer I'd found novels that told of perilous adventures, which might include the heroine being walled up alive, locked in a dungeon, or buried in a ruined tomb. Donata admitted to adoring the novels as a girl, while pretending to her parents that she read only improving books.

I'd enjoyed the stories—harmless entertainment, if farfetched. In them the heroines had found numerous trap doors, hidden passages, and secret staircases at their disposal, no matter where they found themselves imprisoned. The heroines had been extraordinarily lucky that the villains had locked them into places with multiple entrances.

But Egyptian tombs seemed to have been constructed the same way. Apparently, from what I'd read on the subject during our voyage, the builders had given themselves several ways out, so they could seal in their king and then escape. Still more passages had been built to divert thieves to side chambers.

"Show us the map again," I said quickly to Grenville.

Grenville handed me his lantern and we gathered around while he opened his sketchbook and flipped to the drawing he'd made of Marcus's map.

"This must be the tunnel we came down today." I pointed to the line that slanted from the surface to the open square. "This is where Grenville crawled along." That passage ran parallel to the tomb before it angled sharply downward to the cave that had contained the bats. "Which leaves this one."

The third shaft was suspended between the first two, bending from cave to tomb.

"But there must be still another shaft," I said. "The bats have to get out somehow. They don't go through the hole you found first, Marcus, because we had to dig that out. The tunnel that leads down here was also blocked. So either this last shaft connects with one that comes out at the surface, or the cave with the bats has another entrance."

I tapped the third tunnel as I spoke. Though it bent toward the tomb, there seemed to be no opening in the walls of this room to access it.

"We can't dig through solid rock," Brewster pointed out.

"But the Egyptians liked tricks and traps," I said. "My readings said that they left exits for those who buried the king or queen, which is probably what thieves of old found. Let us see if any of these stones can be moved."

We searched. With the desperation of men with one shred of hope, we examined every stone in the walls. Brewster even lifted up Grenville, who was the lightest of us, so he could study all the stones of the ceiling. We spent one candle and lit the next from its embers.

Grenville dropped to the floor as he finished in the last corner and shook his head. "If there is any way out here, then we are not clever enough to discover the trick of it."

Brewster and Marcus also sat down, Brewster with his back to the wall, resting his head against the stones. Marcus sat cross-legged, hands dangling from his knees.

I started to feel despair wash over me, as well as fear. Grenville's idea of us shooting ourselves or each other might come to pass.

No, damn it, I would not give up. My wife waited for me — she would bring forth my child soon, a daughter. I knew she would be a daughter, knew it with all my heart.

I found myself sitting on the floor, my head in my hands. I'd curled up thus at times when melancholia had struck, though it hadn't touched me in a long time. What I experienced at the moment wasn't melancholia, not quite. In those times, I had not cared whether I lived or died.

I cared now. I closed my eyes, shutting out the pinpoint of candlelight, trying to seek calm.

I seemed to see myself walking on the bright sands of the desert, but I carried a little girl in my arms. She was about three years old, and wore in her hair the gold and rubies that we'd found, the jewels flashing in the sunlight.

I carried her down into the tunnel, which had widened considerably, the opening surrounded by people, donkeys, camels and their drovers, and vendors selling souvenirs.

I lifted my daughter to see the beautifully painted birds and beasts on the walls, the colors so resonant that the animals seemed to move. My daughter clapped her hands in delight, then squirmed to get to her feet.

As soon as she touched the ground, she ran down the tunnel toward the burial chamber. I followed in alarm, reaching to catch her before she tumbled through the opening and fell down the drop.

She continued to run, right into the hole, but the drop was gone, the floor of the tunnel dug down to the tomb's level, plenty of light within. At the opening, my daughter turned and held out her hand to me.

I took it. I could feel her fingers, warm and small, against mine, my love for her overwhelming me.

She led me to where I sat now. I sank down, seeming to juxtapose my self of tomorrow with that of today. My daughter knelt at my feet, smiling with red lips, her eyes dark like mine but with the shape of Donata's.

"Here, Papa," she said, and patted the floor at my feet.

I snapped open my eyes. My daughter had vanished, the light that had filled the tomb gone as well.

I dragged in a breath, finding it dry and clogged. I coughed, then got to my knees.

"The floor," I said, my voice a harsh croak. "Check the floor."

The other three men, who'd been sitting in postures of listlessness like my own, scrambled up and began crawling around the room again, brushing dust and sand from the stones.

I moved my hands forward to the exact place my daughter had showed me in my dream.

I pushed, and the stone moved.

Chapter Twenty-Six

Nothing was easy about getting the stone out of the floor.

If we'd had a few iron bars and a fulcrum, we could have lifted it in a trice — as it was, we had rope, candles and lanterns, and the few small hand tools Grenville had brought inside with him. I'd even left my walking stick above, unsure I'd need a prop in tunnels where I could not even stand.

After a very, very long time of chipping around the mortar that held the stone in place, we lifted the block a fraction of an inch, catching it with our fingers . . . only to have it slip out again. We tried again, and again. And yet again.

I grasped it once more, refusing to give in to despair. I would not picture excavators a few years from now digging down here to find our bones, fingers desperately clutching the stone.

I had no idea if the image of my daughter had been a dream, a waking vision, or my own mind trying to show me the irregularity in the floor in front of me. I would not fail her, I decided. I would live to see her, to bring her back and show her the wonders of Egypt.

The stone ground upward enough that Brewster got his big, gloved hands around two corners of it. Marcus caught another corner, and I grabbed the fourth one. We wriggled the block upward, my hope rising with it.

"Grenville, now," I said abruptly.

We'd cut our rope into multiple pieces and knotted them into wide loops. As Marcus and I lifted one side, Grenville quickly slid one loop over the two corners and pulled it tight. While Grenville braced himself and held that, I fixed another loop around the side Brewster held.

Pulling the ropes alternately, two of us on each, we worked the stone out of the floor, slowly, slowly. So must the ancients have hauled the stones upward, one at a time, to construct the giant pyramids. At last, when the stone was almost out, Brewster, Grenville, and Marcus, tipped it until I was able to slide my hands under the bottom and haul it all the way out.

Catching our breaths, we released the ropes and pulled them from the block, hoping against hope that we'd found an opening, and not simply a loose stone.

Our second candle guttered. Grenville quickly touched the flame to the wick of the third candle, and light flared high. Grenville closed the lantern's shield, tied a rope to the ring on top, and lowered it into the hole.

The lantern went down—two feet, four, eight, ten. There it stopped, the lantern clinking on another floor.

"Well," Grenville said, as though we sat in his box

at Covent Garden, waiting for the next performance. "Now to see whether it is another tunnel or simply a deep hole."

He prepared to tie a length of rope around his waist, but I forestalled him. "No, let me."

I had to go down. I don't know why I was compelled to, but I knew it had to be me. I'd promised my little girl.

Brewster lowered me down, knowing it would be useless to argue. At the bottom I groped my way around the small square shaft. On the fourth side, about at my waist height, was another hole. When I inserted the lantern, I saw that it ran straight ahead, as least as far as I could see.

"It is indeed a tunnel," I said. "Shall we see where it leads?"

***

It led a long, long way into the earth. We crawled, the rough stone beneath us cutting into our gloves and knees, the tunnel's ceiling scraping our backs.

We'd gone, at my count, at least a mile when the last candle died. I gazed at the glowing wick as long as I could before it too faded, and we were in darkness.

We continued forward. There was no other way.

The blackness pressed on us, as did the silence. We heard each other breathing, heard the grating of sand on the tunnel floor.

It seemed a long time since I'd stood straight. My knee hurt like fury, so much that I feared I'd ruined it forever.

Donata would have to push me around in a Bath chair, her wasted wreck of a husband. She'd find another lover while I nodded by the fire at home, too feeble to move.

My beautiful Donata. She could stretch out her hand and have any gentleman she wanted. And yet, she'd chosen me.

I pictured her as she'd been the first time I'd seen her, standing in full sunshine in a billiards room, her dark hair soft under a lace cap, cigarillo smoke wreathing her sharp face. "Well, come on then," she'd said in her cool, clear voice.

She'd meant that I should play billiards with her instead of staring at her like a fool. I heard her voice again, the past blending with the present. "Come on then, Gabriel. Be useful."

Her breath, scented with acrid smoke, touched my face. Her eyelashes were sharp points of black.

I decided I very much loved her.

"Guv." Brewster shook my foot.

I realized I'd halted, my mind conjuring images that encouraged my body to lie down, rest, and bask in memories.

"Damnation," I said. I crawled on, every inch agony.

"Talk to us," Grenville said from behind Brewster. "Tell me what you were reading to me on the ship, when I was too ill to comprehend much. The idea about the dark star. As it is so very dark, the subject is apt."

For a moment, I remembered nothing of what he meant. Then I wet my parched lips, thinking it through.

"Laplace's theory," I said, recalling his tome about mathematics and astronomy. "He postulates the existence of a star that has so much gravity in it that even light could not escape it. It would therefore be dark — we'd see only a place of blackness."

Brewster grunted. "Rot. Stars give off light. You

can't have one with no light at all."

"He means it as a mathematical possibility," I answered. As I remembered Laplace's arguments and his neatly written equations, my thoughts focused, the darkness weighing not quite so heavily. "All things, if thrown hard enough, can in theory fly off a world into empty space. The amount of strength needed can be calculated with precision—Monsieur Laplace simply takes the equations to their extreme end. He postulates about a place so full of gravity that it would be harder and harder to throw something from it, until even the corpuscles of light itself could not be hurled away."

"Ah," Grenville said. "That was one of his older theories. I believe he has now rejected the notion that light is a corpuscle, as Mr. Newton called it. Men of science have decided light is a wave and travels through a medium, just as water travels on the sea. So Monsieur Laplace's speculation comes to nothing. If light travels in waves, it cannot weigh anything to be pulled back down by this star with its large gravity."

I had to concede the truth of this. But I rather liked the notion of a dark star, drifting like a strange menace and swallowing all light, like this tunnel did.

We continued, talking about scientific ideas and their possibilities. Marcus proved very well read in both the ancients and the moderns.

Brewster too knew a surprising amount. Though he'd had the barest schooling, he'd been fortunate enough to have a landlady teach him to read as a lad, and had perused many books. He knew a great deal about the worth of things and had a catalog of art in his head that any collector would envy.

I had been an indifferent student as a lad, often

beaten for my lack of interest, but had found the eagerness to learn as an adult. I'd discovered that reading for one's enjoyment was much more satisfying than doing it to please others. I now read everything from Cicero to Daniel Defoe to Donata's harrowing novels by Minerva Press.

It was becoming too dry to talk, but I had something else on my mind that I wanted to know.

"I can forgive you trying to harm *me*, Marcus," I told him. "Your anger at me and my father is understandable. I'll make you answer for nearly hurting Peter and shooting Brewster, but that is another matter. But what about Ibrahim?"

"Who?" Marcus asked behind me, his puzzlement unfeigned. "Who the devil is Ibrahim?"

"You might not have learned his name. He was a Turkish soldier in Alexandria, who was found at the site of the ancient library. Did you kill him?"

Marcus started, then his voice went harsh. "No. I swear to you. I don't harm innocents."

"Huh," Brewster said. "Only blokes what stand in your way."

"You are not an innocent," Marcus said crisply.

"You were seen." I cut into the discussion. "You were there, in the place Ibrahim was discovered."

Marcus rumbled a growl. "Yes, damn you. I do not know how you seem to know these things. I was there. I went to the place where the library supposedly stood, to meet the blasted vendor who sold me the map to this bloody tomb. I'd met him in the market, but was with the bey's guards and couldn't discuss the intriguing map he hinted at. If I could find something worth selling to a museum, I might make my fortune and cease my drudging. I managed to slip away in the night, meet the vendor near the old walls, and get the map. When I was returning, I passed by the site of the library, and nearly tripped over the body of a Turk, mostly buried in sand. I thought to help the poor man, but then I saw he was already dead, his head bloody. I discovered that when I touched him. I also knew that if I were found there with a dead man, his blood on my hand, I'd be arrested and convicted in a trice. So I fled. That is the truth."

I believed him. The story was plausible and his vehemence was real. I could picture him stumbling across the body, pulling a knife as he looked around for the killer, then hurrying away. Ahmed had seen Marcus with the knife, but he probably hadn't seen Ibrahim if the body had already been covered. The night had been dark; both men had turned and gone their separate ways.

"What about the gunfire the night you met with me in the street?" I continued.

Marcus let out another noise of irritation. "Very well, I fired that shot. As I told you, I had to escape from the bey if I wanted to come to Giza and look for this tomb—his idea of employment was akin to slavery. I managed to get out of his house again that night, but one of his men found me. I shot at the man to frighten him off. When he fled, I made for the harbor and hid there until I got onto the boat for the Nile. Not even to annoy you would I stay with that man one moment longer."

Again a plausible tale. "The bey decided I had fired the shot," I told him. "He was ready to arrest me."

"Ah, well," Marcus said. "Then you had a taste of what I suffered with him."

"Which you wouldn't have had to, if you hadn't

followed me to Egypt at all," I said severely. "You must have had other, more important things to do."

"Not really. My only need for the past several years, once I sold my commission, was to find you and take back my inheritance."

"Which, sadly for you, isn't worth tuppence," I said. "My father cheated us both."

Marcus only grunted and fell silent. We crawled on, all conversation dying into the darkness.

The tunnel was endless. I could not remember a time when I was not in darkness and stillness, stones cutting into my skin. The throbbing ache in my leg widened until it blotted out everything — memories, worries, coherent thought. There was only here and now, darkness and agony.

I must have fallen asleep as I went, because a blinding pain flashed through my head, and I jerked open my eyes.

I thought I'd run into the wall beside me, rattling myself awake, but I put out my hand out in front of me and met solid stone. The wall I found was as hard as those to either side, above and below.

"It's blocked," I said, my voice barely working. "There's no way out. Just another wall."

The despair I'd been keeping at bay now swooped in to seize me. I clenched my fists, raging at the desperation, my famous temper now finding release against ton or so of rock.

I banged my fists into the wall, over and over again, my gloves ripping to shreds, my hands bloodying. The others didn't try to stop me. They understood.

I kept pounding. I hated the earth for trapping me, like the dark star trapped all light, keeping me from the lady I loved, the daughter who was my life, my new daughter waiting to appear. Like the light, I fought and fought, needing to escape, even if I shattered myself in the process.

Monsieur Laplace had been wrong, I thought as a white beam struck my eye, momentarily blinding me. The waves of light could not be contained by the heavy darkness, and they exploded away in triumph as I slammed my fist against the loosened dirt.

Heat hit me next, and the smell of sand, wind, and the particularly pungent odor of donkeys.

I pried open my eyes. A hole had opened in front of me. Through it, I could see sunlight, blue sky, and not far away, three regular points of the largest pyramids in the world.

I also saw a woman in a light-colored gown, a long shawl around her shoulders, and a wide parasol over her head, held by a man with skin as dark as Marcus's.

"Good heavens." The voice of Lady Mary joined the brilliant light pouring through the hole. "Must I rescue you again, Captain Lacey?"

***

Lady Mary would have nothing for it but that we stayed the night on her barge, in guest accommodations belowdecks, chambers as sumptuous as her boudoir if not as large. After being entombed in the cramped space, I stretched my arms and enjoyed my cushioned prison.

I accepted Lady Mary's hospitality for the sole reason that my leg refused to bear my weight any longer. I was taken to the river on the back of a camel, riding on a wide saddle, guided by small, wizened man missing most of his teeth.

Lady Mary had stood in the midst of the workmen who had dug us out from the hole, shouting orders in Turkish at the top of her voice. It had been effective—we were surrounded, given water and shelter, and guided back to the river.

We'd come out, it seemed, about half a mile from the pyramids, behind the smallest of the three. Lady Mary had peered into the hole in great excitement after we'd been rescued, demanding to know all about it.

Grenville had given her a smile from cracked lips in his dust-coated face. "All in good time, dear lady. Captain Lacey and I intend to excavate thoroughly." No matter that we'd nearly been entombed alive—Grenville was not about to give up the secrets of our find to rival collectors so easily.

I'd always heard that camels were bad-tempered beasts, but this one regarded me through long lashes like a coquettish young lady and nuzzled me with a damp nose before I was lifted onto the saddle.

The saddle was more like a giant chair with plenty of padding and handholds. I nearly slid off while the camel rose from its kneeling position, back legs first, then front, but I clung on with the last of my strength.

When the camel's porter led me off, I realized why Lady Mary had fetched the beast for me—its gait was soft and rolling, cushioning me from the hard desert in a way a horse, even the pasha's fine Arabs, would never have been able to.

Miguel had to help me from the camel at Lady Mary's barge, and then take me below and get me into bed, which he did with much kindness. The sun was high in the sky and I slept, waking to darkness.

For a panicked moment when I woke, I believed myself back in the silent tunnel. Then I heard voices calling along the river, the jingle of bells as a vendor trotted past with wares, and the soft slap of waves on the hull. I relaxed again, rejoicing that I was aboveground and alive. It had been a close-run thing.

I could barely stand, but Bartholomew, who looked not much better than I did, helped me into my clothes.

Bartholomew told me that he and Matthias had been set upon by Sharkey's men as they'd tried to guard the tunnel's entrance. They'd fought hard, but in the end, they'd been thoroughly beaten and dragged a long way into the desert. When they'd woken, furious and hurt, it had been well past midnight. They'd managed to make it back to the tunnel's entrance but couldn't dig through the rubble. They'd gone back to the pyramids for help, and had just started putting together a rescue party when we'd popped out through the hole that morning.

So explaining, Bartholomew assisted me to Lady Mary's drawing room, where dinner was being served. Bartholomew even handed me my walking stick, retrieved from outside the hole where we'd first entered the tomb.

Lady Mary looked pleased at having me, Grenville, and Marcus at her dining table. The three of us ate steadily, only Grenville managing to remember manners. Marcus and I simply shoveled food into our mouths, washing it all down with wine. I worried about Brewster, but was told he'd eaten plenty of food and had gone to sleep on deck.

Our hostess commanded us to tell her the entire tale, and Grenville complied.

"Mr. Sharkey did this?" Lady Mary said when Grenville told her he'd beaten Matthias and Bartholomew then laughed at us through the rubble.

"Always knew he was a bad 'un, as the Cockneys say. He has a barge, you know, quite expensive, that he moors near mine, but we all know he's not our sort. And now he's tried to murder you." She made a face of distaste.

"Yes," I said tersely. "I believe Brewster and I will have a little chat with him."

***

The next morning saw me, with Brewster, Grenville, and Marcus, approaching a barge moored along the docks that was every bit as sumptuous as Lady Mary's.

I knew Sharkey was there, though we saw no one on deck. He must have retreated here when we burned his house, but more than that, I simply *knew* it.

I wondered why he hadn't taken up his anchor and fled up- or downriver, but the lack of men aboard might explain why. He either hadn't had time to put together a crew, or they'd deserted him.

I intended to climb onto the ship, find Sharkey, lay into him with my fists, and then throw him into the river. Perhaps I'd fish him out again if nothing ate him and drag him to the magistrates. I'd search until I found a magistrate he hadn't corrupted and leave Sharkey under his care.

The gangplank was up. We searched the dock for boards to bridge the gap to the ship or ropes with which we could climb aboard, determined to make the man pay for nearly killing us all.

The tramping of many feet brought us up short. I turned to behold the pasha's palace guard, twenty men armed with swords and rifles, no mercy on their faces. Behind them came the four cavalrymen I'd taught, who looked as grim as the guards.

Without a word to me, they splashed directly into the river, unslinging rope from their shoulders as they passed. The guards threw grappling hooks up to the sides of the ship, then swarmed up onto the deck.

By the time Brewster had boosted me up one of the ropes, one of the guards had dragged Sharkey from his hiding place and thrown him onto the deck.

Chapter Twenty-Seven

I struggled to heave myself over the gunwale, my knee still hurting like the devil. One of my cavalryman friends reached his strong hands down and pulled me aboard. Brewster quickly joined me, followed by Marcus.

"This won't go well for you," Sharkey was saying in English to the lead palace guard. "I'd be worried for your job, mate."

They surrounded him. One guard prodded Sharkey with a rifle butt, trying to get him to his knees.

Sharkey, who'd trained on the dark streets of London, was quickly on his feet, a knife somehow in his hand. He whirled and slashed quickly, slicing into the guard's side.

The guard flinched. Sharkey punched him in the exact spot the knife had cut then spun around and headed for the side.

I got in his way. I knew I was a fool to, even as I saw Sharkey coming at me, his knife gripped solidly in his big fingers.

He cut at me. I tried to dance aside, but my knee would let me do no such acrobatics. I landed on my bad leg, gritted my teeth as pain shot through me, and leveled a punch right at Sharkey's face.

I hit him, to my surprise. He'd expected me to fall, weak and spent, not to land a blow worthy of a pugilist.

My hand stung, Sharkey's face blossomed blood, and he cursed at me. He shoved me aside and I did fall, but Marcus was beside him, his fist now landing on the side of Sharkey's head.

Sharkey was resilient. He broke from Marcus and rushed to the railing, intending to jump. Brewster, moving with his unnerving swiftness, locked his arms through Sharkey's from behind and spun him around. Sharkey darted his knife back to Brewster's thigh. Brewster grunted as the blade sank in, but he did not let go.

The guards fell upon them like a swarm of flies. I heard Sharkey scream.

One of my cavalry friends helped me to my feet. His sword was out, and he put himself in front of me, ready to defend me against any more of Sharkey's treachery.

Grenville had made it to the deck, neat and unruffled. I noted that the gangplank was now down—he'd come up that.

The palace guards jerked Sharkey from Brewster, standing Sharkey upright. Blood poured from Sharkey's nose, his lips were split, and one eye was swollen shut.

A guard pointed at Sharkey with his sword blade and spoke in halting English. "You come. Now."

"You can't touch me, you poxy bastard," Sharkey sneered, blood dribbling down his chin. "Your magistrates know what will happen to them and their families if I'm arrested."

Grenville, who had prudently stayed far from the violence, brushed off his coat sleeves and adjusted his hat. He gave Sharkey a cold stare, a Mayfair dandy at his most disdainful.

"They aren't from the magistrates, old thing," he said, the drawling words cool. "They're palace guard. I believe he means his master, the pasha, wants a word with you."

For the first time since I'd met him, I saw Sharkey's face go tight with fear. Sharkey was pitiless, but he'd met his match in the man busy wresting control of Egypt from the might of the Ottoman Empire.

I had no idea what would happen if Sharkey were taken to the palace. Sharkey might convince the pasha that he should be left alone, to go back to doing as he had been. The pasha might let him, intending to use him in his play for power.

Or, Sharkey might be expelled from Egypt, which meant he'd have to explain to James Denis how he'd managed to draw such attention to himself. No matter where he went, Denis would find him. Or, he might simply be executed.

Sharkey snapped his head around and glared at me. "I knew you was nothing but trouble. Denis sent you to destroy me, didn't he?"

"He did not," I said in a hard voice. "I told you, I knew nothing about you."

"He sent you," Sharkey repeated with conviction. "Don't matter he didn't tell you. He's done wiv me, and he sent you to chuck me out."

His voice rose until the words were a snarl. Sharkey wrenched himself from the guards with the ease of long practice, and launched himself at me.

I saw in his eyes the intent to kill. He'd run into me and take me over the railing, ripping my guts out with his knife as we went. Didn't matter if he drowned in the murk—he'd murder me on his way out of this life.

I braced myself to fight him off. In the same instant, three of the guards stepped between me and Sharkey, leveled their rifles, and shot him in the head.

***

The palace guards searched Sharkey's boat, and I searched it with them. The guards broke into everything—they tore open seat cushions and mattresses, spilled contents of cupboards over the floor then broke the cupboards from the walls to look for compartments behind them. They did not seem to be looking for anything specific, only for money and valuables to confiscate for the pasha.

Brewster, Marcus, and Grenville helped me pick through the mess, and the guards let us without question. Sharkey had kept a treasure here—I saw that he'd not lost much when the house burned.

The guards turned up caches of jewels much like those we'd found in the tomb, as well as solid gold statuettes of dog-headed gods and dignified cats, pectorals of gold encrusted with stones both precious and semiprecious, bones of unfortunate mummies, and more recent trinkets, including a gold coffee service similar to ones I'd seen at the palace.

Sharkey's dead body lay forlornly on the deck. Occasionally one of the guards would stroll to it and spit on him.

"He rob the pasha," the guard who spoke some English told us, his disgust clear.

I was not certain if he meant Sharkey had literally broken into the palace and stolen things like the coffee service, or if he meant that Sharkey keeping the antiquities in his own private stash prevented the pasha from using them as bargaining chips. No matter that treasure hunters up and down the Nile thought Egypt a backward country, handing over its past for nothing, we were all here at the pasha's mercy, and the pasha knew it.

I diligently searched for the Alexandrian book. Sharkey had claimed not to know of the book's whereabouts as he'd beaten Marcus, but he might have lied as an excuse to imprison and hurt Marcus to get to me.

However, we never found it. The guards did a thorough job stripping the boat down, uncovering an entire hoard of precious things, but no papyri at all. Sharkey might not have valued mere words on paper, no matter how ancient. Or perhaps his clients simply hadn't asked for any.

The palace guard finally escorted us off the ship, intending to confiscate the barge itself. Two guards stood over Sharkey's body, arms folded, faces unyielding.

"I know he was a thorough villain," Grenville said as we passed him. "But we could ask that he be given a Christian burial. Even hanged men are sent off with prayers for their souls."

I found the English-speaking guard and repeated Grenville's request. The man gave me a hard look. "He left you to the jackals," he said, his mouth a thin line. "This displeases the pasha. So *he* will be given to the jackals." The man bowed slightly, his look not softening. "Good day."

"Best we go, Mr. Grenville," Brewster said.

"Nuffing more we can do."

Grenville and I realized that Brewster was correct. We departed.

The cavalrymen helped me descend the gangplank, then they took their leave of me. From the way they said good-bye, I knew I'd never see them again. One even took my face between his hands, stared into my eyes, then gave me a nod and turned his back.

I lifted my hand in farewell as the four of them marched away, heading into the city and whatever billet they called home.

"Well, Mr. Denis is out one agent in Cairo," Grenville said as we walked away down the docks, much subdued. "I imagine he will not be happy with us. We could always live forever in Egypt, Lacey. Send for Donata when she's well and we'll eke out our days in tents like the Bedouins. Though I suppose Denis has agents among them too."

I gave him a cursory laugh. "I would not be surprised. No, I will take my lumps. I haven't turned up this book, and my actions got his agent killed. Do not worry, Grenville, I will not let Denis take his wrath out on me or those I love. He knows this."

I also had a feeling that Denis would not be as upset as Grenville surmised at the loss of Sharkey. Sharkey had been a loose cannon, playing his own game. Denis might believe himself well rid of him.

We returned home for a good long rest, but that night found ourselves again on Lady Mary's barge for a dinner she hosted in our honor.

I expected the cream of British society in Cairo to be there but we discovered Lady Mary had invited only Grenville, Marcus, and myself. She'd included Marcus, I suspected, because she was curious about him. Marcus was uncomfortable dining with us, but I urged him to come so I could keep my eye on him. I did not want him slipping away into the aether before we resolved things, if they could be resolved.

To my delight, Lady Mary had also invited Signora Beatrice and Celia, who performed her inviting dances for us.

Lady Mary had dressed tonight in a version of Celia's costume — billowing pantaloons, a bejeweled jacket over her high-collared bodice, thick gold bracelets on her plump arms, and silk slippers turned up at the toes.

"Dear Celia has been teaching me harem dancing," Lady Mary said. She rose and joined the younger woman in the middle of the room, stretching out her arms and moving her feet in imitation.

The result was rather appalling, like a full-sailed galleon listing to and fro, but we politely watched and applauded. Signora Beatrice's eyes sparkled with bright mirth.

Celia finished, bowed low to Lady Mary, who tried to copy the bow in return, her bosom sagging unfortunately as she did so.

Celia bowed to us gentlemen, giving Grenville a blatant come-hither look, and departed the room.

Lady Mary, oblivious of the look, waved us all to the dining table where she'd made certain Grenville was seated at its head and next to her. Signora Beatrice ended up beside me, which was to my liking, Marcus opposite her.

"Celia is such a lovely girl," Lady Mary said as the food was served. "I had hoped that Miguel would make a match with her, but unfortunately nothing has come of it."

Miguel, who was even now pouring wine in our glasses, looked pained. I sent him a sympathetic glance, which he accepted with a nod.

"Spaniards can be such snobs," Lady Mary went on, as though he could not hear her. "I've pointed out that Celia is not a native woman, not even a Mohammedan. She is a Venetian, like Signora Beatrice. Quite respectable. Of course, she would have to cease dancing for gentlemen if they were together. But Miguel has declined to pursue the suit." She shook her head, long-suffering. Miguel quietly finished serving the wine and departed.

Grenville murmured something appeasing, and I again caught Signora Beatrice's amused expression.

After supper, we adjourned to the deck. The weather was warm tonight, the stars a canopy of beauty.

Celia joined us, dressed now in a modest frock with a high neck and long sleeves, something my own daughter might wear. I saw Miguel, who'd come out with us, give Celia a wistful glance, but she ignored him.

As the party wound on, we drifted into groups to contemplate the stars or chat. Lady Mary determinedly followed Grenville, who with equal determination made certain I or Marcus was with him at all times.

Signora Beatrice was at the rail alone, and I moved to her. Before I reached her, Celia materialized at her side. In the deep shadow, Beatrice turned to her, and Celia touched her hand.

The look they exchanged was long and full of meaning, and I understood exactly why Miguel had been rebuffed. Beatrice might have lost the love of her life when Chabert died, but she seemed to have found love anew. Celia obviously returned the affection.

Why then, I wondered, had Celia given Grenville the significant look? It had been the glance of a lady telling a gentleman she would not mind if he wanted to meet with her in private. Did Celia truly enjoy the company of men, only pretending to be devoted to Beatrice?

No, as I watched the two ladies in the dark, thinking themselves unobserved, I found it easy to deduce that Celia had a fondness for Beatrice equal to that of Beatrice for her.

Then why try to lure in Grenville?

I leaned on the railing, facing the river, and came to an abrupt realization. Beatrice had been a courtesan. As much as Lady Mary admired her and pretended that Beatrice's past did not matter to women of the world, Beatrice had made her living by pleasing gentlemen for payment.

She'd told me of her love for Chabert, and likely she truly had loved him, but she'd first met him for the purposes of seduction for reward.

Beatrice had intimated that she was finished with such things, that her old life was over. But why should I suppose she spoke the truth? She hadn't out-and-out told me that, in any case. By her own admission, she had Celia now to please a gentleman's physical longings, while Beatrice supplied the sophisticated conversation.

I saw, as I watched them, not a pair of ordinary women who'd stumbled into affection for each other, but a well-rehearsed team who knew exactly how to pull in a mark for mutual benefit.

And in that moment, I knew what had happened to the Alexandrian book.

Chapter Twenty-Eight

Suspected, rather. Now to prove it.

I turned and sought out Miguel, who for a change, stood by himself, peering into the darkness on the other side of the river.

"Captain," he said in his pleasantly accented English when I reached his side. "How might I assist you?"

I said nothing for a moment, gazing with him at the far bank, where the Egyptians of old had built cities for the dead. I had nearly met my own death out there.

I remembered Miguel's worried face when he'd leaned down to help me out of the hole. He'd been distressed for me and my friends. A compassionate gentleman.

"You can give me the Greek book," I said in a low voice. "The one by Aristarchus, from Alexandria."

Miguel sent me a look of profound astonishment. "What do you mean?" He lifted his spread hands. "I have not this book—I know nothing of it. How would I know what it is?"

"You are a scholar," I said. "An artifact from the Alexandrian library would be extraordinary treasure to you—far better than gold statuary or jewels. You would know what the scroll was—I imagine you are able to read it."

Miguel said nothing. He returned his gaze to the west bank as though seeking solace from the ancient dead.

"Celia seduced you," I said, working it through my mind. "Whether on her own or at Signora Beatrice's behest, I am not certain. Perhaps they thought to obtain money from Lady Mary through you. Lady Mary had come to visit Beatrice to tell her of my interest in the book. You go where Lady Mary goes. I am fairly certain a man of your intelligence would see through Celia's ploy, but it gave you the opportunity to go belowdecks and steal the book. I had been thinking Lady Mary had taken it. Then I remembered that where Lady Mary goes, you follow."

Miguel remained silent for a few moments longer. When he spoke, his accent had softened, and his English was perfect.

"I have tried for a long time now to remove myself from under Lady Mary's thumb," he said, no more struggling with words. "I took what I believed her kind offer of employment because I had no money, nowhere to go. My wife's passing robbed me of my senses for a long time, and I lost my post at the university in Barcelona. I was once a highly respected man of letters, Captain. Now I fetch and carry for a boorish Englishwoman whose wealth and power cannot compensate for her very shallow mind. She does not act from kindness, I discovered to my dismay, but from a love of controlling others. She has her hand around my throat, and she toys with me day and night."

"Are you lovers?" I asked with some sympathy.

"No." Miguel's look turned to disgust, then relief. "Thank God she sets her sights on young and prominent men, like Mr. Grenville. He is, as you say, rather long in the tooth for her tastes, but his fame and fortune outweigh that fact. This book will set me free, Captain. I will not only have the reward for it but be restored in the eyes of learned men."

"It is not yours," I pointed out.

"Nor is it yours," Miguel said, his anger rising. "You want to hand it over to an unscrupulous collector, who will lock it away and gloat when he looks upon it. You have no claim on this book. I feel no shame keeping it from you."

"It belongs to Signora Beatrice," I said severely.

"It belongs to no one." Miguel's eyes flashed in the darkness. "It belongs to scholars, those who seek knowledge. It was written in a cradle of learning, in a time when learning was meaningful. Now a book that explains the mechanism of the universe is valued not for its information but because it is old and came from a famous place. So be it. I will turn that value into my freedom and work to copy, translate, and publish the information inside."

A noble goal, and what Chabert had wanted. I ought to simply give the damn thing to Miguel and wish him well.

"The man who sent me to find the book," I began slowly, "told me to offer any price for it. I could buy it from you and let you walk away. If you take my offer and disappear tonight, I will not divulge that you stole it. I can arrange to have it found where it will have no connection to you."

Sharkey was dead and would make a convenient scapegoat. I would claim I had found it on the ship and pocketed it before the palace guards realized what it was.

I felt a bit unclean as I proposed this—it was Signora Beatrice's book, entrusted to her by the man who found it, the man she'd loved.

However, I agreed with Miguel, as much as I thought him wrong for stealing from Signora Beatrice. The book was a special thing from an amazing period in history—when all the world had gathered in Alexandria to study in peace.

Should the scroll not be returned to a library, a museum, for scholars of today to examine? By selling the book to me, Miguel could be quit of Lady Mary, could stand with dignity once more.

Miguel's expression, if anything, grew more outraged. "If I thought you would value this book, I might take your money and go. But you will hand it to the dilettante who hired you. He will lock it in a case to admire alone, until it crumbles to dust and is lost forever." Miguel drew himself up. "It was kept, treasured, all this time, waiting to come to light again. I will not let it be returned to darkness."

He reached a trembling hand into a pocket inside his coat and brought out a small canvas bag.

"Good Lord." I bent to it. "Is that it?"

Miguel turned so that his back shielded what we did from the others. He opened the bag and showed me a corner of rough, browned paper rolled tightly in on itself. I saw Greek letters on the papyrus but he hid it in the bag again before I could read them.

The sight of the scroll made my mouth go dry. I'd just seen paper and writing from the Hellenistic age, when art, learning, music, and philosophy had been at its height, moments before ignorance and darkness had swallowed the world for a thousand years.

"Take the money, Miguel," I urged. "Go to England. I will make certain you have access to the book. I promise you."

Denis could by all means grant me this favor for the trouble I'd been to.

Miguel hesitated, and for a moment, I thought he would agree.

But being Lady Mary's dogsbody must have worn him down. His lip curled into a sneer.

"I will not be bought like a slave," he said in a clear voice. "Your master will not have the book, nor will the duplicitous Signora Beatrice. Chabert protected it for knowledge's sake, and she has kept it like a trophy."

Miguel lifted the canvas bag high, snatching it out of my reach as I lunged for it. He held the bag aloft, moonlight flashing on the canvas, then he hurled it into the Nile.

The bag burst open as it fell, the papyrus shattering as the wind caught it. The brittle paper fluttered westward, toward the land of the dead, then lost momentum and rained to the water below.

I was ready to rush down the gangplank to the murky river and rake up as much of the paper as I could find when the waters began to roil. A hungry crocodile rose up, snapped his mouth over the fragments, and sank down again in disappointment.

"Bloody hell." The words dragged from my throat. I clung to the railing, my legs giving way. I found myself on my knees on the damp deck. "Damnation, man, you've just …" My voice died. I couldn't even form words to express my dismay.

The others had noticed Miguel's grand gesture

and were closing on us.

Miguel straightened his spine and looked Lady Mary in the eye. "I am finished with you."

He held her gaze as she gaped at him, the haughty imperiousness in his stance making me wonder from what lofty family Miguel had sprung. The Spanish had lost much when their country had become a battleground between France and England, fortunes drained, families broken. Now a scholar poured tea and carried things for a vain Englishwoman, who did not even use his surname — I speculated that she couldn't pronounce it.

Miguel turned on his heel, marched from the deck and down the gangplank, and was lost to darkness.

"Well," Lady Mary said in confusion "He certainly can be bad-mannered, can't he? I've had to admonish him about it before."

***

I never saw Miguel again. He disappeared from Lady Mary's employ, leaving without a word. Whether he'd returned to Spain or continued to travel the world, I could not know.

But I had many things to do. Now that Sharkey was dead and the book lost, and Marcus had ceased trying to kill me, at least for now, I settled in to enjoy the remainder of my stay in Egypt.

We found no more treasure as we excavated the tomb, but as I'd hoped, the paintings were copied then chiseled out whole and prepared for transport to the British Museum. I reveled in every moment of the excavation, every tiny fragment of painting or revealed hieroglyphs a joy to me. I copied out whatever hieroglyphs I could find, intending to see what I could make of them.

We were allowed to keep the jewels we'd found.

The cache on Sharkey's boat, which was much grander and more extensive, had been presented to Henry Salt by the pasha. Salt was so pleased with the pasha's gift to England that our find paled in comparison. And so, we kept our treasure, dividing it into the equal shares we'd agreed in the tomb. We each gave Bartholomew and Matthias a trinket, which they took in delight.

I felt compelled to tell Signora Beatrice what had happened to Chabert's book. She was saddened, but resigned. "It was cursed," she said. "It brought no pleasure to anyone. Poor Chabert."

The morning after I'd visited her to explain, Signora Beatrice set sail upriver again, with Celia, continuing her wandering.

Marcus and I formed an uneasy truce. He confronted Brewster one day as we worked at the tomb, putting himself in front of the man until Brewster finally conceded to listen to him.

"I wish to offer my abject apologies," Marcus said. "You are a good man, and I hurt you. The fact that I did so inadvertently is no excuse. If I had not been certain that only violence would do, you would not have suffered."

The speech was pretty, and I wondered how long Marcus had practiced it. It sounded sincere, though, no matter how rehearsed.

Brewster regarded Marcus for a long time. "Make no mistake, Mr. Lacey, by no stretch of the mind am I a *good* man. I was born a villain and always will be. You're a fool to think otherwise." He shrugged. "The captain now, *he* is a good man. No matter what you want to fink."

"I am coming to suspect that," Marcus said dryly. "At least, all his friends say so."

"He's rash and sometimes a great fool," Brewster went on, knowing full well I was within earshot. "But I'd leap in front of your gun again, if I had to. Remember that."

"I will indeed, Mr. Brewster." Marcus did not sound as meek as he might. "Please convey my apologies to Mrs. Brewster as well."

"Ah. Well." Brewster moved uneasily, and rubbed his nose. "My Em, she's not as forgiving as me. I'll tell her, but I can't answer for her if you darken my door. As much as your life is worth, I'm thinking."

"Tell her anyway," Marcus said. He touched his forehead in a salute and walked away.

I caught up with him. "What will you do?" I asked. "When your stay here is at an end? Continue to follow me and try to make my life a misery?"

Marcus sent me a wry smile. "I will return to England when you do. As you suggest, I will seek a solicitor and prove that I am Gabriel Lacey, rightful heir to the Lacey estate. Will you try to stop me?"

"If your story is true, then no," I said. "If you are a confidence trickster, then I will fight you. But know this." I made Marcus halt, and we faced each other under the hot blue sky. "If you are my cousin, regardless of whether your father was a legitimate child or a by-blow, you shall not lose by it. You do not have to be a rightful heir to win my friendship or my trust. Family." I echoed Sharkey's words. "It is important to me."

Marcus studied me for a time, his brows drawn, as though he decided whether to believe me sincere or not. Then he shrugged.

"We shall see what happens," he said, and stuck out his hand.

I took it. "We shall see."

Our handshake was a little more firm than necessary, and we each waited to see who would give way first, but I had not expected otherwise.

***

I made a nuisance of myself exploring the pyramids when I wasn't at our tomb, though I could not bring myself to enter dark passages where I had to crawl. It would be a while before I could do such a thing again.

Even so, I marveled at the pyramids' construction, and to my delight, I did get to meet the great Mr. Belzoni.

He returned from his journey to the Red Sea and began digging around the pyramids, looking for more entrances and burial chambers. He found them, to the annoyance of the wealthy aristocrats who did not like being outdone by a former circus performer. His wife, a small, slim, tightrope dancer who dressed in man's clothes, was a tough but friendly woman who was happy to point out to me all that her giant of a husband was unearthing.

Sunny October waned, and I became anxious to depart, wanting to be at Donata's side when my daughter was born.

We returned to Alexandria on the first of November. There we met Sergeant Porter and his wife—Mrs. Porter and Mrs. Belzoni had much in common, I noted. Porter had uncovered an intact tomb of one of the ancient bulls, and was quite pleased with himself.

He listened with interest to my adventures and admired the jewelry. I'd carefully pieced it back together, using Grenville's drawings and some guesses. In the end I had a small diadem of rubies and gold and a necklace of lapis lazuli, carnelian, and gold beads. Grenville had a similar collection. Brewster had elected to string every jewel and piece of gold into one long strand to lay around his wife's neck when he returned. He enjoyed picturing her response.

Porter shook his head when I told him about being sealed into the tomb. "A man doesn't know what he's made of," he said, voice going quiet in sympathy. "Until he faces the darkness. I am pleased you survived, Captain."

Before we departed, Grenville and I visited Haluk, who'd given us his hospitality the day we'd arrived in Egypt.

He again received us in his colorful sitting room, the tall Karem serving us.

"What happened regarding Ibrahim's death?" I asked. "Before I left, I had heard that the magistrates decided a man from a foreign ship had done it."

"Yes," Haluk said, nodding comfortably. "They could not find out, and so they made up a story. The bey, he does such things."

"I have been thinking on it," I said, cradling my small cup of coffee. "Ibrahim was meeting someone. He did not even tell his closest friend who it was, and so I think it was a lady. Or at least Ibrahim must have believed so."

There was a clatter of metal and a soft splash. Karem had dropped the coffee pot. Swiftly, and without apology, he dropped to his knees and began to wipe up the spilled coffee from the carpet.

I'd pondered the question as I'd helped with the tedious chore of looking through the rubble for more gold or rubies, the sun beating on my neck, the end of my turban swinging against my cheek.

"It is unlikely a young lady such as your daughter

would be able to slip away from your house," I said. "Even if she were truly enamored with Ibrahim and not disgusted by him as you implied. But Ibrahim might be eager enough to believe she would run off with him. Perhaps someone else met him, warned him and his friends to stay away from her, argued with him, struck him."

My words fell on dead silence. Grenville nodded thoughtfully. Karem remained in a crouch, unmoving.

"Or the magistrates have it right," Haluk said, clearing his throat. "A man from a foreign ship fought with him."

"Ahmed, Ibrahim's friend, is a strong lad. A good fighter. I imagine Ibrahim was much the same." I set down my coffee. "I doubt the woman's father would be much of a match for him. Ibrahim became violent, and the man defended himself as he could. A rock was the best weapon he could use in his sudden fright. Perhaps the man did not mean to kill at all, only to fend off an attack."

Haluk's eyes were wet with tears. He opened his mouth to speak, but Karem rose to his full height, his head lifted, his stern face filled with dignity.

"Do not accuse my master of such things," Karem said to me in fluent French. "Even if you choose fine words, we know what you mean. He had nothing to do with it." He struck his chest with his forefinger. "*I* killed Ibrahim."

Haluk jumped to his feet, and Grenville and I struggled up from the floor. Haluk spoke to Karem in Turkish, his words impassioned. Karem remained stoic.

Haluk turned to me. "I have done as you say. I did not mean to—you are right that Ibrahim was strong and agile, more than I understood. He tried to kill me. He disdained me because I had the courage to speak against the sultan. I lifted a rock, tried to fight …"

Karem stepped in front of Haluk, cutting off his speech. "Do not listen. It happened as he said, but *I* met Ibrahim, I fought, I wielded the rock. I covered the body when I knew he was dead, hoping he would not be found."

Karem could be telling the truth — or Haluk could be. Karem was more robust than Haluk, but he was aging. Ibrahim would have been able to best either of them.

I lifted my hands. "I am not a magistrate. I wanted to tell you my thoughts on the matter. That is all. The verdict was that a foreign man committed the deed but managed to escape. Let the conclusion stand."

Haluk and Karem stared at me. Haluk wet his lips. "You would keep your silence about so grievous a thing?"

I regarded the two men, one a father who would do anything to protect his daughter, the other a retainer who would do anything to protect his master.

Ahmed would be unhappy that I could not find the true killer of his friend, but he would go on, fighting battles for the glory of the Ottoman Empire. He'd take a wife one day and have children of his own. Perhaps then he would understand.

"I have a daughter," I said. "She is eighteen, and very beautiful. I would go to hell itself for her."

Haluk nodded. "Yes."

"So the story is at an end," I said.

Haluk nodded again, sadness in his eyes. Grenville and I said good-bye to him, and we took our leave.

"So you will say nothing?" Grenville asked me once we'd returned to our lodgings. "You usually are so keen to bring a killer to justice."

It depended on the crime and why it had been done. I'd faced this sort of decision before.

"Why would the magistrates listen to me, a foreigner, accusing a wealthy Turk?" I asked. "Even if that Turk is here in disgrace? Besides, if Haluk is arrested, it will not only be he who suffers. What would become of his wife, his daughter? His servants? Karem? The laws here can be harsh. The death was accidental, I am certain of it."

"Which is why Karem tried to take the blame," Grenville said. "In his opinion, he had less to lose."

I believed Karem when he'd said he'd covered up the body. He would do such a thing, to try to shield his master. His agitation when he'd found us in the place Ibrahim had been killed had not been feigned, but he'd hidden it well by pretending to be upset only for our sakes. He likely *had* been distressed that we'd been pulled into the mess—I remembered the sincerity in his eyes when he'd apologized to us at the time.

"There is no evidence," I said to Grenville. "None at all. And so, as I said, that story is at an end."

Grenville nodded, and we agreed to say no more about it.

***

The next day, we, along with Marcus, took ship for England, again on a vessel of Captain Woolwich's line. We paused in Malta, where I returned the books to Grenville's friend, and Grenville gave him a stone with hieroglyphs on it, similar to the seal I'd bought in the market in Alexandria. We left the man poring over it, eyes alight, but not before he graciously invited us for a long stay any time we wished.

The rest of the voyage was uneventful. Grenville took to his bunk. I wrote up my journal for Gabriella, and reflected on all I'd seen. I talked with Marcus, the two of us sitting in the ward room on rainy days or on deck in full sunshine on fair ones. I learned much of his past, and told him much about mine.

At long last, as November drew to a close, we sailed up the Thames, ending where we'd begun.

On a rainy, foggy, November London day, I presented myself at Number 45 in Curzon Street, and asked to see James Denis.

Chapter Twenty-Nine

Denis's house hadn't changed at all since I'd last been in it, which had been in sunny June. I was shown to his study on the second floor, where Denis sat behind a desk that was empty save for a book open before him. A pugilist footman stood at the window, watching with sharp eyes as the slimmer, wiry butler ushered me in.

Denis glanced up and waved me to a seat with the flick of his fingers.

I settled myself in the armchair that waited in front of the desk, resting my hand on my walking stick. Before I could speak, Denis closed his book, set it aside, and gave me a full stare with his dark blue eyes. Again, I marveled at the weight of ages in those eyes, in the body of one so young.

"I understand that you have come to tell me you were unable to obtain the Alexandrian book."

I did not let myself be surprised that he already knew. "I made a valiant attempt," I said. "I saw the book with my own eyes. Then it was gone."

I gave him a brief summary of what had happened—I did not mention Miguel by name, referring to him only as a servant. I had no wish for Denis to scour the earth looking for him to express his displeasure.

Denis watched me as I spoke, his fingertips together. I could see that he did not altogether believe my tale, but he did not argue.

He lifted his shoulders in a smooth shrug. "It is no matter. I considered it farfetched that you would find the book but thought I would take a chance. The fact that you saw it at all is somewhat surprising."

I stared at him, my anger mounting. "Farfetched? Thought you would take a chance?" I surged from the chair, and the pugilist tensed. "I was at much trouble looking for that blasted book. I fought for my life, was nearly caught in a fire, had your miserable agent wall me and my friends into a tomb, for God's sake. And you claim you did not seriously believe I could find it? Why send me looking for it, damn you?"

"I do regret the dangers to your life." Denis spoke coolly, no hint of apology in his voice. "I forget how determined you can be. Mr. Sharkey acted without my consent. He had been doing things against my wishes, ignoring my instructions, for some time."

"Well, he's dead now," I said in a hard voice. "I saw him shot by three rifles, all pointed at his head. I imagine his bones have already been picked over in the desert."

"He is indeed dead," Denis said. "My new agent in Cairo confirmed it."

Of course, Denis would have had a man to slide into place the moment Sharkey was gone.

Did he do it on purpose? I wondered dimly. Wait for me to understand what he'd done, so he could enjoy my outburst of rage?

I closed the space to his desk and slammed both my fists to its surface. The pugilist started forward, but Denis held up a hand, forestalling him.

"Damn and blast you," I said clearly. "You didn't send me to fetch an ancient book—you sent me to deal with Sharkey. You knew bloody well I'd never let such vermin best me. I was to make certain he was taken care of. Why the hell didn't you simply ask me?"

Denis regarded me calmly, but that only made me angrier. "Because you would not have done it," he said. "You would have torn up my instructions and ignored them. You would have decided that dissension in my ranks was my own affair. A search for an ancient book would be much more to your liking. And I confess I would like to have put my hands on it." Denis's eyes narrowed. "Are you certain this servant threw it overboard?"

"I watched him," I said, my fury not abating. "A crocodile ate the remains."

Even as I spoke, I wondered. Miguel had shown me a corner of papyrus with Greek writing on it. An ancient document, I was certain, especially in light of the way the brittle pages disintegrated.

But had I seen the Aristarchus? Or simply an old Greek scroll that Miguel had been studying, or had prepared in case someone searched him?

Was Miguel, even now, in some library in Spain or France or Amsterdam studying the scroll, copying it out, treasuring it as he'd said he would?

I could picture him doing so quite easily. The man had been far more intelligent than Lady Mary gave him credit for. He'd planned, bided his time, acted.

I snatched up my walking stick. I was finished with people manipulating me.

"I have an appointment in Oxfordshire," I said firmly. "Good day to you."

Denis nodded without rising. "My felicitations, Captain." He flicked his fingers again, and his butler rigidly opened the door for me. "Please give your wife my best wishes."

***

My anger dissipated as the miles to Oxfordshire fell behind me. I traveled with Bartholomew alone, Grenville remaining in London to put his house to rights. He also, I suspected, wanted some private moments with Marianne.

Brewster also remained in London, returning to his Em with his gifts. He told me that Denis had said he deserved a rest, though Brewster vowed he'd be back watching over me as soon as he could. He didn't trust any of Denis's other men to do it right. I knew that I owed Brewster much, and I would stand him all the ales he'd earned when I returned to London.

Marcus had accepted my offer to stay in my rooms in Grimpen Lane for a time. He would be close to Lincoln's Inn for when he started proceedings to recover his inheritance. Marcus still did not quite believe I'd be willing to let him take over the house in Norfolk, but we could argue about it another time.

The weather grew sunnier as we journeyed west and north, though it was cold, morning frost coating the ground.

I descended the coach at the front door of Pembroke Court rather stiffly, already missing the desert's heat. Donata's father's majordomo greeted me cordially, with the same sort of deference and respect Karem had shown Haluk.

I barely acknowledged him or the rest of the staff who'd turned out to welcome me, hurrying as fast as my leg would let me to the suite of rooms upstairs.

My wife reposed on a chaise in the winter sunshine, her dark hair cascading across her shoulders. Though she'd covered herself with a thick shawl, her distended belly could not be hidden.

She looked up at my step, and the sudden dart of joy in her eyes gladdened my heart. My lovely lady was delighted to see her battered and broken husband.

"Good heavens, but you are sunburned," Donata said as I came to her and kissed her lips. "But there is lightness in you. It seems that three months under the hot sun was good for you, Gabriel."

I could not think of a word to say in response. I wanted to crush her in my arms; I wanted to hold her in the night. I wanted to sit beside her and tell her everything.

All I could do was seat myself on a chair next to the chaise, pull out the slim box I'd carried all the way from Cairo, open it, and lay the contents on her white coverlet.

Donata stared down at the fire-colored rubies, the deep blue of the lapis, the burnished, ancient beauty of the gold.

"Oh, Gabriel," she breathed. "This is ... I've never seen ..."

The fact that I could render my wife of the many opinions speechless pleased me.

"Found buried far beneath the earth," I said. "I will tell you all about my adventures discovering them." I touched the diadem. "This is for you, for your hair." It would gleam like fire in the darkness. I laid down the comb Haluk had given me, ostensibly from his wife to mine. "This is also for you, from a Turk who loves his daughter."

Before Donata could begin her questions, I moved my fingers to the lapis lazuli and gold necklace. "This is for Gabriella."

"Yes." Donata brushed it, her hand meeting mine. "Perfect for her. She will adore it. What is this?"

She lifted the seal and the copies of the hieroglyphs I'd taken from the tomb. "For Peter," I said. "He will enjoy puzzling out the writing."

Donata smiled. "He will indeed. And this one?" She moved to the smallest strand of jewelry, gold and lapis beads strung on a gold chain.

"For our new daughter," I said. My touch moved to Donata's abdomen and the life inside.

Donata raised her fine brows. "Your time in the desert has made you clairvoyant, has it? How do you know it will not be a son?"

"I know."

I remembered the vision I'd had in the tomb, of a little girl with dark hair, brown eyes, and her mother's face. She'd laughed at me, stretching out her hand. *Here, Papa,* she'd said, her voice as warm as daylight.

"I know," I repeated with conviction.

Donata sent me a questioning glance. "I ought to put down a wager. But we will discover which of us is correct soon enough." She touched my face, then her practicality faded, and her eyes softened. I saw pain in them, loneliness, and annoyance that she'd missed me so much.

I gathered her into my arms, showing her how

much I'd missed *her*.

"You'll stay, won't you?" Donata whispered, her hands tightening on my back.

"Unless you have me abducted and taken away, yes," I said. I smiled at her, and she returned it, a wicked look in her eyes. She'd enjoyed besting me.

"I'll be here until there is one more of us," I went on, laying my hand on her abdomen again. "That is our next grand adventure."

End

Author's Note

Thank you for reading! Captain Lacey's adventures will continue in Book 12, *A Mystery at Carleton House*.

The Alexandria Affair was first conceived, in concept if not in detail, soon after I began writing the Captain Lacey Regency Mysteries. Once Grenville brought up the possibility that he would return to Egypt and take Lacey with him, I knew I had to one day write this book.

I went into the story knowing I could not include many of the recurring characters who have become familiar over the books, as it would be unrealistic for all Lacey's friends to simply turn up in Egypt. I decided to return to the original characters, Lacey and Grenville, having them solve crimes together, with the footmen, Bartholomew and Matthias, assisting. I added Mr. Brewster, Lacey's bodyguard provided by James Denis, as Denis would never think to let Lacey roam the world without one of his men to keep an eye on him.

Egypt in the early 1800s was at a crossroads. Muhammad Ali, the wali, or governor, of Egypt, had taken control in 1805. Albanian by birth, he was a soldier who rose to command armies and then was granted the governorship of Egypt.

Muhammad Ali declared that the Ottoman Empire was dying and that he would build a kingdom on its ruins. He nationalized the agriculture of Egypt and pushed for modernization, inviting Europeans to bring him Western ideas, technology, and medicine. He allowed the early archaeologists to take what they could find of ancient Egypt, sparking heated rivalries among them.

Modern archaeologists cringe at the methods used in the early years of excavation, the tombs basically plundered for treasure to be displayed in museums and private collections throughout Europe, with artifacts then considered of no value shoved aside or destroyed. A terrific description of early archaeology of Egypt and the rivalries of the period can be found in the book, *The Rape of the Nile,* by Brian Fagan.

Archaeologists were somewhat hindered at this time by not being able to read hieroglyphs. The Rosetta Stone, found by one of Napoleon's soldiers in 1798, had not yet been deciphered at the time of *The Alexandria Affair* (1818). The Rosetta Stone has three scripts: Greek, hieroglyphs, and demotic (a simpler form of ancient Egyptian writing), each a copy of the same text. Jean-Francois Champollion finally deciphered the stone in 1822.

Therefore, Lacey and his friends would not know the Egyptian names of the pharaohs or queens in the tombs they found or visited, or be able to read the elaborate inscriptions on the walls or the papyri. At this time, knowledge of ancient Egypt came mostly from Greek writings—Herodotus, who'd visited Egypt in the fifth century BC, was still used as an authority.

The City of Alexandria itself was at a crossroads. Once famous for its scholarship, library, and huge lighthouse—one of the Seven Wonders of the ancient world—Alexandria had long been in decline. Wars, earthquakes, and invasions had cut the city off from the Nile and severely altered its geography, until by Captain Lacey's time, there was nothing left of the Hellenistic city.

The pasha, Muhammad Ali, began an extensive renovation of Alexandria, which included cutting a canal from the Nile, expanding his navy in the port, and building lavish buildings. All this renovation was just beginning when Lacey visited, and continued throughout the nineteenth century, rendering Alexandria a modern cosmopolitan city.

Captain Lacey could see only what was visible in Egypt in 1818—not all the monuments were cleared and accessible as they are today. I also used the spelling for names of people and places, such as Aboukir and Rosetta, that would have been used in Lacey's time.

Captain Lacey may well return to Egypt, perhaps with his growing family, to see what changes have occurred over the years.

Meanwhile Gabriel has much to do in London with his friends and family in *A Mystery at Carleton House*.

To be kept up to date with new releases, join my newsletter here: http://eepurl.com/5n7rz or check my website: www.gardnermysteries.com

About the Author

Award-winning Ashley Gardner is a pseudonym for *New York Times* bestselling author Jennifer Ashley. Under both names—and a third, Allyson James—Ashley has written more than 85 published novels and novellas in mystery and romance. Her books have won several RT BookReviews Reviewers Choice awards (including Best Historical Mystery for *The Sudbury School Murders*), and Romance Writers of America's RITA (given for the best romance novels and novellas of the year). Ashley's books have been translated into a dozen different languages and have earned starred reviews in *Booklist*. When she isn't writing, she indulges her love for history by researching and building miniature houses and furniture from many periods.

More about the Captain Lacey series can be found at www.gardnermysteries.com.

Made in the USA
Middletown, DE
15 March 2020